Praise for Georg...

Finding Home

"Georgia Beers has proven in her popular novels such as *Too Close to Touch* and *Fresh Tracks* that she has a special way of building romance with suspense that puts the reader on the edge of their seat. *Finding Home*, though more character driven than suspense, will equally keep the reader engaged at each page turn with its sweet romance."—*Lambda Literary Review*

Lambda Literary Award Winner *Fresh Tracks*

"Georgia Beers pens romances with sparks."—*Just About Write*

"[T]he focus switches each chapter to a different character, allowing for a measured pace and deep, sincere exploration of each protagonist's thoughts. Beers gives a welcome expansion to the romance genre with her clear, sympathetic writing."
—*Curve magazine*

Mine

"From the eye-catching cover, appropriately named title, to the last word, Georgia Beers's *Mine* is captivating, thought-provoking, and satisfying. Like a deep red, smooth-tasting, and expensive merlot, *Mine* goes down easy even though Beers explores tough topics."—*Story Circle Book Reviews*

"Beers does a fine job of capturing the essence of grief in an authentic way. *Mine* is touching, life-affirming, and sweet." —*Lesbian News Book Review*

Too Close to Touch

"This is such a well-written book. The pacing is perfect, the romance is great, the character work strong, and damn but is the sex writing ever fantastic."—*The Lesbian Review*

"In her third novel, Georgia Beers delivers an immensely satisfying story. Beers knows how to generate sexual tension so taut it could be cut with a knife....Beers weaves a tale of yearning, love, lust, and conflict resolution. She has constructed a believable plot, with strong characters in a charming setting."—*Just About Write*

By the Author

Visit us at www.boldstrokesbooks.com

RIGHT HERE, RIGHT NOW

by
Georgia Beers

2017

ISBN 13: 978-1-63555-154-9

This Trade Paperback Original Is Published By
Bold Strokes Books, Inc.
P.O. Box 249
Valley Falls, NY 12185

First Edition: December 2017

Credits
Editor: Lynda Sandoval
Production Design: Stacia Seaman
Cover Design by Ann McMan

Acknowledgments

With each book I write, I'm amazed by how many people help me along the way, whether I ask or not, whether they know it or not. This book is no different.

Thank you to Bold Strokes Books and the staff there for making this process much easier than it could have been, especially Len Barot and Sandy Lowe, who walked me through, step by step. I so appreciate your patience.

To my niece, Katie Benko, for answering all my questions about Philadelphia and pointing out some fun places and details. I owe you dinner, Kate.

My books are so much better than the first drafts I hand in, and that's thanks to my editor extraordinaire, Lynda Sandoval. I have learned so much from her over the years. Whether it's an easy edit or a global restructuring (words no writer wants to hear, trust me), her instincts are impeccable and she's always right. Well, maybe 95 percent of the time...Thank you, Lynda, for making me a better writer.

To Dr. Holly Garber, who's been my friend since we were five years old, for answering all my annoying medical questions.

I've got a pretty good routine going by now with this job, but I still talk to a handful of people every day, and they still help me to relax. Thank you, Rachel Spangler, Melissa Brayden, and Nikki Little, for being around when I need you. Whether I want to celebrate with you, cry on your shoulders, or need you to smack me back into action, your friendship means a lot. I'm keeping you guys.

I know he can't read and has no idea what I do for a living, but I feel oddly compelled to thank Finley, my sweet and loving dog, for keeping me sane over the past year. I don't know what I'd have done without him. He teaches me unconditional love every single day. He is my heart.

Last, but never least, thank you to you, my readers. Your support means more than you know.

RIGHT HERE, RIGHT NOW

CHAPTER ONE

I, Lacey Chamberlain, am not a morning person.

There. I said it.

I never have been a morning person, even when I've tried (cough/college/cough). When my alarm goes off in the morning, what I really want to do is hurl it across the room so that it shatters (silently, of course) into a million pieces, allowing me to stay in the warm coziness of bed until I'm good and ready to get up. Around ten or so. Maybe ten thirty.

Luckily for my financial well-being, I'm structured and I'm a rule follower, which means, in actuality, when my alarm goes off, I have no choice but to obey it and get my ass out of bed. I'm never happy about it, but I do it. Because I have a job.

Leo, on the other hand, is all about the morning. The terrier mix I rescued two years ago scrambles up from the foot of the bed every morning, as soon as the second alarm begins its obnoxious ringing. He knows I always hit the snooze button. Once. That's all I allow myself. So, when the alarm goes off the second time, he sees that as his cue for morning doggie lovin', which I live for, I have to admit.

"Okay, okay," I mumbled to him. I was still half-asleep as I simultaneously tried to love him and keep him from poking his tongue in my mouth. "Dude. Ease up. I love you, too. I swear."

This game went on for a good ten minutes, me covering my head with my down comforter as Leo scratched at it madly with his tiny paws. I peeked out just enough for him to see me and dive for my face before I pulled the covers back up. It's our daily routine, and after a few minutes, I'm usually laughing and almost awake. Almost.

Two hours and two cups of coffee later, I packed Leo into the car along with my messenger bag filled with client folders, and a travel mug filled with yet more coffee, and we headed off to work. The drive is about twenty minutes, and I always use it to mentally go over my schedule for the day. Whether I have people to meet or just paperwork to do, I lay it all out in my head while I drive. Leo was seat-belted into the passenger seat, his sweet brown eyes scanning the scenery as it flew by. I learned the hard way to belt him in…one day, as we sat at a red light, I thought I'd be nice and slide the window down a bit for him so he could stick his little nose out. I neglected to put the child lock on, however, and all it took was him standing on the button before the window was down far enough for him to jump out. And he did. I watched it happen in slow motion, I swear to God. I leaned to grab him, but I missed. I can't believe he didn't break a leg—it was a long way down for his ten-pound body—and it's a miracle he didn't get flattened by a car as he darted across two lanes of traffic. The beeping horns, screeching tires, and shouts from his terrified mommy were apparently enough to scare the bejesus out of him, though, because he doesn't seem to mind the belt at all.

It was a really beautiful, not-yet-spring day in suburban Philadelphia. The sun was shining, which always makes me happy, so I slid on my Ray-Bans, sipped my coffee, and felt pretty close to fully awake. While the nights can still get pretty cold in early March, the daily temperatures had been hitting the high fifties, and that told me spring was just around the corner. Thank God. I hate being cold. You think I'd be used to it after thirty-three years in the same city, but sadly, I'm not. I live for spring because it means summer is coming, and summer means warmth. I'm like an old lady; I really should move south.

I swung my car into the parking lot of Dogwood Landing, the commercial building where my office has been since my father started it when he was thirty. He'd retired two years ago at sixty-five, and I took over fully, having worked side by side with him for almost nine years. As I aimed my car at my usual space, I thankfully saw a flash of bright yellow out of the corner of my eye and slammed my foot on the brake just in time to narrowly miss having my front bumper ripped off by that little bastard who works at the hardware store on the first level of the building. My nose crinkled up as I growled, causing Leo to look at me with alarm.

"That kid and his muscle car are going to kill somebody one of these days, Leo," I muttered, staring after him. In all honesty, it was the exact same line I muttered almost every day. His name was Kyle, but I'd nicknamed him Nascar Kyle. He was about twenty, and he'd worked for Mr. Archer in his small hardware store since before he graduated from high school. He was actually a really nice kid when he wasn't behind a steering wheel. I didn't know what happened to him when he plopped his butt in the driver's seat, but I knew I didn't like it.

When I looked forward again, I grimaced. My good mood was fading fast. There was a moving truck in my usual parking space. In fact, it was taking up three spaces. I took a big breath and blew it out slowly as I maneuvered my car into a spot I never parked in.

"I don't know, Leo," I said, as I slipped the gearshift into park. "I am not in love with where this Monday is going so far. Are you?"

Leo cocked his tiny brown-black head, his mismatched ears pricking up as he listened to me, and I couldn't help it. I grabbed his face and kissed it. Several times. Loudly. "You are my love," I told him, the first of about fifty-seven times I'd mention it that day.

I threw my messenger bag and my purse over my shoulder, clicked Leo's leash onto his harness, locked my car, and headed in.

The building is old. Hell, it was old when my dad started his business here thirty-seven years ago. But it's not run-down. The management company does a really good job taking care of it, and they respond quickly when there's a problem. The rent is reasonable, and the location is terrific, so I can't complain. There's also a security code to be entered in order to get through the door, but that door was propped open by a box. I'm usually a stickler about security, but I couldn't realistically expect the movers to punch in a code every single time they needed to carry something up, so I let it slide.

My office is on the second floor, and as Leo and I hit the stairwell, we were met by two burly men pushing a handcart. They grunted greetings as they passed. I reached our floor, went through another propped-open door, and stopped in my tracks.

Boxes.

Boxes and boxes.

Everywhere.

Leo and I maneuvered our way around them like we were working an agility course until we got to our own door, which was open, just the way Mary likes it.

My office is actually two. Sort of. There's a smaller area immediately inside the door. Sort of a reception space. That's where Mary's desk is, along with things like the printer/copier/fax behemoth, the coat rack, and four chairs for people who are waiting to see me. I don't think more than two chairs have ever been occupied at once. In the corner is a small coffee station and a mini fridge. Clients can use the single cup Keurig to make themselves some coffee. I also keep bottled water in the fridge and a selection of tea bags for the crazy people who don't drink coffee. Beyond Mary's desk is a doorway that leads to my larger office.

"There's my little munchkin," Mary said, immediately bending down in her chair so she could lavish attention (and too many treats) on Leo. He, of course, ate it up—figuratively and literally. He's no dummy, that boy of mine.

"Yeah. Hi there," I said, with a little wave, when Mary finally looked up at me.

"Oh, hi, Lacey. Are you here, too?" she asked with a smirk. Mary Kirk worked with my father and has known me since I was a kid. When my dad retired, she wasn't ready to, and it seemed nothing but super smart to keep her around, as she knows the ins and outs of many of the clients better than I do. She's in her sixties, her bob a chestnut brown that she gets touched up every four weeks like clockwork. She's small, friendly, and frighteningly efficient. I'm reasonably sure the office would crumble around my ears if I didn't have her. *Especially at this time of year*, I thought, as the phone rang.

"Chamberlain Financial," Mary said, in the almost musical tone she uses when she answers the phone. "How can I help you?"

I headed into my office, Leo opting to stay with Mary and the treats. Not unusual. She has a little dog bed under her desk that he loves to nap on. He spends more time with her during the day than with me, greeting the clients and keeping away burglars, I'm sure.

Things were starting to get really busy, well on their way to the chaos that is late March/early April for me and every other accountant in this country. The fact that I was there before nine was a big clue, as I prefer to come in closer to ten or eleven and work until six or seven. But when April 15 is closing in fast, I can find myself working fourteen- or fifteen-hour days, and then taking work home and putting in a couple more hours in my jammies. I had nine client visits lined up that day, plus a huge pile of returns to complete and file.

I took off my coat and hung it in the tiny closet in my office, the tiny closet crammed with pamphlets and supplies and a change of clothes (I've been known to fall asleep at my desk). A glance out the window showed me the movers working hard, this time a large drafting table being carried between them. Back out in Mary's area, I asked, "Were the movers here when you got here?"

"They were just starting, I think," she replied, her eyes never leaving her computer screen. Leo was curled up in her lap. "They're going into the office next door."

"Really?" My eyebrows rose. The office next door had been empty for over a year. It was about three times the size of mine, maybe more, and it had its own full bathroom—the only reason I ever considered maybe moving one door down, but I couldn't justify the rent increase, and I didn't really need that much space. Now the option was no longer available, which was probably for the best. I could stop thinking about it. I had, however, been enjoying the quiet of having nobody occupy it. "So much for the silence, huh?"

"We'll see." Mary shrugged. "Might be nice to have some neighbors, though."

"Maybe." I moved to the doorway and watched the movers carry the drafting desk past. I could hear a male voice from inside the other office telling them where to put it and I was tempted to go say hi, see exactly what was happening over there, but the phone rang. A glance at Mary told me it was a client, so I headed to my office and began my day.

❖

The music started up just after lunch.

I was in the middle of talking with Mr. Robichaux, a man older than my father who was very hesitant to let a woman do his taxes when my dad announced his retirement. I'm not exactly sure what he said, but Dad got Mr. Robichaux to keep his business with us, and I've done a pretty good job, if I do say so myself. But "Single Ladies," much as I and all the world love Beyoncé, wasn't a terrific soundtrack for Mr. Robichaux's tax filing, and the disapproving look on his face made that pretty clear.

I held up a finger. "Hang on one second. I'm sorry. Excuse me." I opened my door just enough to stick my head out so I could ask Mary to take care of the nuisance, but she was on the phone. With a sigh, I turned back to Mr. Robichaux, whose bushy gray eyebrows had formed a stormy V at the top of his nose. "I'll be right back."

The hallway was still an obstacle course of boxes, some stacked four or five high, and I wove my way around and between until I reached the door of the next office. The movers had obviously finished, but there were three people flitting around inside like worker bees. I knocked on the doorjamb, but nobody looked up from what they're doing, probably because they couldn't hear me over the music. There was a woman in the back corner putting things in the drawer of a desk. She was African American and looked to be in her mid-twenties from where I stood, her head bopping to the beat. The bottom half of what I could only assume was a guy stuck out facedown from underneath a table. The third person was a young man, tall and lanky with glasses and tousled dark hair in need of a trim. He was standing in front of the largest whiteboard I've ever seen, his hand closed around a variety of dry erase markers. None of the three noticed my presence.

"Excuse me," I said, raising my voice to be heard over the music, and finally the girl and the whiteboard guy looked in my direction. Under-the-table guy cracked his head loudly and dropped an F-bomb. The whiteboard guy approached me, his expression neutral.

"Can I help you?"

"Yeah, um, I'm in the office next door." I jerked a thumb over my shoulder. "I'm with a client and..." I glanced around for the source of the music, but couldn't find one. "The walls here are pretty thin..." I waited for him to catch up, but he simply blinked at me.

"The music, Brandon," the woman said, shaking her head. "I told you. Turn it down."

I nodded and shot her a grateful look.

"Oh. Sure. No problem. Sorry." The whiteboard guy moved to a computer, clicked the mouse a couple times, and Beyoncé quieted right down. Then he returned to his whiteboard without so much as a second glance at me.

"Okay," I said, because I could think of nothing else. Under-the-table guy was back, well, under the table. The woman in the corner gave me a smile, though, so at least one person in the room might not be an android, and I nodded at her. "Thanks."

Mary was still on the phone when I returned, Leo snoring loudly at her feet. I rolled my eyes when she looked at me and headed back to Mr. Robichaux, who had, thankfully, not left.

"I'm sorry about that," I said as I sat back down behind my desk. "New people are moving in next door."

Mr. Robichaux grunted in response, his usual reply to any sort of small talk, so I got right back to the numbers, which immediately helped me relax.

The rest of the afternoon flew by. There were no more disturbances from next door, aside from the occasional bump against the wall or slight shake of the floor as something heavy was obviously dropped. Sounds to be expected on moving day, I supposed. I could hear voices through the wall at times. Excited conversations. Laughter. One squeal (of delight?). There were definitely more than three people there at different stages of the day, but I was too busy to go introduce myself, especially since our first meeting had consisted of me complaining about their music. I preferred to wait for a fresh day.

Mary headed home at five thirty. Leo and I were there until almost eight. When we finally packed up our things and I shut the door behind me, the lights were still on next door, illuminating the hallway that was dimmed for the night. The music had gotten louder again over the past hour, but I really had no right to complain when it was after business hours. I gave Leo's leash a gentle tug, and as I stepped farther into the hall, I could see the office door, its window freshly logo'd.

Just Wright Marketing & Graphic Design

"Interesting," I said out loud, but that was the last thought I had, as my brain was fried from such a long day. Plus, I was starving. "Come on, Leo. Let's go home and find some dinner."

CHAPTER TWO

Tuesday morning dawned cold and rainy—so much for impending spring. I was already not in the greatest of moods when I braked slowly to a stop and simply stared at my usual row of parking spaces. No moving truck this morning, but there were four unfamiliar cars parked one next to the other in the row that was usually pretty empty. Except for the baby blue BMW convertible. That one was parked in my spot. And enough into the next spot over to prevent me from parking there either. A glance at the license plate told me immediately who I was to direct my silent anger toward.

JstRite

I shook my head. There were no assigned spots, so I didn't have any real reason to be mad. It just harkens back to my being a very structured person. I like routine. I find a parking spot I like, I park in it every day. Just like I have been for the past two years. It was my dad's unofficial spot. Now it's my unofficial spot.

With a shiny BMW in it.

"Looks like this Mr. Wright certainly knows how to make an impression," I said to Leo. Then I chuckled. I couldn't help it. "See what I did there, Leo? Mr. Wright? Funny, huh?" I chuckled some more at my own joke as I steered my Toyota two spaces down to a new spot, mentally challenging myself with facts and solutions. *If you get here earlier, you can probably snag your spot before Mr. Wright and his fancy car arrive for the day.* I snorted, which caused Leo to give me a look, because we all know I'm not coming in any earlier. Damn it.

I unclipped Leo from his seat belt, grasped his leash and my messenger bag—which bulged with work I'd taken home—and headed inside, hurrying through the rain and drenching one foot in a puddle I'd seen too late. I wasn't happy to find a piece of wood wedged in the door, keeping it open so I didn't have to use the security code. Not cool. I kicked the wood out and let the door shut completely. Once in the stairwell, Leo and I both took a moment to shake ourselves free of rain and to shiver against the low forties that the day wasn't getting out of, according to the cute meteorologist on the morning news. Then we headed up.

As soon as I opened the stairwell door to the second floor, my senses were assaulted. First, my ears cringed. I don't actually know if ears can cringe, but it sure felt like that's what mine were doing at the onslaught of Taylor Swift reverberating down the hall. Then my nose wrinkled at the smell of something unfamiliar, but…kind of yummy. Eggs? Bread? Not bacon, but something close. Ham?

The door to Chamberlain Financial was open, and I absently realized that might have to change from here on out if the music was going to be a regular occurrence. *Please don't let it be a regular occurrence.* Mary sat at her desk, a slice of what looked like pizza in her hand, a smile on her face as she munched away.

"Good morning, Lacey," she said in her ever-pleasant tone. Then, as usual, she devolved into baby talk as I let go of Leo's leash, and he bounded over to see her.

"You know," I said to my dog, "you could at least wait until I'm sitting at my own desk before you drop me like a hot potato for your mistress here."

Leo, of course, paid me no attention, his focus completely on whatever food Mary had.

"What is that?" I squinted. "Pizza? In the morning?"

"Breakfast pizza," Mary clarified. "Scrambled eggs, cheese, and diced ham. The new neighbors brought it over." She used the slice to gesture in the direction of the music.

"How long has the noise been going on?"

"Oh, that was on when I got here."

I inhaled slowly, then let it out. Was this how it was going to be now? I pointed at Leo, told him to stay, and headed down the hall with determined steps.

They'd done a ton of work since I'd been there thirteen or fourteen hours ago, and it stopped me in my tracks.

The first thing I noticed was color.

There was color everywhere. Bright. Cheerful. Lots of oranges and greens. All the laptops had colored covers. The chairs had red, blue, and hot pink seat cushions. The windows were wide open. Not open, but devoid of blinds, all of which had been pulled all the way up to let the daylight in. Despite the gray and rain, this space felt jovial and inviting. To my left, they'd set up a sort of food station with a large table covered in a lime green tablecloth, a mini fridge, a red Keurig, and two stacks of brightly colored coffee mugs. The breakfast pizza box was there as well, a stack of orange paper plates next to it.

In addition to the three people from yesterday, there were two more who seemed very busy. Another woman, a stunning redhead who was either talking on a Bluetooth or to herself and gesturing with big arm movements as she laughed at whatever she was hearing, and a handsome young man with thick, wavy dark hair any animated Disney prince would kill for. He squinted at an enormous computer monitor and never even looked in my direction. I wondered if he was Mr. Wright, and I pictured him in the BMW convertible, that mane of hair being tousled by the wind.

I was still taking it all in when the volume of the music decreased suddenly, and I looked over to see the woman from yesterday grimacing at me from a different desk than before.

"I'm so sorry," she said, as she crossed the room to me. "I told Brandon we have to keep it down, but he's in his own little world sometimes." She shot him a look as he paid us zero attention and rolled her eyes good-naturedly. "I'll do my best to keep the volume down during business hours."

"I'd really appreciate that," I said.

She stuck out her hand. "I'm Gisele. Gisele Harris."

I put my hand in hers. Her grip was firm and she paired it with a friendly smile. "Lacey Chamberlain."

"Oh, that's a great name. It's nice to meet you, Lacey." Her eyes moved to her right as she asked, "Are you hungry? There's breakfast pizza left."

"No. Thank you. I'm good." Gisele was nice enough, but I was still slightly aggravated that Brandon hadn't thought there might be others in the building who didn't want to rock out to his tunes first thing in the morning.

"Well, come on over if you change your mind," Gisele said.

"I'll do that." I cleared my throat. "Also, I'm not sure if it's you guys, but the door at the bottom of the stairs can't be propped open. It's for security purposes."

Gisele nodded. "I'll tell these guys."

"Thank you." I took one more look around, my eyes stopping on the redhead. She was still talking animatedly, but her large eyes were focused directly on me. Even through the black-rimmed glasses, I could almost feel her gaze. As she spoke to the person on the other end of her call, she raised an eyebrow and one side of her mouth quirked up as she continued to hold my gaze. Whether intended or not, it was very sensual. Sexy even, and I felt my face flush. Suddenly, I was roasting like a red pepper in my winter coat I hadn't taken off yet, and the sudden urge to flee hit me like a slap. I swallowed hard, gave a lame wave to Gisele, and hurried out of there as if a swarm of wasps were chasing me.

Back in the office, I took a deep breath and removed my coat. Leo looked up at me, chewing, and I gave Mary a look, silently telling her I knew she'd given him some of her pizza crust. She pretended not to see it.

The phone rang as I made myself a cup of coffee. Mary gave me a heads-up with her eyes. I headed back to my office, coffee in hand, dog dissing me yet again by staying with my secretary, and my day began.

A steady stream of phone calls, returns to file, and face-to-face appointments made my morning fly by, and the next thing I knew, it was nearly 1:00 p.m., and I was pretty sure my stomach was eating itself. I'd put nothing in it but coffee since the chicken salad sandwich I'd made at 9:00 last night.

I hit my intercom. "Mary, I'm going to order some lunch. Want anything?"

"Nope," she said, and it was obvious her mouth was full. "I'm good."

"Oh. All right." I dialed ChopStix, my favorite Chinese place and a number I had programmed into my contacts on my phone. Don't judge me.

"Hello, Miz Chamberlain. Your usual?" It always freaked me out at least a little bit when they knew who I was before I uttered a sound. Or that they knew what I ordered: chicken lo mein, steamed rice, two spring rolls.

"Yes, please, Julie." There was a bit of satisfaction knowing this would be either lunch and dinner or lunch for the next three days.

"Be there in twenty."

The whole conversation took less than two minutes. Efficiency at its finest.

It was a good time to relieve my poor bladder of the four cups of coffee that had been sitting there for far too long, and I headed out to Mary, who was in the middle of taking a bite out of what looked like a turkey sub from D'Amico's Italian Deli.

"When did you get lunch?" I asked, knowing if she'd left, she'd have stashed Leo in with me.

"I didn't," she said, holding a hand in front of her mouth as she chewed. "The new neighbors brought it over when they borrowed the bathroom key."

I furrowed my brow. "Doesn't that office have a bathroom?"

"It's not working."

"I see." I glanced at Leo, sitting at Mary's feet, watching her with laser-like focus. "Um, why does Leo have mayonnaise on his chin?"

"I have no idea," Mary said too quickly, not looking at me.

I shook my head. "You're going to lose visiting privileges, mister," I scolded him. He ignored me, like he always did when food was nearby. I headed for the door and noticed the empty nail on the wall. "Have they not brought the bathroom key back?" I asked.

"Oh. No, I guess not."

I sighed. *Fine. Back to the world of color, music, and endless food.*

Imagine Dragons was playing this time when I approached the door to Just Wright Marketing & Graphic Design, but at a tolerable level. The door was open, and the people inside flitted around like worker bees accomplishing various tasks. I rapped my knuckles on the doorjamb and the guy with Disney prince hair glanced my way, a thick, dark eyebrow raised in expectation. I decided to nip that in the bud by striding across the office, hand outstretched.

"Hi. Lacey Chamberlain. I'm in the office next door." I jerked my chin to my left.

Disney Prince looked momentarily confused by my introduction, but recovered quickly and shook my hand. "Patrick Cabello. Hi."

"You can call him Pantone," said Gisele from her back corner of the room. "Everybody else does."

"As in the color chart?" I asked, recalling something vague from a college art class I took forever ago.

Patrick—err—Pantone nodded. "Exactly." He returned his attention to his monitor, but Gisele was coming my way, so I didn't have to stand there like an idiot.

"Is the music too loud?" she asked me, a slight grimace crossing her pretty features.

"No, no, not at all," I assured her. "I'm actually here for my bathroom key. Somebody borrowed ours?" Gisele furrowed her brow, and I explained: "Each floor in the building has a couple of bathrooms, and they're designated to specific offices. So, you, me, and two other offices in this stretch share the one at the end of the hall." My eyes wandered to the door of theirs, back by Gisele's desk. "Until yours is fixed, I imagine. We all have a key to our designated restroom so random strangers from outside don't wander in to use the facilities, you know?"

Gisele nodded. "I get it, but I'm not sure who borrowed it. Pantone?" After a beat or two, she asked, "Did you borrow the bathroom key?" He shook his head, his eyes never leaving his monitor. "Brandon?" she called out. He was at the opposite corner of her desk. "Bathroom key?"

Apparently, eye contact was not big at Just Wright because he didn't look up either as he answered, "Alicia has it."

With a nod, Gisele said, "Hang on," and headed back to where I'd seen the redhead on the phone earlier. She was nowhere to be found now and Gisele made a show of looking under papers and folders, in drawers. Hands planted on the desk, she looked up at me with an expression of sympathy. "I'm going to guess she put it in her pocket and forgot she had it."

"Oh," I said, because what else could I say?

"I'm so sorry. She should be back in an hour or so…" Gisele let her voice trail off because it was obvious that she, too, wasn't sure what else to say.

I shrugged. "Okay, then. I'll try back later." I give a sort of half-smile because I wanted to remain friendly. It wasn't Gisele's fault the sexy redhead had left with my key. I headed down the hall to the stairwell on the other side of the wing. It took me down to Archer's Hardware. Bill would let me use his restroom. It was the least he could do to make up for the dozen times a month Nascar Kyle nearly killed me with his ridiculous car.

❖

I sat at my desk, eyeballing the remains of my Chinese food at 8:45 that night. Initially, I'd been trying to decide if I should heat it up in the microwave and work for another hour or pack it all up and go home before my brain short-circuited from overwork, leaving Mary to find my lifeless body in the morning. But now I didn't feel great, and even the thought of more lo mein did not make my stomach happy. I blinked at the containers across the room and wondered if I didn't feel well because I was hungry or because of what I'd eaten. *Eat? Don't eat?* It was a simple decision that shouldn't have taken more than a second or two, but I sat there, staring, squinting, decisionless.

I swallowed, feeling that slight, scratchy irritation that marked an impending sore throat. Which, for me, meant I was probably coming down with something. No wonder I was so tired.

A knock on the door of my office startled me out of my health analysis, making me realize that I'd left the door ajar. I always close it when I'm there after hours. Despite the keypad at the entrances to the building, it's not hard to get in, as evidenced by the propped-open door that morning. I must not have latched it properly, and it swung open before I could even get to my feet.

There stood the redhead from next door, her hair falling around her shoulders in waves the color of the sunset, her black pantsuit with the jacket sleeves rolled up to just below her elbows making her look like she'd just gotten dressed instead of it being long past business hours. The glasses were missing, which only served to amplify the blue of her eyes. In her arms was Leo, looking just as happy as he could possibly be.

"What the hell?" I said, and jumped up from my chair. "How... what...?"

The redhead chuckled from somewhere deep in her throat as she turned her face to my dog and he licked her nose. "I was working and looked down to see I had a visitor," she said. "Honestly, he scared the crap out of me at first. I thought it was a raccoon or something. I'm surprised you didn't hear me squeal like a little girl."

"I'm so sorry," I said, taking him from her arms and trying not to notice his reluctance. The redhead smelled amazing, though, like peaches and cream, so I couldn't really blame him.

"It's no trouble at all. I met him earlier when I borrowed your bathroom key, which…" She reached into the pocket of the black blazer and pulled out the key, let it dangle from her long fingers. "I then took off with. My apologies." She wrinkled her nose and made a face that would make me look silly, but only made her seem fun.

I took the key and tossed it onto my desk, then turned to kiss on my dog, horrified that I hadn't even noticed he was missing. I was way too tired.

"He's got some great energy, that little guy. I might need to borrow him in the future for brainstorming sessions."

I had no idea if she was serious, but before I could say a thing—thank her, introduce myself, speak in tongues because I was too tired to remember my base language—her cell phone rang. She pulled it from the pocket of her blazer and glanced at the screen.

"Sorry, I've got to take this." With a wave, she hurried out the door as I heard her call a cheerful greeting into the phone.

I stood there staring after her, for longer than I needed to, stuck in a trance of fatigue. Finally, I stepped to the door and closed it with a click, then set Leo down.

"Dude, seriously?" I said to him as he looked up at me with the sweet brown eyes that won me over when I first saw him at the shelter. "You can't just leave like that." Leo cocked his head to the side as if thinking this over. "I'm not kidding. You could get lost. You could get hurt. You could give Mommy a stroke."

I gathered my things as I scolded him, having decided I was just too exhausted to look at any more numbers. I fastened Leo into his harness, slung my bag over my shoulder, and hung the bathroom key back up. Then I locked up the office. In the hall, I could hear the redhead talking animatedly with whoever was on the other end of the phone, speaking a bit louder than regular volume, as people tended to do on cell phones. It sounded like an early morning business call, her voice fresh and energetic. I tried to tamp down my envy as I fought the temptation to peek in the open door, see who else was in there; I could make out the low hum of another conversation happening as well, but my exhaustion won out.

"Come on, Leo, before Mommy falls asleep right here on the floor." I'd had enough for one day, and whatever creeping crud I had was going to take over much faster if I didn't get some rest. Leo and I drove home, I made some tea and downed a handful of cold medicine. I should have eaten, but my stomach eighty-sixed that idea. Instead, I crawled into bed and Leo curled up in the crook of my knees, his usual spot. I glanced at the clock. It wasn't even ten yet, so I hoped a full eight or nine hours of sleep would head this cold off at the pass.

Wishful thinking.

CHAPTER THREE

When my alarm went off at seven the next morning, I was pretty sure somebody had snuck in during the night and stuffed my head full of cotton. I squeezed my eyes shut, my face in my pillow, and willed the alarm to be a dream sound. Maybe it was really only two in the morning, and I could sleep for several more hours.

Leo's warm and wet kisses told me it was no dream. It was morning, I had six clients to meet with today, and I was definitely sick. I sat up slowly and Leo cuddled in close, pushed his wet nose against my neck. "Good morning, little guy," I croaked, wincing, my throat on fire.

This was the worst time of year for me to be sick, and I grumbled in annoyance about it the entire time I got ready. A hot shower helped a little bit, but I wanted to stand in it for hours, not minutes. I had no desire to style my hair or put makeup on, but I did both, not wanting to scare away clients with my Death Warmed Over look. I made tea instead of coffee, chose the strongest English breakfast tea I had, as I needed the caffeine, but also something to soothe my throat. A touch of honey helped, but not enough.

It was going to be a long day.

Like yesterday, the day was gray, damp, chilly. I longed for spring, especially when I didn't feel well and wanted nothing more than to burrow under my down comforter and go back to sleep. But it wasn't quite spring yet, and I had too much work to do to even think about taking a sick day. I turned in to my office parking lot, and as I lamented my sad, sad life, Nascar Kyle cut off the guy in front of me, causing him to slam on his brakes, which made me slam on mine. Leo gave a little yelp as he was thrown forward but stopped short by his seat belt. My front bumper was a scant inch or two from the rear bumper in front of me. I glanced up to see the other driver looking at me in his rearview mirror. He gave a little wave of apology, and I waved back my forgiveness.

"Not your fault, sir," I said aloud in my empty car. "Welcome to my world."

Again, the baby blue BMW was in my spot, but I had no energy to muster up any anger. "Stupid Mr. Wright," I muttered instead, then shrugged. I parked four spots down from my usual, gathered my things and my dog, and headed inside.

Mary was just biting into a delicious-looking cherry cheese Danish when she looked up at me and her face fell. "Wow. You look awful," she said.

"Gee, thanks."

"You sick?" She set her pastry on a small paper plate. A glance at our little coffee area told me we had neither those plates nor tasty-looking Danishes.

"Unfortunately, yes." I gestured at her plate as I removed Leo's harness and he zipped right over to hop into Mary's lap. "Where'd you get that?"

Unsurprisingly, she jerked her chin toward the far wall. "They needed the bathroom key again." She smiled as she looked down at her lap where Leo sat, watching intently as she chewed.

"Don't give him any of that," I ordered, pointing at her.

She made a face that said, "Please. Who do you think you're dealing with?" But I knew her, and I fully expected to find Leo with cream cheese on his face later.

In my office, I dumped everything on the floor next to my desk and fell back into my chair, my body feeling as exhausted as if I'd been there for ten hours already. I allowed myself three minutes to just breathe, but that was it. My first client was due any minute, and I needed to prepare. She was new, a referral from a longtime client, and I wanted to make a good first impression. I hauled my ass up out of my chair and straightened up the office. Then I called up her information on my computer and was ready when Mary buzzed me.

"Lacey? Sharon Antonelli is here for her appointment."

"Great. Send her back."

I loved when we did the intercom thing. It was so professional (and so unnecessary, as we were barely twenty feet apart, but whatever. It was fun). I stood up and met Sharon Antonelli at the door of my office, my hand outstretched. She grasped it firmly and we shook.

"It's so nice to meet you," I said. "Please. Sit." I gestured to the two chairs across from my desk.

"Well, Richard Bell speaks very highly of you." Sharon Antonelli was in her fifties, maybe, well-dressed and very put together. In her simple yet elegant gray pencil skirt and burgundy silk top, she gave off an air of sophistication. Of class. She was an independent contractor for the ad agency she worked for, so she had expenses and things to itemize. Over the phone, she'd told me she could probably manage to file on her own, but simply didn't want to deal with it. Her previous CPA had retired last year, so here she was.

"Richard's great," I said, as I took my own seat behind my desk. "He was a client of my father's and then when my dad retired, he trusted me to take over. So, I speak very highly of him as well." I hit a couple keys on my computer. "Okay, let's talk about your expen—" My sentence was completely obliterated by an obnoxiously loud whirring sound coming from the other side of the wall behind Sharon Antonelli. She turned to look as I squinted.

What the hell? I thought, but kept it to myself, as I didn't think swearing around my new client was a smart move. Abruptly, the sound stopped.

Sharon turned to look at me, her perfectly tweezed eyebrows raised up in question.

"I have no idea," I said. "I apologize."

We got back down to work. A good five minutes went by before it happened again, catching both of us off guard enough to make us jump in our chairs.

I sighed quietly and held out a placating hand toward her. "Please excuse me for one minute." Determination in my steps, I walked out of my office, through Mary's area—both she and Leo looked up at me in surprise—and out in to the hall. The door to Just Wright Marketing & Graphic Design was standing open, because of course it was, and I didn't bother knocking. Nobody would hear me over what sounded like the sound of a jet taking off. Instead, I marched all the way to the back of the office where the whiteboard hung on the wall shared with my office. The redhead, Brandon, and Pantone Patrick were all standing around a card table they'd apparently set up. On it were bowls of fruit, sliced or chunked or whatever, a pitcher of orange juice, and a large container of yogurt. In the middle of it all stood a blender, one of those high-end ones that could make a steak into a milkshake if you ran it long enough.

"Excuse me," I said loudly, but not loudly enough, as nobody even looked my way. I tried again, louder, pretty sure the combination of my shouting and the chainsaw-like screaming of the blender was about to make my head explode.

The redhead noticed me then, and her blue eyes widened in surprise. She immediately hit a button that turned the blender off, and the ensuing quiet was bliss. "Hi there," she said, unassuming. I simply blinked at her as my ears adjusted to the change in sound. Undeterred, she smiled, accentuating the cleft in her chin and the perfection of her cheekbones, which I would've taken time to notice if I didn't feel like I just wanted to lie down and go to sleep. She wore a bright lime-green top that was perfect against her creamy skin and sunset hair. "We have to come up with a pitch for marketing this thing," she indicated the blender with one hand, "so we're making smoothies. Want one?" She held up a glass filled with what I wanted to admit was a delicious-looking pink concoction—strawberries, maybe?—but I was too frustrated at the cluelessness of the three of them.

"No," I said. "No, I do not want a smoothie." I swallowed as I walked toward their whiteboard and put my palm against it. "This wall," I said, and had to clear the frog out of my throat, "is shared with my office. This one." I patted it. "Right here." Another pat. "Shared wall." I moved my hand to my forehead, massaged it with my fingertips. "Over there, right now, on the other side of this *very thin* shared wall, sitting in a chair in my office, is a new client who wants me to do her taxes for her. I'm hoping maybe I can talk to her about some investments as well. But thanks to your eardrum-busting blender, I can't hear a thing she's saying to me. Not a word. So, what I *do* want is for you to please, *please* keep it down." My head was throbbing, as if a little man was inside my skull and going to town with a sledgehammer, and I just kept talking. "First my parking space. Then the security door. I've asked more than once about the music. Now the blender. This is a place of business, and

I don't think I'm asking a lot." I took a breath and adjusted my voice so that it was less irritated and more of a plea before I added, "Look, I don't want to have to ask to talk to the guy who owns this company, but I will if I have to."

Brandon gave a snort, which had my eyes snapping up to glare at him as he smiled and looked away. Pantone Patrick was gazing at his shoes. I couldn't be sure, but he seemed to be hiding a grin as well. The redhead, however, gave me direct eye contact as she held out her hand.

"We haven't been properly introduced," she said, her voice calm, a subtle smile on her face. "Alicia Wright. The guy who owns this company."

Yeah, I know. I should've seen that one coming.

I stared at her outstretched hand, and wrapped a hunk of my hair around my forefinger to twirl, a habit I'd had since I was a kid. As I felt my face heat up, I closed my eyes and slowly shook my pounding head back and forth, then put my right hand in hers. "I'm so sorry," I croaked. "I…" I shook my head again, no words springing forth to help me dig my way out of this.

Alicia Wright, on the other hand, seemed perfectly comfortable with the situation. Of course, why wouldn't she be? *She* hadn't embarrassed herself. Nope. Just me. Suddenly, the inconsideration of the loud noises didn't really compare to my automatic assumption that this company would be run by a man. What kind of feminist was I anyway? What kind of lesbian?

A lousy one, the little voice in my head replied.

"I sincerely apologize for the noise…" Alicia Wright let her sentence dangle and was looking at me expectantly, my hand still held warmly in hers. It took me longer than it should have to recognize she was asking my name.

"Oh. Lacey. Lacey Chamberlain."

"I'm so sorry, Ms. Chamberlain. We're not used to sharing office space, so it's taking us some getting used to. I promise we'll try to be better." Reaching around with her other hand, she picked up a clear plastic tumbler full of that pink smoothie. "And if you don't mind my saying, you look like you could use some extra vitamins today." Before I realized what she was doing, she'd let go of my hand and her own had drifted up to my face where she gently brushed some of my hair off my forehead. "You look really exhausted," she said, and her voice was soft, seeming to hold genuine concern as she handed me the cup.

Too mortified to analyze any further—or let her continue to touch me because that was weird and awesome at the same time—I muttered one more apology, turned on my heel, and fled that office as quickly as I could. My heart was pounding and my head felt foggy, but for different reasons than my cold. It wasn't until I was safely back in my own space, standing in front of Mary's desk, that I noticed I had the smoothie in my hand.

"Oooh, that looks good," Mary commented, and I set the cup on her desk without another word. Thank God, Sharon Antonelli was still sitting across from my desk. I literally shook my head to rid it of everything that had just happened—not a great idea, given the head cold from hell—and headed back into my office.

Sharon Antonelli sat where I'd left her, scrolling on her phone. She glanced up at me, her face open and friendly. "Mystery solved?" she asked.

"High-speed blender. They're a marketing firm, and I guess the blender company is their client."

Sharon nodded as if this type of thing occurred every day in her office. "I want one of those things. A friend of mine has one and makes a shake using kale and bananas, but it just tastes like bananas. Kale is so good for you, but that's the only way I'll eat it."

"If it tastes like bananas?" I asked with a grin.

"If it tastes like anything that's not kale."

We both laughed and then got back to her taxes. The blender remained quiet.

The rest of my day was nonstop, and thankfully, there were no more sounds of rockets launching or dance parties or firecrackers going off next door, so I chalked it up as a win for me, even though a small sliver of shame still held on in the back of my mind. My head continued to stuff throughout the day, and by four o'clock, I was pretty sure it weighed more than the rest of my body. Keeping it upright on my neck took massive effort on my part. I downed another dose of cold meds, wanting desperately to go home but knowing there was no way. I had so much to get done and not enough time or energy to do it.

I had two evening appointments still to go and I wasn't at all sure how I was going to pull that off. A knock sounded on my door, and before I could call for the visitor to enter, the door opened.

"I heard you were under the weather." Leanne Markham stood in my doorway, a white plastic bowl in one hand. Her dark hair was pulled back in her daily ponytail, her lab coat peeking out from under her jacket.

"And how did you hear that? Are you psychic now?"

"Sadly, no, but I know how to get information out of your secretary."

Mary's "ha ha" came from the outer office, and I smiled.

"Come in," I said, waving to the empty chairs. "I've got some time before my next client."

"I'm going to guess you've eaten next to nothing today, so I ran home and grabbed some of this for you." She set the bowl on the desk in front of me and peeled away the lid. The steamy gloriousness of Leanne's chicken soup wafted up, and I closed my eyes, trying to sniff but failing miserably. "I made it last night." She pulled a spoon from her pocket and handed it to me. "Eat."

She didn't have to tell me twice. I dug in, surprised that it was hot, but also not surprised. Leanne was a caretaker.

We'd been together once. It lasted for nearly two years. More than dating, but we never managed to get any further along than simply talking about the future. We never lived together, but we spent time at each other's places and that worked for a while. As fate would have it, our individual businesses took off at the same time. My dad retired, and I took over his company. Leanne is a doctor, a general practitioner, and she hit the ground running with her practice. We had trouble finding time for each other. Actually, no. That's not quite the truth. We had trouble *making* time for each other, Leanne more so than me. When I finally called her on it, she told me that she thought we'd make better friends than partners. When I asked her why, she said it was obvious that I was too routine and set in my ways to make that significant a change. "It takes so much effort to pull you an inch out of your comfort zone, Lace."

I wanted to argue with her, I really did. But instead, I agreed with her. Because she was right. I spent several weeks crying over the fact that what she really, indirectly, had said was I was boring. I never mentioned that to her, but it's what I'd heard. Took us a while, but our friendship held on and grew stronger, and now she was one of my closest confidantes. Weird, I know.

Leanne grabbed a seat and watched me eat for a moment before asking, "So what's new?"

I shook my head, savoring a bite of soup before swallowing it, a little surprised I could even taste it but grateful that I could. "Just busy."

"It's that time of year for you, and I'm sure you're working way too many hours, which is why you're sick now."

"Yes, Doctor. I'm aware."

"You need to pay more attention to what you eat, Lace."

"I know."

I was saved from further scolding by a loud sound that shook the floor, like something very heavy had fallen. Leanne's eyebrows went up just as I heard a muffled, "Sorry!" come from the other side of the wall. Alicia, I was pretty sure, and I didn't mean to, but I grinned.

"What the hell was that?" Leanne asked, turning in her chair.

"My new neighbors."

"They finally filled that office, huh? I didn't think they ever would. How long's it been empty now?"

"Over a year. Year and a half, maybe?"

"Who moved in?"

"A marketing and graphics company. A loud one. They're young and hip and they like to work to music and make smoothies and they eat like pigs. And they're loud. It's like Google moved in next door."

Leanne just blinked at me for a beat before asking, "What are you, eighty-seven years old? They sound fun. I want to work there."

With a groan, I let my head drop down a bit. "I know. I'm so bad."

Leanne's chuckle made me feel the tiniest bit better. "No, you're not. You're just routine and set in your ways, my friend. You don't like change."

I opened my mouth to argue, but Leanne's expression looked almost like a dare, and I shut my face. She was right and we both knew it. Which didn't mean I was unfun. Did it?

My intercom buzzed and Mary told me my next appointment had arrived.

Leanne stood to leave, shaking her head with a grin. "That intercom still cracks me up. She's literally *right there*."

"Hey, we run a professional operation around here. Intercoms are professional." I snapped the lid back onto the now-empty bowl and handed it to her. "Thank you so much. I needed that."

"You're welcome." Leanne took the bowl and kissed me on the head. "Don't work too late tonight. Go home and get some rest."

I almost said, "Yes, Mom," but that was never a thing that went over well with Leanne, as she was fifteen years my senior—another aspect of why we didn't work—and had never found it funny to have our age difference pointed out in jest. Instead, I smiled and said simply, "I will." I followed her out and greeted my next clients, the Carlsons, a newly married couple who'd come directly from their jobs, judging by the business attire they were both wearing. I directed them to head into my office and have a seat as Mary stood and donned her coat.

"I'll see you in the morning," she told me, then added as an afterthought, "Oh. Leo is next door."

My eyes flew open wide. "Wait, what?"

"Yeah, he loves that redheaded woman. What is her name again?" She gazed at the ceiling.

"Alicia," I supplied.

"Yes! Alicia. Every time Alicia comes to borrow the bathroom key, he runs right over to her. She says he's got great energy. He followed her out earlier, and when I called him, she said not to worry, that he was fine and she'd bring him back later. She's so nice. I like her." With a little wave, she was out the door, leaving me standing there absorbing the fact that my neighbor had "borrowed" my dog without my permission.

I marched my ass right out into the hall, down it, and stopped in front of the closed door of Just Wright Marketing & Graphic Design, which had been painted a bright and cheerful red in the past day or two. I could see through the glass, around the logo. Four people were seated around a table in front of the enormous whiteboard. Alicia was standing in front of it, pointing with a marker and saying something I couldn't hear. Leo was in her arms and looked stupidly happy to be there. Alicia said something, Leo gave a little yip, and the people seated all laughed. I couldn't help it. I smiled.

"All right," I said to the empty hall. "It's okay." I could admit to myself that I was a little jealous Leo was so happy at Just Wright, but he's a social guy who loves to be around people, and people love him. And I had the Carlsons waiting for me. I headed back to my office, making sure to leave all the doors open so I could see straight out into the hall from my desk chair. I sat down, shot one last glance toward the hall, then turned my focus to my clients.

Two hours later, I had made it through both client meetings and had at least made a small dent in the pile of work I needed to finish by the weekend. But I was exhausted. Leanne's chicken soup was long gone, and I knew I should eat something—should have eaten something way before now—but my stomach again felt a little wonky. I set my pen down, propped my elbows on my desk, and let my face rest in my hands.

When I registered the gentle tap on the doorjamb, it took me a moment to comprehend whether I'd actually fallen asleep. I didn't think so, but wasn't totally sure. I looked up at Alicia Wright in her black-rimmed glasses, Leo in her arms. I could see his tiny nub of a tail sticking out from behind her bicep, wiggling like crazy.

"Well, hello there, my tiny guy," I said, ridiculously happy to see his furry face. Alicia set him down and he ran to me—the best feeling in the world, really. He leapt up into my lap before I had a chance to bend down and grab him, and he put his front paws up on my chest so he could lavish my face with his kisses. "I missed you," I said to him, devolving into baby talk before I realized it. "Yes, I did. Yes, I did." A couple moments of this went by before it occurred to me that Alicia was still here. A glance in her direction showed me that she was leaning against the door frame, arms folded across her chest, an expression of sheer amusement on her face.

"I hope you don't mind that I borrowed him," she said. "Mary said you wouldn't, so…" She let her voice trail off. "He's just so adorable and was terrific for our brainstorming session."

I continued loving my dog as I listened. "I was a little surprised," I said honestly. "But it's fine, as long as you keep your door closed. Otherwise, he might bolt."

Alicia said, "Oh," and gave a quick nod. We both sort of blinked at each other for a beat until she pushed off the door frame, stood up straight, and said, "Come have a drink with us." It was as though she'd blurted out a secret, because we both looked kind of surprised.

"I'm sorry?"

She jerked a thumb over her shoulder in the direction of her office. "We've had a long day over there and we're going to go out for drinks. A lot of times we do that right in the office, but we all feel like we need to get out of here, you know? You've been here as long as I have today. Come with us."

"Oh, no," I said immediately. "I've got more work to do. And then I need to go home." I unintentionally punctuated that with a cough. "Thank you, though." Was that an expression of disappointment that zipped across her face? I wasn't sure.

"You do sound pretty stuffy. I bet a shot of whiskey would help." She gave me a wink.

"So would a shot of NyQuil," I responded with a grin.

"Whiskey would taste a hell of a lot better."

I was shocked to feel myself wavering. "You make a fine point," I said, although I didn't actually enjoy the taste of whiskey, so I'm not sure why I said it except…Alicia.

"We're just going to that place down the sidewalk a bit. Boomer's, is it?"

Boomer's was a quick two-minute walk, and I could easily lock Leo in the office for a bit. There was something about Alicia, something about her face, her demeanor, that tugged at me. I held up a finger. "One. Only one drink."

I thought she'd already been smiling but was quickly proven wrong when her entire face lit up. Those blue eyes sparkled; it was obvious, even behind the sexy glasses. "Fantastic! The others already headed down. Let me go lock up and I'll meet you in the hall." And she was gone.

"This is a terrible idea," I said quietly to Leo, as I looked at all the work scattered across my desk. Leo cocked his head at me and I kissed his nose. "But I'm still going. You stay here and hold down the fort, okay? I won't be long."

He had everything he needed, so I left the lights on, stuffed several tissues into my purse, and locked both doors behind me.

Alicia came out her own door at the same time and we smiled

down the hall at each other. For a brief instant, I had a vision of the two of us in high school, standing at our individual lockers, tossing glances at one another without anybody around us noticing. I tried not to stare as Alicia walked toward me, but I had to force my own eyes away and I pretended to be engrossed by the ring of keys in my hand. So interesting, they were!

"Ready?"

I nodded and followed her down the stairs and out into the chilly evening.

Turned out it was karaoke night at Boomer's. Which meant it was super loud. The guy singing "You're So Vain" couldn't possibly have been more off-key. I actually did a little stutter step in the doorway, as if my head was revolting and physically yanked my body to a halt. But Alicia's warm hand slid down my arm and closed around my wrist, and she pulled me gently toward her and pressed her lips near my ear.

"Just one," she said.

I nodded. A) I'd made a promise, and B) her proximity was doing things to me. I couldn't have left if I'd wanted to. I followed her, noticing she had yet to let go of my wrist, and we stopped at a round table where the rest of Just Wright sat. Alicia directed me into the chair next to Gisele, then headed toward the bar. I watched as she found a spot and squeezed in. The man to her right immediately turned on his stool and struck up a conversation with her. She smiled widely, genuinely, and spoke back.

Fun fact about me: I have zero gaydar. It's true. Unless somebody is a walking stereotype, I'm never really sure which team they play on, and with Alicia, it was especially difficult because she was touchy. That tended to tip the scales for me. But they could be tipped just as easily in the other direction. So Alicia practically touched her lips to my ear and she almost held my hand on our way in. The scales tip. Then she goes to the bar and a man obviously flirts with her and she obviously flirts back. Scales tip the other way.

"How are you feeling?" Gisele's voice pulled me back to the table and out of my own head.

"Like my head weighs three hundred pounds."

"Oh, man. I'm sorry. But I'm glad you're here." Her smile was sweet and friendly and it occurred to me that probably nobody ever met Gisele without liking her immediately.

Alicia returned with two whiskeys, neat, and set one in front of me, then sat in the chair to my left. She held up her glass until I picked up my own. "To the end of your cold."

"I'll drink to that."

We clinked glasses and I sipped. I hate whiskey. Did I mention that? It's awful stuff, like lighter fluid burning its way down my throat. It doesn't really taste any better than NyQuil, to be honest. But I know it's good for what ails you, as my grandma would say. And also, the fact that it was suggested by and then purchased by Alicia made it somehow more palatable. Not much, but a little.

Alicia made a face as she swallowed her drink, and I grinned at her.

"Why are we drinking whiskey?" I asked, raising my voice over the girl singing "I Will Survive" so Alicia could hear me.

"Because you're sick and this is supposed to help." She held up her glass.

"You're not sick. Why are you drinking it?"

"I like it."

I laughed. "No, you don't."

"No, I don't. But I didn't want you to drink it alone." Her smile was soft.

"That might be the sweetest thing anybody's ever said to me."

Alicia's eyebrows went up. "You need to get out more, my friend." She bumped me with a shoulder and suddenly, I didn't feel so sick.

Wait. No, that's not true. I still felt sick. But I also felt…happy being out with these people. Happy being out with Alicia. I'd stepped out of my comfort zone of routine and the world hadn't crumbled. On the contrary, I found myself actually having fun.

"Tell me about how you got Leo," Alicia said, pulling me out of my head and scooting her chair closer to me. Suddenly, all I could smell was that peaches-and-cream scent of hers.

"Well." I took another sip of the whiskey because, despite the unpleasant taste, I was starting to feel warm inside and my throat didn't hurt quite so much. "I'd been single for a while, living on my own. We had a dog when I was a teenager, but he died when I was twenty-three and my parents didn't want another. I wasn't ready for one of my own at that time either. But about two years ago, I started thinking about it. I knew I wanted something small—my place isn't that big—but wasn't sure where to start. I visited a local shelter just to get a feel for how it's done."

Alicia shook her head as she grinned. "Yeah, I can't do that."

I furrowed my brow. "What? Rescue?"

"No. 'Visit' a shelter." She made air quotes around the word "visit." "I would end up bringing them all home."

"Yeah, well, Leo was there and I had to have him. It was the weirdest thing."

"Really? How so?"

I thought about it, sipped the whiskey as I tried to recall that day in detail. "It was like he was mine. Like he was already mine and was just waiting for me to come get him."

Alicia propped an elbow on the table and leaned her head against her hand. "That is *so cool.*"

"It really took me by surprise."

"I'm not kidding when I say he has great energy. Everything gives it off, but some more than others, and some have more positive energy than others. That's why I snagged him earlier. He's great for creativity. I have no idea why."

"You have any pets?" I asked, realizing I knew next to nothing about Alicia Wright.

She shook her head and her red hair bounced lightly. "My schedule's kind of crazy."

"Yeah, that can make it hard. I lucked out with Leo being okay in my office. Perks of being your own boss, right?"

"Definitely." Alicia held up her glass and we clinked again, then each emptied our glasses.

"Speaking of, I should go get my boy and finish up some work." I didn't want to leave, but the responsible part of me had somehow escaped her binds and gag and was now poking at the part of me that yearned to stay right here, right now, with this woman.

Alicia earned extra points by not trying to stop me. "I'd love for you to stay, but I know you've got stuff to do. You promised one, and you kept your promise. Thank you for that."

That soft smile again. God, she was beautiful.

"Thank you for the invite. Sometimes I need a nudge."

"I'm making a mental note."

"Uh-oh."

Our gazes held as I stood. I turned to the rest of the group and waved my good-byes, feeling the tiniest bit rude for not having conversed with them at all. Next time.

I'm pretty sure I wore a stupid grin the entire walk back to my office, even as I coughed like an organ was about to come up. I hadn't had that good a time in longer than I could come up with, and I tried to ignore the fact that I was mentally making a list of reasons I might have to see Alicia tomorrow...

Chapter Four

By that Sunday, I was actually starting to feel somewhat human again. I lounged on my parents' couch with a glass of Sauvignon Blanc and alternately chatted with my dad and watched him watch MSNBC. Well, mutter at MSNBC was a more accurate description of what he was doing. I rarely caught a whole sentence, but heard lots of "Sons of bitches" and "Hell in a handbasket, this country."

I sipped my wine, then called out, "Mom, can I help?"

"Nope. You just relax right there. You're finally feeling better. Don't jinx it. Drink your wine and talk to your father. I'm fine." I never saw her—the dining room was in my line of sight, and the kitchen was around a corner from that—but I could hear her just fine, along with the sounds of dishes clattering and pans being moved. I could picture her flitting around the kitchen like a pro in her yoga pants and tunic top, humming to herself or to the little satellite radio she has on the counter. She tended to zero in on one musical artist at a time and then play the crap out of them nonstop until she moved on to the next. She was currently on Adele, which I didn't mind at all. She actually had a Nicki Minaj phase not too long ago. That was...weird.

"Leo," I called to my dog. "Are you bothering Grandma?"

"He's fine," my mom responded. "Leave him be."

I grinned and took a sip of my wine.

"You take care of Robichaux?" my father asked, snapping me out of my reverie. His eyes never left the TV, but he was listening.

"Yes. Earlier in the week. That man does not like me."

"That man doesn't like anybody. You're not special." He glanced at me then, and I caught the twinkle in those blue eyes of his that I am continually annoyed I didn't inherit. My stupid older brother got them, though. *So* not fair. "Everything else going okay? You need help? I know you've been sick. Don't let anybody slip through the cracks."

"Leave her alone, John," my mother said as she brought a stack of plates out and set them on the dining room table. "She's got it under control."

"I know she does," my dad said, a tiny hint of defensiveness in his tone. "I'm just asking."

"She doesn't need you to ask. She's got it."

I grinned at my mom and mouthed a *thanks*.

She blew me a kiss and went back into the kitchen.

"Don't worry, Dad. It's all good. I've kept up with all my appointments, even with this cold." I didn't tell him I'd almost fainted on Friday and Mary forced me to pack up my things so she could drive me home. I was kind of surprised she hadn't called him and told him herself, but I think over the past couple of years, her loyalty has shifted from him to me, especially once I proved I was able to run the place on my own.

"I can send your brother if you need help."

"No," I said, too quickly, and my dad looked at me. "I'm fine. I don't need any help." My brother Scott and I were so very different in so many ways, it was often hard to believe we had the same genes. We were very different physically—he's got sandy hair and those damn blue eyes and he's a very tall 6'4"; I have dark hair and dark eyes and I'm a very average 5'5". Both our parents have light hair and my mom's eyes are hazel, so Scott took great delight in spending our childhood trying to convince me I was adopted. I believed him on more than one occasion, as little sisters tend to do.

My big brother is spontaneous, a fly-by-the-seat-of-your-pants kind of guy who tends to put himself first, one of his few bad traits. Don't get me wrong; he's a good guy and he's crazy smart. I've always wanted to be like him. I mean, doesn't every little girl want a big brother who's tall and gorgeous and looks out for his younger sister, *and* want to follow in his footsteps a bit? Like I said, though, we're really not that much alike at all. I'm okay with that.

But it doesn't mean I need his help running my business.

"He's good with numbers," my dad was saying. "You know

he is. He could blow through a stack of those returns like there's no tomorrow."

I made myself count to five before saying, in a very controlled voice, "Thanks, Dad. I appreciate the offer, but I'm fine. I don't need Scott's help."

My dad grunted, and I wasn't sure if it was directed at me or the television.

"Honey?" my mom called to me, saving me from more of this frustration. "I can use you now."

I jumped off the couch like it was an ejector seat and took my wine into the kitchen to help my mom.

"You did good," she said, as she pointed at the refrigerator. "Get the salad dressings out."

"Thanks."

I helped set the table and the three of us sat down. My parents are a little old-fashioned—well, actually, it's my mother—and Sunday dinner has always been a thing for us. Ever since I can remember, we've been together on Sunday afternoon, eaten a late lunch/early dinner together, and just had some family time. As Scott and I got older and started to develop our own lives and relationships, we drifted away from Sunday dinner. But over the past six or eight months, I've been doing my best to show up. It makes my mom ridiculously happy, so it's worth it.

"Somebody finally moved into that empty office next door," I told my dad as I forked a slice of chicken breast onto my plate. I could feel Leo under the table, lying across my foot.

"Yeah? About damn time." Dad made a crater in his mashed potatoes and filled it with gravy. "What kind of company?"

"Marketing and graphic design."

"Big? That's a pretty roomy office."

"Five or six people, it seems," I said, trying to count up Alicia and her staff in my head. "They're nice enough. Kind of noisy, though."

Dad grunted as he chewed. "You got too used to having that space empty."

"I so did," I agreed with a chuckle. I gave them the rundown of the less-than-ideal issues we'd hit over the past week, starting with the parking and ending with Leo being a traitor. Strangely, I felt more and more petty the longer the list grew.

"Leo can't help it if everybody loves him," my mother said, and I felt him leave my foot at the mention of his name, almost certainly moving over to my mother's feet instead. "It's not his fault."

"I know," I said, and told them how Alicia had borrowed him on several occasions.

"Just be a good neighbor, Lacey. It doesn't take any work." My mom was pretty easily the kindest, sweetest person I'd ever known—which was mostly awesome, but once in a while frustrating because she always, *always* sees the good in people first. That means she can get her heart hurt quite easily. I've spent much of my life making sure she stays insulated from the awful parts of humanity if I can help it.

"I know, Mom. I'm doing my best."

❖

Thank God my cold only held on for a week and change. By Thursday of the following week, I was feeling infinitely better, with only a bit of residual stuffiness in my head. As long as I stayed hydrated, the headaches left me alone.

Until I headed to the waiting area to get my next client and found my path almost completely blocked by a stack of boxes as tall as me. No—three stacks, I realized, as I sidled past them so I could see Mrs. Harrington sitting in a chair, a manila folder on her lap, waiting patiently for me.

"Mary, what the hell is all this?" I whispered.

Mary was typing away on her keyboard, glanced up, then returned to her screen as she spoke. "Those are for next door. There's nobody there right now, so they told UPS to leave them here when their door is locked."

I poked the inside of my cheek with my tongue. "So now we get to run an obstacle course in our office until they decide to come back and get their stuff?" I muttered, my tone still low, so as to keep Mrs. Harrington from hearing. "Terrific." When Mary didn't respond, I looked her way and noticed the plate on her desk. "Where'd you get the pizza?"

"Alicia brought it over earlier," she said absently.

"Mm-hmm." I had to admit it was kind of brilliant. Just Wright Marketing & Graphic Design was bribing my secretary with food.

Constantly and consistently. And she was letting them. "Would you please stick a Post-it on their door and ask them to come get their boxes as soon as they return?"

"Will do." Mary's voice was cheerful, and I shook my head and tried to hide my grin.

"Mrs. Harrington?" My client looked up at me and I smiled. She was a favorite of mine, in her third year as a widow but always smiling. She told me after her husband had passed that she couldn't bring herself to be too sad because that would overshadow the fifty amazing years she'd had with him. She chose to stay as positive as she could instead. I admired that, even as I was sure, if it were me, I'd probably still be in bed, under the covers, avoiding the world and letting my grief drown me. She was much stronger than I, and I gave her a little wave. "Come on back."

I saw several more clients throughout the afternoon, and it wasn't hard to tell when somebody at Just Wright had returned. The sudden loud music told me it was probably Brandon, Master of Grump, as I'd nicknamed him. Only in my own head, of course.

Good, I thought, despite being assaulted by the music yet again. *At least the damn boxes will be gone.*

Imagine my surprise when I headed out to make myself a cup of coffee at around seven, and all three stacks of boxes still filled up my waiting room. Mary had gone home about an hour earlier, but I'd been with somebody, so hadn't had a chance to say anything other than good-bye. I sighed as I entered the hallway and walked down to Just Wright, Leo on my heels. The door was open, but I knocked on the frame.

Nobody heard me over the music, of course, and, remembering my mom's admonition to "be a good neighbor," I took a deep breath and tried to smile as I walked in.

The whole staff was sitting around the card table by the whiteboard, laughing and joking, this time with little clear plastic cups instead of smoothies. Each cup filled with something pale and bubbly.

"Lacey!" Alicia said happily as she saw me, and my mission in marching over here—the boxes still in my office—dimmed a bit. I couldn't decide if she was that good at shifting my focus or if I was just that easy. "We landed a huge account today. Celebrate with us." Leo immediately ran to her and hopped up into her lap before anybody could tell he was going to, which made her giggle with delight. Yes, she actually giggled. "Did you come up here to congratulate me?" she asked my dog, who responded by bathing her face in kisses—kisses she freely accepted which, I had to grudgingly admit, earned her points, as people who avoided dogs or love from dogs immediately raised my suspicions. Alicia looked up at me, her blue eyes sparkling with happiness. "Seriously. Have some champagne." She gestured to the bottle sitting on the table as the guys chatted among themselves.

"Yeah, join us," Gisele said and poured some of the lovely, bubbly liquid into a cup for me, handing it over before I could protest further.

I half-heartedly held it up and muttered a "congratulations" before taking a big gulp. Too big, but I didn't want to stay. I couldn't. I had more work to do.

And the boxes. *The boxes!*

But the champagne was delicious, the cool feel of it sliding down my throat kind of wonderful.

"Sit," Alicia said, her hand running up and down Leo's back as she indicated an empty chair with her chin. "You sound much better."

"I am." It was really nice of her to notice, and I let myself get distracted for a second or two by those blue eyes before declining the invitation to join them. "I really can't. I've got another client due in soon." I cleared my throat. "Listen, did Mary leave you a note on the door?"

Alicia furrowed her brow in thought. "A note?"

"Yeah, when you guys were all gone."

"Oh, I only just got here about an hour ago." She looked around the table. "Who was back first?" When the staff paid her no attention, she increased her volume. "Guys." They stopped talking and met her gaze. "Who was back first?"

"I was," Brandon, Master of Grump, said.

"Was there a note on the door?"

Brandon sipped his champagne, seemed to make a show out of thinking really hard. "There might have been…"

Alicia sighed, but good-naturedly, and returned her focus to me. "What did the note say? Do you need something?"

"I do, actually. There are about fifteen large boxes of yours that UPS delivered to my office because yours was locked." I paused, glancing around at them in the hopes I wouldn't need to say another word. No luck. "Soooo…I need somebody to get them out of my reception area so there's room for my, you know, clients." I glanced at Brandon. "Did you not see the note?" I kept my tone as light as I could, cocked my head as I waited for him to answer.

He looked at Alicia and she raised an eyebrow at him. He sighed then, and said, "Yeah, I saw it. Sorry."

Alicia turned her gaze back to me, she said, "I apologize. Is it okay if we get them first thing in the morning?"

Deciding to pick my battles…and a bit blinded by that smile of Alicia's, I agreed. Alicia's gratitude seemed genuine, though, so that made it a bit more bearable. A very tiny bit. I thanked her and turned to go, calling Leo to follow me.

He didn't.

When I turned around, he was looking right at me, completely content on Alicia's lap. She had rolled both lips in and was biting down on them to hide her smile, but I saw it and gave a good-natured roll of my eyes.

It took my having to literally walk around the table and physically pick Leo up out of Alicia's lap to get him to leave with me.

At least the traitor had good taste.

❖

It was Friday, and we'd passed the mid-March mark on the calendar. That meant one more month and my crazy work schedule would ease up in a massive way. You'd think I'd be used to this, to tax season. I'd been involved in some way since I was a teenager helping my dad, so I'd seen at least fifteen tax seasons. Maybe more. It was funny how the same pattern emerged each year. I could map it out at this point and found it almost comforting.

The holidays would pass, and the new year would begin. The phone calls and appointments would start to trickle in, and I'd get this fun sense of excitement for my job, a renewed vigor of sorts. Not that the rest of the year didn't have its bright spots, but this was a different kind of excitement, like preparing for a marathon. By mid to late February, I started to get the tiniest bit tired, especially when clients began calling in a panic because they didn't think they had all the paperwork they needed to file. Then March shows up and by then, I'm more than a tiny bit tired. I'm bone-weary. But I push through to the beginning of April, when I'm sporadically entertaining the idea of throwing myself off a building just so I can get some sleep.

On April 15, I tend to work right up until midnight (I've been known to go to three in the morning if I've got something on the West Coast to deal with). And it's all downhill after that.

Oh, there's still a lot of work after that all-important date. Lots of people have extensions. But the mad rush is over, and I usually take the first weekend after April 15 to completely disconnect from work. I sleep, watch movies, read a book, eat a cheeseburger, do everything I haven't been able to do for the previous three months. It's like getting out of prison.

So, passing the middle of March was a good thing, because it meant I was that much closer to the end of the season when I could breathe again. I narrowly avoided getting T-boned by Nascar Kyle, parked six spaces away from what I now referred to as my old parking spot, and tsked as I found the security door ajar yet again. I refused to let it sour my mood, however. My Past the Middle of March Happy, I called it, and did my best to hold on to it as I kicked the piece of wood away, closed the door tightly before Leo and I headed up the stairs.

The Happy stayed grasped in my fingers until I got to my reception area.

My reception area full of boxes.

Still.

And then I dropped the Past the Middle of March Happy right there on the floor where it shattered into a million tiny pieces.

"Son of a bitch," I muttered, before realizing that my first appointment was seated in a chair to my left. I threw Mr. Kennedy a grimace of apology, handed Leo off to Mary, and marched down the hall, still wearing my coat and still carrying my messenger bag.

The music was on, but at a bearable volume, which surprised me. The red door was closed, so I knocked on the glass, then let myself in without waiting for permission.

As always, the atmosphere inside Just Wright was cheerful. Happy and colorful and fun, but I had to put up my force field because I didn't want to be distracted away from my mission this time. I saw Alicia out of the corner of my eye as she looked up at me, but it became clear right away that she was talking on her earpiece. That was probably a good thing, and I moved right over to Brandon's desk. He added to my annoyance by keeping his eyes on his computer screen and not acknowledging me at all, even though there was no way he didn't see me standing right in front of him. A beat went by. Two. I heard Gisele call from the back corner.

"Brandon." She said it quietly, but with a firmness that told me she totally got that he was being a jerk.

Brandon sighed. Loudly. Then he hit one last key on his keyboard. Loudly. And *then* he looked up at me. "Hey."

I poked the inside of my cheek with my tongue while I counted to five in my head before I said, "Hey. There are still a large number of boxes in my reception area. Could you come get them please?"

He gave a nod, then turned back to his monitor. "Just give me a sec."

"Now." My tone got his attention and when his eyes snapped to mine, I pasted on a half-smile and added, "Please." I didn't understand the rudeness, the unprofessionalism. I really didn't. And I'd had enough. "What is your problem with me? Did I do something to you? Piss you off in some way I know nothing about?"

He seemed completely shocked that I'd called him out. He opened his mouth to speak, closed it again. When he finally spoke, he didn't look at me and his voice was very soft. "Just...be careful. Around her. Please." And before I could ask him what the hell he was talking about, he headed out the door.

I could feel Alicia's gaze on me even as she continued with her phone call, and I sent a glance her way, but I didn't think she'd heard my conversation with the Master of Grump. I followed Brandon out the door and watched as he silently hauled the boxes away, not uttering another word.

I felt better once the boxes were gone, though I also felt a little weird, both about Brandon's cryptic words and about having stomped in there like I'd been ripped off somehow. I shrugged both off for now. I'd learned long ago that being a female small business owner meant nobody was going to stand up for me but me, and if I wanted something—or wanted something done—I had to go get it or do it myself or be a hard-ass about getting it taken care of for me. I didn't enjoy being that person, but it's what I had to do to be a success. I imagined Alicia Wright knew that as well.

The rest of the day went pretty quickly, probably because I had back-to-back appointments for the entire afternoon. Mary stayed until after six. Given she'd come in at seven that morning, I finally kicked her out. Leo and I were planning on a long night.

I was contemplating what I wanted to order from ChopStix when I heard the gentle rap on the outer door. I'd begun keeping that closed at night and the door to my office open so I had a clear line of sight from my desk to the main door. I watched as it pushed open and Alicia Wright entered, a bottle and two clear plastic cups in one hand and a large white bag in her teeth. She pushed the door closed with her free hand and smiled at me as she took the bag out of her mouth and approached.

"Hi there," she said, as she came into the room. Leo, who'd been crashed in the corner, finally noticed her presence and jumped up like his bed had suddenly become electrified. "I know you're busy, but I'm going to guess you haven't eaten. Plus, it's Friday night and you should be able to have a cocktail on a Friday night, even if you're still working. You can't go to happy hour, so I'm bringing happy hour to you."

I sat there, speechless, and just took her in as she set things on my desk. She must not have had any client meetings today because she wore soft-looking jeans, a navy blue long-sleeved top, and a lightweight scarf in a dark blue and light blue paisley print. She looked casually elegant, her hair falling in sunset-colored waves around her shoulders. I watched her hands as she pulled containers out of the bag, and I knew she'd gotten the food from ChopStix.

I opened the containers she set in front of me. Chicken lo mein, steamed rice, two spring rolls. She pulled up one of the chairs opposite my desk and sat down, opened her own containers, and then handed me a fork. I looked at my food, then looked up at her, a question in my eyes.

"Mary helped me," Alicia said, a sexy glint in her gorgeous blue eyes. "I wanted to do something for you to apologize for the boxes. And Brandon." She grimaced. "So I asked Mary what I could do, and she said you work late during this time of year and you forget to eat."

"She knows me well." I dug my fork into the rice and put a huge scoop into my mouth. That's when I realized I'd eaten nothing all day but an apple.

Alicia opened the bottle, which I saw was the remainder of the champagne from yesterday, and filled both cups, leaving just a small amount. She handed one cup to me, then held hers up in a toast. "Here's to new offices, new friendships, and the removal of boxes, albeit late."

I touched my cup to hers, then sipped. The champagne was still bubbly and the carbonation danced on my tongue.

Alicia sat down and Leo immediately jumped into her lap. I scolded him, but she waved me off. "He's fine. I don't mind."

I swallowed a mouthful of lo mein and studied her. "What's the deal with Brandon anyway?" I finally asked. Because I had to. I needed to know who I was dealing with and if I wanted to avoid him like the plague in the future.

Alicia took in a long, slow breath, let it out, took a bite of what looked like cashew chicken to me, and chewed. "Brandon is…" She gazed off into the distance. "I've known him for a long time. He's brilliant. I couldn't ask for a better right hand at my company. He catches things I don't. He's got fantastic ideas. He's…I don't know what I'd do without him." She sipped from her cup. "That being said, he's also overprotective and a bit…socially inept."

"Overprotective of what?"

"Me." She shrugged and went on before I could question further. "He's tough," she said, and I tried not to notice that she didn't try to reassure me. "But I'd be lost without him."

A thought occurred to me then. "Are you guys—?"

Alicia's eyebrows shot up. "Oh, God, no. No. Not at all. Not even a little."

"Never?" I asked, as her protests seemed…almost unnecessarily firm.

"No." That one was the firmest. "He's not my type."

"Got it. Thank you, by the way," I said, pointing at the food with my fork. "This is great. I was just about to order this very meal, as a matter of fact."

She held up her glass. "Cheers to good timing, and you're welcome." We ate in happy silence for a while, and I was surprised by how comfortable it was, how not awkward.

"Where was your office before you moved here?" I asked finally, wanting to talk with her but keeping an eye on the clock. I really needed to get back to work.

"We were in the basement of this warehouse-type building. It was small, cold, and had no windows, which was really not at all conducive to creativity."

"Ah, that explains the blinds open all the time."

Alicia gave me a grin. "When you've been without daylight for a long time, you want all you can get."

"Is that why you moved?"

"We should've moved sooner, but you see all the stuff we have. A move is such a daunting task. It's huge and takes a ton of organization. But I needed a money person. I'd been doing all the books and accounting myself, which was killing my schedule as far as searching for clients, so I hired Justin. And when he came on board, it was super obvious we needed more space."

"So, he was your moving catalyst?"

"Exactly." She finished her champagne. "But it was the right thing, hiring him. We've increased our business by nearly twenty percent so far this year."

"Wow. That's impressive."

"Thanks." Her expression was one of obvious pride. "What about you? Have you always been here in this spot?"

I nodded as I finished my second spring roll and crumpled up the wrapper. "My father began this business, like, three decades ago. Right here in this very office."

"Seriously?" Alicia's eyes went wide, like I was dazzling her with a fairy tale or magic trick of some kind.

"Yup. I started to help him when I was a kid. Then I sort of picked up on the job, found not only did I like it, but I was good at it, and he hired me full-time. When he decided to retire, I took over."

"How long ago was that?"

"Two years, roughly. Mary worked for him, and she wanted to stay on for a while."

Alicia's head bobbed up and down. "That explains why I've seen so many elderly clients come in here. They were your dad's."

"Yes. I have his clients, and I'm picking up new ones on my own all the time. I get quite a few referrals, which is awesome."

"Right? Referrals are the best because it means somebody likes your work enough to recommend you to somebody who trusts them. It's very validating."

"Totally validating."

We finished eating and began cleaning up our mess. I finished my champagne and there was enough left in the bottle for Alicia to give us each what amounted to maybe three more sips. We touched glasses again and emptied the cups.

"All right," she said at last. "I'm going to let you go back to work. I feel better about doing so knowing you've eaten some dinner and experienced a tiny bit of happy hour."

"You can rest easy," I said with a nod, playing along.

"I'm relieved."

"Good. Alicia, this was great. Again, thank you so much for keeping me company for a bit." I felt like I could now finish up my work in a short span of time and go home. I felt relaxed. Content. Happy. I didn't want to get into all of that and send her running off into the hallway screaming, so I simply smiled at her.

"You're very welcome." Alicia took the empty champagne bottle and the cups, squatted so she could kiss Leo on the head, then looked at me. Her eyes darted off to the right as if she was suddenly shy. "I'll see you later."

"Bye." I gave a little half-hearted wave, strangely sad to see her go but more than happy to watch her ass in those jeans as she left. The door clicked shut behind her, and I looked down at Leo, who was looking up at me with accusation in his eyes. "Yeah, I'm sorry your girlfriend left. You're gonna have to get over that." I patted my thigh, and he took a moment to think about it before hopping up into my lap. "Just a bit more work to do and we'll go home," I told him, kissing his head right in the same spot Alicia had.

CHAPTER FIVE

By the end of the last week in March, I'd hit my not-quite-insane-but-awfully-damn-close level of work stress. My workload was larger than even I'd anticipated, and I absently thought about the idea of hiring somebody next tax season. An assistant of some kind. An intern, maybe. Leanne knew a woman in administration at one of the local colleges. I jotted myself a note to ask her about it.

It was Wednesday, just after lunch, and I'd been seeing clients nonstop since nine that morning. I finally had an hour between the Hardings, who'd just left, and the Newcastles, who'd be in at one thirty. My brain wasn't quite fried, but it was a little bit mushy, and I dug in my messenger bag for the apple I'd tossed in there that morning. Normally, I'd take this hour to catch up on email and paperwork, but I decided I wanted to decompress a bit, give my head some downtime, so I stared out the window as I ate, watching the people come and go in the parking lot below and trying not to hear the bassline thumping through the wall I shared with Just Wright.

I took in a deep breath and let it out slowly. I'd been doing my best to be more flexible, to relax a bit more around the antics of the staffers at Just Wright, around the things they did that annoyed me, ever since Alicia had coaxed me to have drinks with her. I figured it was the least I could do. Sure, it could've been her subtle way of bribing me, thinking I'd do exactly what I was doing: not complaining about the noise/inconveniences/irritations caused by her people, but I couldn't make myself believe that about her. She'd been far too genuinely nice.

Though she hadn't brought me dinner again, Alicia still popped in on occasion. Sometimes to bring food to Mary, sometimes to borrow Leo for a brainstorming session, sometimes just to say hello. She never stayed to hang out with me—probably sensing how busy I was—but I saw her at least a couple times a week.

I liked that. Maybe too much. I wondered if she did, too.

My mind was just about to jump onto that merry-go-round, which would drive me nuts, I knew, when there was a rap on my door, causing Leo to jump up from his bed with a little yip. The door swung open wide, and there stood my brother in all his handsome glory.

"Hey there, Lace-Face," he said, as if I were ten again. That nickname changed to Brace Face when I was thirteen, for obvious reasons. When the metal came off, it was back to Lace Face. He was dressed in his usual suit and tie; today's was gray with a white shirt underneath and a blue-and-silver-striped tie. He needed a haircut, but I'd always liked his hair a tiny bit too long. His blue eyes sparkled as he crossed the office, kissed the top of my head, and plopped himself into one of my guest chairs, uninvited, parking one ankle on the opposite knee. Leo went back to his bed and curled up, and I made a mental note to reward him for that later. "That little bastard in his Charger almost killed me on my way in."

I gave a nod. "Happens to me at least three times a week."

"What year is that car? Sixty-eight? Sixty-nine?"

I gave him a look. "How the hell should I know?"

Scott looked at me for a beat before saying, "You look tired."

"Uh, yeah, Captain Obvious, it's March twenty-seventh. Of course I'm tired."

He took his time scanning my office, his eyes roaming over my photos, my diploma and certificates on the wall, the scattered papers on my desk.

His slow perusal made me feel impatient. "What do you need, Scott?"

His sandy eyebrows rose slightly. "What, I can't just pop in on my little sister for an impromptu visit?" His tone was all innocence.

"You absolutely can," I said. "Except it's tax season, and I'm slammed, so…" I left the sentence dangling, my meaning clear.

He sighed in defeat, and I was surprised he'd given up so easily. He must be busy. "Dad asked me to stop by, see if you needed help. Looks like you might."

"He did not," I said, but my expression of disbelief was lame and I knew it. Because of course he did.

Scott shrugged. "I told him you had it under control, but he insisted. You know how he is."

"I do."

Scott made a show of running his gaze over the mess on my desk, then the stack of customer folders and manila files on the floor, and raised an eyebrow. "You're sure, though?" His concern was actually kind of sweet.

"I'm sure. Promise."

At that moment, Leo sprang from his bed and shot across the office to the door before I could even comprehend it. I followed him with my eyes and saw Alicia standing in the doorway, an uncertain expression on her face, a paper plate in her hand. She picked Leo up, kissed his head.

"I don't mean to interrupt you and your client," she said, lifting one shoulder. "I just came over to drop off some pizza, but Mary must already be at lunch?" She posed it as a question, clearly hesitant to intrude.

"Oh, no worries," Scott said, and popped up from his chair almost as fast as Leo had. He crossed the room, hand outstretched. "I'm Lacey's big brother, Scott, just here to make sure she's not drowning in tax returns."

"Believe me, your sister holds her own." Alicia held my gaze for a beat while my heart swelled from her support, before turning to Scott and shaking his hand. "Alicia Wright. Lacey's neighbor."

"Ah, so you're the one who moved into that perpetually empty space." Scott's eyes never left Alicia's face. Not that I could blame him, though I tried to shoot laser beams at him with my eyes.

"Guilty as charged."

"And what do you do next door, Alicia Wright?" Scott's flirtatious tone was so glaringly obvious, I almost felt sorry for him. But Alicia smiled warmly and answered his question. I could take a lesson from her in how to deal with my brother.

"Marketing. Graphic design. Promotions. Advertising."

"A little bit of everything, huh?" Scott leaned against the door frame, making himself comfortable.

"Listen, you guys, I've got a ton to do here, so if you don't mind..." I kept my voice light and pleasant. No reason not to, right? I just didn't want to be privy to this conversation any longer.

"Oh," Alicia said. "I'm so sorry. Um, we're working on a pitch session at one thirty. Could I borrow Leo? You know how much we love having him over there." That face she made, that hopeful, kind, gorgeous face of hers made it impossible for me to say no. She made me weak. I freely admitted it.

"Sure," I said with a nod and then forced myself to turn my focus to my brother. "Hey, don't you have to get back to the office?"

"I've got a little time," he said, offering me the sparest of glances before going back to Alicia. "And we're looking for a new marketing firm to rep us. Why don't we get out of Lacey's hair and go over to your place and you can impress me?"

I swear to God, it took everything I had not to groan out loud at Scott's obviousness. You almost had to feel sorry for the guy.

"Sure. Let's go." Alicia shot what seemed like a genuine smile in my direction. "I'll bring him back in a bit," she said, holding Leo up enough so I knew she was talking about him and not Scott.

I nodded and took a bite out of my apple to show how fine I was. Perfectly okay. Not bothered at all. *Nope. I'm good. It's all good.* The second they shut my door behind them, I wanted to throw up.

❖

"That was nice of Scott to stop by," Mary said later, as she donned her coat and gathered her things.

I grunted, then realized how much like my father that made me sound and decided to use my words. "Oh, yeah, it was awesome. Dad sent him to check up on me."

Mary knew it was true and didn't bother to try and convince me otherwise, so she got points for that. Instead, she glanced at the puppy calendar she'd hung on the wall. "We're in the home stretch."

"We are. Thank God. Thank you so much for staying late tonight." It was almost eight, and Mary had stayed through my client appointments.

"I'm happy to help."

"And you know what to do if you come in here tomorrow and find I've slit my wrists, right?"

"Yup," Mary said and ticked off the list on her fingers. "You want to be cremated. You want 'Born This Way' played at your memorial service. You want your ashes scattered along the Schuylkill Banks. Which I'm pretty sure is illegal, by the way."

"You'll figure it out," I said with reassurance.

On her way out, one hand on the knob, Mary turned back to me. "Maybe use pills instead? Blood would be really hard to get out of that carpet."

"Good point. I'll think about it."

She winked at me and was gone.

I sat back in my chair, trying to summon up the energy to tackle five more returns so Leo and I could head home. Speaking of Leo, I missed having him and his big-dog-in-a-little-body attitude sitting in my office with me. I heard no music thumping through the wall I shared with Just Wright, so I wondered if they had mostly cleared out for the night. I was just about to get up and check when there was a knock on the door and in sauntered Alicia, Leo flying past her to leap up into my lap and kiss me on the chin.

"Well, hello there," I said to him, through almost-closed lips. "I missed you, too."

Alicia gestured to my face with a finger. "Is that how you avoid him French kissing you?"

I nodded. "Took me months to perfect it," I said, talking without moving my lips. She smiled that smile I'd grown to look forward to. Then I wondered if she'd used it on Scott as well. "I hope my brother didn't take up too much of your time." I didn't look at her as I said it.

"Actually, he took me to lunch," she said, and when my head snapped up to see her, she wasn't looking at me.

"He did?" I hoped it didn't come out too shocked or disapproving, but I wasn't sure.

"He's quite the charmer."

"Yeah, he's something, that's for sure."

Alicia gave me an odd look. "He's looking for some marketing direction for his company, so I'm going to pitch to him next week."

"That's great." My tone said otherwise, but I couldn't seem to help it.

"Do you…have a problem with me working with him?" Her brow furrowed, and I had the almost irresistible urge to smooth it out with my thumb. Instead, I wrapped some of my own hair around my finger and twirled.

I shook my head. "No, of course not. Just normal brother/sister competitive stuff. Ignore me. I'm just tired." It wasn't a lie. It just wasn't the whole truth.

"I can imagine." Alicia's eyes were the color of a robin's egg, I noticed, as she took in the stacks and piles I had let build up on my floor, on my desk, on the credenza behind me. "Seems like you never catch up."

"I do eventually. Oh, and thanks for having my back with Scott earlier. My dad sends him to check up on me when he thinks I'm getting 'overwhelmed,'" I air-quoted. "Equal parts well-meaning and annoying. But your words meant a lot."

"Well, they were true. You are one of the hardest working women I've ever seen."

"Only for another couple of weeks." I smiled past my fatigue.

"You should go home."

I scoffed in response.

"Seriously, though. You're exhausted. What's it going to hurt if you leave now?"

"I always work late at this time of year, said every tax accountant ever."

"Is there a rule that says you have to?"

"My rule does, yes." Her pushing chafed a little, but only because my level of fatigue left me with few coping skills. I could feel my stomach tightening.

"Well, your rule is silly if it leaves you to collapse on your desk."

"I do it every year sans collapse. I'll be fine."

"Ah. You're one of those people."

I squinted at her. "One of what people?"

"A this-is-how-it's-always-been-done-so-I'm-not-changing-it person."

This, on top of the whole thing with Scott, wormed its way under my skin like a splinter, and I just looked at her. She'd been smiling a bit, but as I watched, the smile faded and there were several moments of silence. Regret bloomed in my chest. I'd made Alicia uncomfortable. It was obvious. Which...why wouldn't she be? I'd been rude for no other reason than I was too tired to practice my manners, and I was senselessly jealous she'd spent time with my brother. Honestly, she wasn't the first girl I'd liked that my brother had swooped in on and whisked away with his broad shoulders and blue eyes and smooth talk. I flashed back to Emily Garcia, a girl in high school that I had a crush on. Scott ended up taking her to the senior ball and then dated her for the next year or so. I hated him for that. And I wasn't too happy with Emily either—not that she'd even known I had a crush. Seemed silly, in hindsight…but I couldn't help my teenage feelings.

"Well," Alicia said, as she backed toward the door, "I don't want to distract you from your work, so…" She jerked a thumb over her shoulder. "I'm just going to go. But…" She hesitated as if she wasn't sure she should say what she was thinking. Finally, she gave in. "Don't stay too late, okay?"

My irritation evaporated immediately because the concern in her voice felt genuine, and I was touched. "Thank you, Alicia."

She smiled softly, and with that, she was through the door, closing it behind her.

I glanced at Leo and he stared back at me. A laugh burst out of me. "Yeah, we both have a crush, don't we?" Okay. I'd admitted it. To myself at least. I had no idea what Alicia would think about that if she knew. I was making the assumption that she was straight, though, and didn't really have any intention of telling her. And if she started dating Scott, my crush would disappear faster than a piece of steak in Leo's dog dish. I decided I'd enjoy the little fantasies that had started to infiltrate my thoughts.

But later.

I reached for a folder and got to work.

With a much-needed goofy grin…

❖

Around the third year I was working full-time for my father and it got to be the end of March, I learned something interesting. It was another symptom of being overtired, of stretching myself too thin: weird-ass dreams. So weird that I often sat up in the middle of the night and wondered what kind of drugs somebody'd slipped me without my knowledge, because I was obviously tripping.

I was able to chase them away with an over-the-counter sleep aid during that last month of craziness, and after a year or two, they seemed to go away on their own.

Until that night.

I worked until almost ten. Leo was snoring so loudly in his bed when I started packing up my things that I felt awful waking him up. He was like a toddler, all blinky and confused. Once we got home, I put him on my bed and he curled up in a ball against a pillow and went immediately back to sleep. I zipped through an edited version of my nightly routine as fast as I could, not bothering to remove my makeup or any jewelry, simply brushing my teeth, stripping, and sliding under the covers. I didn't remember actually turning off the light, I was so tired.

My dream was full of people that night. Brandon (scowling, of course), Gisele, Pantone Patrick, Mary, my dad, Alicia, Scott, George Clooney, Leo, and Maroon 5. I have no idea what was happening in my brain, but it was weird. Maroon 5 was giving a concert. Sort of. We were in a tiny, tiny bar with a tin ceiling and dim sconces on the walls. The bartender was Taylor Swift—I had no idea why—and I ordered a Manhattan from her. I'd never had a Manhattan in my life, so why I chose that drink, I couldn't tell you. Alicia and Scott were dancing, as were Mary and George Clooney and a bunch of faceless extras. Since the only member of Maroon 5 I knew was Adam Levine, the other guys' faces were blurry, like on *Cops* when they conceal the identity of bystanders to a crime.

Anyway, I was busy watching the band and sipping my Manhattan when Alicia approached me, her hand outstretched.

"Dance with me?" Her expression was soft, inviting, and it made Dream Me all tingly inside. I was lifting my hand to place in hers when a large man hand beat me to it, and then Scott was whisking her back onto the dance floor. She didn't look upset by it, though. She was thrilled, her face a glowing mask of glee and happiness.

"Yeah, you'll probably never get that one," Taylor Swift informed me from behind the bar. She wore very short denim cut-offs and a white V-neck T-shirt and was surprisingly tall. With a white bar rag, she dried a clear glass.

"I'm sorry?" I said.

"She's totally out of your league, like most girls you crush on. You know that."

I gave her a look that I was pretty sure said something to the effect of, "Seriously? Dating advice from Taylor Swift?" But I didn't actually say it out loud.

"You know I'm right," she said as she set the glass down and picked up another one. "You can't compare to your brother. You never could. I mean, God, *look* at him." She stopped drying the glass and just stared at Scott with this dreamy look on her face.

"Shut up," I muttered, and drained my glass. I turned to set it on the bar and another one was all fixed and waiting for me.

"Come on," Taylor said. "Think about it. You live in his shadow. You have your whole life. At school. At work. With girls. The only reason he didn't try to steal Leanne for himself was because she was over forty."

Despite the fact that I was pretty sure that was true, I scowled at her. "I hate you, Taylor Swift."

"Yeah, everybody says that, but they lie. They all secretly love me." She gave me a cute little shrug as Maroon 5 broke into Taylor's song "Love Story." "See?" Then she flounced off to wait on some faceless customer at the end of the bar.

On the dance floor, Alicia was glowing. She was so happy as she swayed in my brother's arms. Her cheeks were flushed, her hair tousled and perfect. My chest tightened as he made his move and she tipped her head up to receive him. I shouted in protest and threw my glass at a wall, and as it shattered, my eyes snapped open to see the ceiling of my bedroom.

I lay there for a minute or two, steadying my breathing, not wanting to move for fear of waking myself up further. It was still dark out, which meant there was time left for sleeping. I was afraid to look at the clock, so I managed not to. I was also afraid to revisit the dream but couldn't manage that as well, and it flooded through my brain. Alicia and Scott dancing, looking so happy in each other's arms, as words flew through my head.

She's totally out of your league. Like most girls you crush on.
You can't compare to your brother. You never could.

I blew out a big breath and turned on my side, yanking the covers up over my shoulder.

"I really do hate you, Taylor Swift."

Chapter Six

The hallway reeked of bacon when I arrived at work Friday morning. Don't get me wrong; I love bacon. I mean, who doesn't? But the residual smell of it is cloying and greasy and it lingers for a long time. It also made me hungry.

"Good morning, Lacey," Mary said as I entered the reception area and dropped Leo's leash so he could scoot off to her. She shoveled a forkful of something into her mouth.

"Let me guess. Omelet day? BLTs for breakfast?"

"Eggs in a hole," Mary said gleefully as she chewed. "They've got an electric frying pan over there and they're cooking away. I bet they'll make you one."

I thought about it. I did. But then I got a flash of Alicia dancing with my brother, and my stomach soured a bit. "I'll pass," I said, heading through to my office. I turned and tossed over my shoulder, "I dreamed you were dancing with George Clooney last night."

"I was?" She heaved a big sigh. "Oh, I wish I could've seen that dream."

I wish I could unsee it, I thought as I unpacked my crap. Except for Mary's dance with George. That part was memorable.

Clients came in a steady stream all day long, and as my three o'clock left the office, my three thirty entered, large plastic bag in hand, just after he passed Alicia in the hall.

I was making myself a cup of much-needed coffee near Mary's desk. "Go on in, Mr. Baker. I'll be right there. Coffee?"

He shook his head and went into my office.

Alicia popped her head through the door and whispered, "Was that bag full of…?"

"His receipts that need to be itemized? Yes. That's exactly what it is." I blew out a big breath. Mr. Baker did this every year.

"And he just expects you to take care of it?" Alicia's voice was laced with awe.

I tipped my head back and forth. "He was a client of my dad's, and this is how they always did it, so…"

She gave me a look and pointed a finger at me. Aside from arching an eyebrow, she said nothing, but I heard the silent, "See?" Then she winked and went to her own office. Only in that moment did I realize I had again used the this-is-how-it's-always-been-done excuse.

I twisted the ends of my hair with a finger as I waited for my coffee to brew. She was right. It was the way my mind was wired, thanks to my dad. Maybe I needed to try and do a little…rewiring. An interesting idea, to say the least, and not something I'd ever really thought about before. I could hear my dad now: *if it ain't broke, don't fix it.* But things changed. Times changed. I was pretty sure Alicia viewed those as good things.

Hmm.

My coffee finished, I doctored it up and walked with determined steps into my office, and for just a split second, I faltered at the sight of Mr. Baker's bulging plastic bag full of scraps of paper. Yeah, maybe Alicia was right. Maybe change was better. Sometimes. Maybe.

❖

Are you eating?

The text was from Leanne and not at all a surprise, as she knew me well, and the end of March/early April was about when she started to check on me daily. I asked her why once, and she said she was simply making sure I hadn't keeled over from exhaustion or starvation or dehydration or a caffeine overdose or any number of health hazards I subjected myself to at this time of year. Her words, not mine.

About to. Just finished with Mr. Baker.

The emoji she sent was one with wide, horrified eyes and it made me laugh. *How long this year? My money's on two hours.*

I scoffed. "I wish," I mumbled as I typed *Three and a half.*

Leanne sent the same horrified emoji. Four more times. I laughed again.

I'm bringing you a salad on my way home. Don't argue.

I would never argue against a woman delivering food right to my door. I'm not an idiot.

I had purposely scheduled Mr. Baker as my last appointment because I had no idea how long he'd take. It really varied every year, depending on how good a job he did categorizing his receipts. This year, he'd totally dropped the ball. I was glad for that now, though, because my eyes burned from squinting at all the faded print, and I had an ache in my wrist from overuse of my adding machine, so I didn't feel bad taking a break. A salad sounded awesome. The only thing that would make it better would be a glass of white wine.

Half an hour later, Leanne sat in the chair across from my desk and ate her own salad and I dug into the one she'd brought for me. Mine was bigger and had more stuff in it, including some chicken, bacon bits, hard-boiled egg, and some sharp cheddar that made my mouth sing. I only realized how hungry I was—and how badly I needed some vegetables—after I stuffed the first bite into my mouth and the flavors exploded on my tongue.

"Oh, my God. I so needed this," I said, as I chewed.

"I know. I've met you," Leanne said, with a grin.

Not for the first time, I realized how lucky I was to have a friendship with Leanne. I'd seen so many partnerships end in anger, even hatred, and it was so sad and so hard to watch, like a train wreck or a car accident that you just couldn't look away from. That's not to say that our breakup was easy, because no breakup is, and ours was no different. But Leanne knew me better than most people and I knew her as well. There was a nice cushion of comfort to that.

We were laughing about one of her (unnamed) regular patients, one she'd dubbed Mrs. Hypochondriac, when there was a rap on the door that caused Leo to jump up out of his bed and sprint that way.

"Leo," I called, standing up from my chair. But I got no further as Alicia Wright walked in and scooped him right up, then sauntered into my office with my dog in one hand and an open bottle of white wine in the other.

"Hi there," she said hesitantly. "I don't mean to interrupt…which it seems like I'm always doing lately." She wrinkled her nose.

"Not at all," Leanne said, before I could answer. "I was just making sure Lacey, here, ate some actual food while she was working." She stood up and held out her hand. "Leanne Markham."

Alicia set the bottle on my desk and shook Leanne's hand. "Alicia Wright. I'm the new neighbor."

"Ah," Leanne said, as if she completely understood, and I wracked my brain trying to remember if I'd said anything to her about all the issues that had come with finally having neighbors. Or about going to the bar with her.

"Listen, I've got an appointment in a bit, and a client left this with me this afternoon." Alicia pointed to the bottle of what I could see now was a very nice Sauvignon Blanc. "I had a quick celebratory glass with him then, but it's Friday and I don't want to leave this opened over the weekend or it'll get gross."

"Is that a technical wine term?" I asked, while accepting the fact that I was happy to see her.

"Absolutely. Google it." Alicia gave me that grin. She looked amazing in crisp navy blue slacks, matching heels, and a cream-colored top that made me want to reach out and rub the fabric between my fingers. Silk, possibly? Her hair was bouncy and her eyes glittered, as did the silver necklace and matching earrings that seemed to catch any ray of light in the room and amplify it, making her bright and sparkling, like she was made out of sunlight. As always, she looked like she'd just showered and gotten ready for her day, not like it was after seven in the evening and she'd been wearing the same clothes and makeup for eleven hours. I had no idea how she did it, but I wished I could learn.

I glanced at the clock. "You've got a client meeting this late?"

"It's a dinner meeting." She was still holding Leo and put her nose up to his as she said, "I'm meeting your brother over at that new steak place in Olde City."

Leanne's eyebrows rose; I could see them out of the corner of my eye as I stared at Alicia for a beat too long, then tore my gaze away to focus *very* intently on my salad.

"Carmichael's," Leanne said.

"Yes! That's it." Alicia probably looked Leanne's way. I didn't know because I didn't look. I didn't want her to see my face, didn't want her to recognize the fact that I was jealous. I knew it, but I didn't need her knowing it. It was weird. And I wasn't twelve.

"I was there last week. The Delmonico was to die for." When I finally moved my gaze to Leanne, her face was open and friendly as she said, "I hope you got reservations, though. It's really busy."

"Scott said he did, so…" Alicia glanced my way. I could feel it as I shoved more lettuce into my face. "I'll be paying, though." Her voice sounded injected with artificial humor. "Can't have the client buying me dinner, not if I want his business."

Hmm. Well, that seems pretty clear. I chewed some cheese as I felt a tiny surge of relief wash through me, and finally decided to look at her. Her beautiful blue eyes were intent on mine, almost pleading for… something I couldn't—or didn't want to—comprehend.

"I hope you enjoy it," I said.

"Me too." Alicia kissed Leo once more on the head, then set him down. "Okay, I'm off. Enjoy the wine. It was nice to meet you, Leanne."

"Same here," Leanne said. To her credit, she managed to stay quiet until the door clicked shut behind Alicia before muttering, "Wow." Then she got up, went to my closet to find two paper cups, poured us each some wine, and sat back down. "Drink that. It's good stuff."

I nodded and took a sip. She was right. It was good. Really good with an acidic sharpness that danced with my taste buds.

Leanne grinned, and her expression said she knew something.

"What?" I asked.

"You're jealous."

"No, I'm not."

Leanne rolled her eyes and continued to grin. "Why do you argue with me? I can read you like a book."

I shot a sneer her way and took another sip of wine. "Fine," I conceded, as Leo jumped up into my lap, no doubt waiting for a nibble of cheese. "Fine, I'm jealous. Okay? Happy?"

Leanne continued to grin, even as she sipped her wine. Her brown eyes smiled at me over the rim of her cup. She swallowed and asked, "What are you jealous of?"

"The same thing I've been jealous of my entire life," I said, resolutely. "My brother."

"What about your brother?"

I narrowed my eyes at her, annoyed that she was pushing me to say it. *"Fine,"* I repeated. "I'm jealous that Alicia is into him."

Leanne nodded slowly and sipped her wine, her expression pensive.

"What are you thinking?"

She shrugged. "Nothing, really. She just seemed to…look at you a lot."

I furrowed my brow.

"It just seemed to me that she was more…into you." As I stared in disbelief, she drained her cup.

"She's going out to dinner with him," I pointed out.

"Because he's a client," she answered. Then she stood up and tossed her cup and empty salad container into the trash. She shouldered her bag, came around my desk, and kissed the top of my head. "Whatever. I could be wrong. Just thinking out loud." Then she rapped on the desk with her knuckles. "Don't stay much later. Go home and get some sleep."

"Thanks for the salad," I called, as she exited the office and shut the door behind her.

Then I sat.

And sat.

And sat.

And I stared off into space and replayed Leanne's words. She had to be wrong, didn't she? Alicia wasn't into me. Was she? How could she be? *I mean, look at her.* She was smart and funny and sexy and absolutely gorgeous. And she had my smart, funny, sexy, absolutely gorgeous brother interested in her.

"She pops by," I said softly to Leo, as I stroked his back. A few beats of silence went by. "But no more so than any neighbor. Right?" Leo looked up at me. "She made me a smoothie that one time." Leo cocked his head as if waiting for more. "She did bring happy hour to me when I was stuck working. And dragged me out with her." My confused brain then decided to toss me a memory. The memory of that first day when she told me I looked tired and then brushed my hair off my forehead with her warm, gentle fingers. I had forgotten about it, but it came screaming back.

Could Leanne be right?

Because it was impossible for me not to, I pictured Alicia having dinner with Scott. The fancy restaurant, the elegant food and wine, the candlelight dancing off the copper in her hair, him being his usual, charming self. Then, of course, my dream came raging back and I wondered if Carmichael's had a dance floor where Scott could hold Alicia in his arms and sway to the…

"Ugh. Stop it. Just stop it." I squeezed my eyes shut and shook my head. "Enough."

It was all so much for me to process, and I was much too tired to do it intelligently. With a sigh, I gave Leo a bite of chicken, finished up my salad, and cleaned up my trash. It was time to go home. My brain was fried, my eyes were scratchy, and my body was bone tired. Even Leo seemed extra low-key. I set him down on the floor and he immediately stretched out and fell on his side like road kill.

I gathered my things, gently scooped up my dog, and kissed his furry little face.

"Let's go home, Leo. We'll be back here soon enough." A glance at the pile of folders on my floor tugged a groan from my throat. "Like, tomorrow."

❖

I never asked Mary to work on the weekends, even though I knew she would in a New York minute. It just didn't feel right to me. It was my business, they were my clients. I paid Mary pretty well, but that didn't mean I expected her to give up her life for three and a half months of the year like I did. That wasn't fair. And honestly, knowing I *could* call her if I needed to and she'd show up inside thirty minutes was enough.

Leo was as tired as I was, and it made my heart swell with love for my little guy. He was curled up in his bed and stayed there through my first three Saturday clients, apparently having little to no energy for greetings, or even to do more than to lift his head. I had a vision of him doing that, muttering a very basic "hey" and going right back to sleep, and it made me grin.

I'd actually slept really well the night before, so I felt good. Fresh and clear and happy to deal with numbers and finances and government rules, and I spent the day working eagerly and efficiently. My last client for the day, a young woman named Kendra who worked in sales for a pharmaceutical company, had a ton of expenses and deductions and questions. She was much more organized than Mr. Baker, so that helped a lot, and when I finished her return and told her she was due a $2,174 refund, her eyes filled with tears. She got up from her chair, came around my desk, and wrapped me in a grateful hug.

"You don't understand," she said, as she sat back down and pulled a tissue from the box on the corner of my desk. "I'm going through a divorce. I just moved into an apartment. I totaled my car last month and need to get a new one. I feel like everybody in my life wants money from me right now, and I was pretty sure the government was going to be no different. *I'm so relieved!*" Her eyes welled up again, but she grinned at me, and I grinned back.

"Well, I'm glad to have helped." I stood up and we shook hands across my desk. "You hang in there, okay?"

"I'm doing my best," Kendra said, and I walked her through the reception area and opened the door for her. "Thanks, Lacey."

"Sure. Take care." I watched her walk to the stairwell door, which was being held open for her by Alicia Wright, who must have also been on her way out. She wore a bright blue top, and when she turned and met my gaze, her eyes softened noticeably.

"Hi there," she said, a smile breaking across her beautiful face.

She's happy to see me, my heart told me.

She had dinner with your brother last night, said my head.

It was business, countered my heart.

Taylor Swift hates you, too, said my head.

Low blow.

"Hey," I managed, in a light tone, despite the head/heart battle raging.

"You're working on a Saturday again," she said as she came back in from the stairs and approached me.

"Tax season," I said, then asked, "How was dinner?" much to my own horror, because it popped out without permission. And because I didn't really want to know. I groaned internally at myself.

Alicia gave a moan of pleasure and dropped her head back, exposing her long, elegant throat. I swallowed hard as she pressed a hand to her chest and closed her eyes. "Your friend wasn't kidding. *To die for*. I had a strip steak that could not have been cooked more perfectly. The wine list is huge and impressive." Her face was dazzling as she spoke, animated and excited, making it impossible for me to look away. "They have their own pastry chef on-site, and the dessert menu is *so* unique."

"Sounds great."

"Oh, it was stellar." When she opened her eyes, she fixed them on me, pinning me in place.

"Good." I tried to turn to go back into my office, but my feet stayed riveted.

"We should go some time."

That was unexpected. "I'm sorry?"

"You should go there. With me. Some time."

"I should?"

She nodded and for the first time since I'd met her, Alicia Wright seemed a bit...uncertain. Nervous, maybe? I wasn't sure, but a faint wrinkle had appeared on her forehead and she blinked several times, then shifted her weight from one foot to the other as I studied her.

"You want to go to Carmichael's for dinner with me." I stated it, didn't ask it.

She nodded again, but as I watched, a calm seemed to settle over her. Her eyes cleared.

She smiled that beautiful smile, and I threw caution to the wind. "Like, on a date?"

She nodded yet again. "Yes."

The words were there, in my head, but I didn't say them. Instead, I just looked at her and, somehow, she knew what I was thinking.

"Your brother is a *client*, Lacey. You...would be my date." Alicia took a step toward me. My feet still wouldn't move, and I let her into my space, let her close enough to breathe my air. She lifted a hand and, just like before, gently pushed my hair off my forehead, tucked it behind my ear, her fingertips brushing the sensitive skin there. The scent of peaches and cream filled my nostrils as she moved in even closer and her fingers slipped into my hair. I was still absorbing that fact as she leaned in, pressed those perfectly full, glossy lips to mine, and kissed me.

It was gentle. A little bit tentative at first, like she was testing the waters. She tasted like peppermint and excitement, and she pulled back just a smidgen to look into my eyes, as if gauging my reaction. Then she kissed me again.

My hands rose on their own and settled on her waist as I gave a little back, pressing my body gently against her, deepening the kiss just a touch, not wanting to scare her away, but not ready to be done yet. I held on.

Finally, she broke the kiss and took a small step back. When I opened my eyes, she was smiling tenderly. She rubbed her thumb across my bottom lip, raised her eyebrows, and backed away toward the stairs. "Just think about it," she said, as she stepped through the stairwell door. Then she gave me a cute little wave and was gone.

I stood there in the hall and watched the door close behind her before her words echoed in my head.

Just think about it.

As if I'd be able to think about anything else.

I brought my fingers up to my lips and felt the smile appear. I continued to stand there for I don't know how long, replaying that kiss in my head over and over.

When I was finally able to make my legs move again, I turned to go back into the office. Leo was sitting in the doorway, looking at me with what, I swear to God, appeared to be accusation.

"What? I didn't do anything." I shut the door behind me. It was the truth. I did nothing but stand there and be kissed. "I would never in a million years have made that move," I said to Leo now, as he followed me back to my desk. The fact was, I hadn't really thought such a move was even a possibility. Despite all of Alicia's friendly-bordering-on-what-could-be-considered-flirting gestures, I was pretty sure she was either straight, out of my league, or both. Then I remembered Leanne's comments and rolled my eyes, because she had been right. "I really should probably listen to her more," I muttered. "Don't tell her I said that."

Concentrating on work after that proved to be very difficult, not surprisingly. My head kept tossing me images of Alicia's face as it moved closer to me. I had sense memories of her mouth against mine, the softness of those lips, the tiniest touch of the tip of her tongue. If I closed my eyes, I could still feel her fingers at the back of my head, delving into my hair, tugging it gently. The forms on my computer screen might as well have been in Latin for how clear they seemed to me in that moment.

I got up and went out to the reception area to make myself some coffee. Maybe that would help me focus. Mug in hand, I went back into my own office, walked to the window, and sighed sadly when I saw no baby blue BMW in the lot. Yes, I actually sighed. Loudly. Like a schoolgirl. It was funny to me now that I'd had such a problem picturing Brandon or the mysterious Mr. Wright in that car, but the image of Alicia sitting behind the wheel, top down, sunglasses on, wind blowing through her sunset hair seemed utterly perfect and wildly sexy.

"I'm going to have to say yes to this date thing, Leo. You know?"

My terrier mix was curled up in his bed and didn't even bother to lift his head as he looked at me with his big brown marble eyes. He was obviously not interested in offering up any agreement.

I flopped back into my chair and sipped my coffee. Catching a lock of hair with my finger, I twirled it as I thought. Or tried to think. I really couldn't form anything coherent. I simply replayed that moment in the hallway over and over, obsessively.

"Okay," I finally said, and it must have been loud because Leo did lift his head. "Enough." I looked at him as he studied me. "It was just a kiss, Leo. That's all. No big deal. God knows it's been a long time since I've experienced one, so it's no wonder I'm dwelling. Right?" This time, Leo cocked his head, as if actually contemplating what I'd said. "So. Enough. I'm putting that kiss in a box up on a high shelf so I can get back to work. Sound like a plan?"

Leo yawned, then set his head back down and sighed just as loudly as I had earlier.

"Nice."

❖

I managed to keep that box tucked away up on its very, very high shelf in my mind until Sunday afternoon. That's when I lost all control, gave everything a good shake, and that box came happily tumbling off its shelf to spill all over the room.

My mother made a pot roast, which filled the house with the warmest, homiest smell on earth. Nothing made me feel more relaxed and content than that scent. I was helping her set the table as Leo sat in my father's lap.

"Goddamn sons-a-bitches," he mumbled at the TV, and I slid a look to my mom, who rolled her eyes good-naturedly and smiled.

"Don't you be teaching my boy to swear, Dad," I called to him. "He's very impressionable, you know." He didn't respond, but I saw his shoulders move as he chuckled.

We were just sitting down to eat, the pot roast with potatoes and carrots on a platter in the center of the table, a plate of warm rolls just out of the oven next to them, when we heard the side door open and my brother's voice called out, "Did I make it in time? Or did Dad eat all the meat already?"

The faces of both my parents lit up, something I was used to, as they didn't see Scott nearly as often as they saw me. Leo stood up from his spot under the table and barked as my brother entered the room, shedding his jacket. He tossed it onto the couch, then crossed into the dining room and bent to kiss my mom.

"Smells amazing," he said as he got himself a plate from the kitchen, then dug into the platter of meat and potatoes.

Scott and my dad launched into a rousing political discussion, which I would have found even more tedious if they'd been on opposite sides (which has happened in the past). Luckily, the entire family had similar opinions of the current administration, so my mother and I simply nodded and ate while Dad and Scott went on and on. Mom would throw me a glance every so often and wink at me or roll her eyes and I'd grin and we'd continue to eat. It was like Girl Code.

"And work?" my dad asked, as he shoveled the last bite of his roast into his mouth and reached for the platter and seconds.

"Work is great," Scott said, with his usual enthusiasm. Both my parents' kids loved their jobs. I think that made them happy. "We've won over several new clients lately, but we're looking to expand that even more."

"Marketing," Dad said, almost as a grunt.

"Exactly." Scott took a sip of the beer he'd grabbed from the fridge. "So, I've been dealing with Lacey's new neighbor." He pointed at me with his fork as he turned to look at me.

And here we go, I thought, making no comment.

"Oh," my mom said. "I didn't know that. Did you, Lacey?"

I nodded. "I did."

"She really has a great handle on what we need," Scott said. "I think her firm is going to be a big help." I knew from the tone of his voice that things were about to take a turn. Scott isn't terribly subtle. But I smiled to myself and ate some potatoes, letting him run with whatever he thought he had. "Plus, she's so hot."

"Scott," my mother admonished.

"What? It's true." He bumped me with a shoulder. "Right, Lace-Face?"

I nodded again. "She's very pretty."

"We went to Carmichael's Friday night." He left out the part about it being a business dinner, and I clenched my jaw to keep from stepping in. I didn't want to look like I was trying to dampen his excitement.

"That new place?" my dad asked. "Pricey."

"It is. And she paid. She's kind of a modern woman that way."

I couldn't keep it in anymore. I had to poke at him. I couldn't help myself. "Wasn't that a business dinner?" I asked innocently, as I met his eyes. "I mean, it's kind of standard practice for the business person trying to win the account to buy, isn't it?"

Scott shrugged. "It was a combination. A little business…" He waggled his eyebrows in a way that made me want to punch him in the throat because of the sheer sexism of it. "A little not business."

My father chuckled.

"You should see her, Dad." Scott gave another look that I couldn't even describe but knew it meant he wasn't talking about anything to do with Alicia's business prowess.

"Yeah?" my dad asked.

"Oh, yeah."

And I suddenly felt like I was in a men's locker room.

"I'm hoping we can have both a working relationship and a personal one," Scott said then, and that was it.

I'd had enough.

I tossed my mother a look of apology, though she probably had no idea why. "That might be hard," I said, taking my last bite of dinner.

"Oh?" Scott turned to me with expectation, his whole demeanor giving off an air of superiority, like he couldn't wait to hear what his silly little sister had to say. "Why's that?"

I set my fork down and dabbed the corner of my mouth with my napkin, taking my time until I knew everybody at the table was waiting for my answer. Then I pushed my chair back, stood up, and collected my dishes. I stepped away from the table. On my way to the kitchen, I passed behind Scott, leaned toward him, and said simply, "Because she was kissing *me* in the hallway yesterday."

I heard my mother give a little gasp and my father guffawed loudly, and it was totally worth it. So completely, utterly, totally worth it. It wasn't often I got to one-up my brother, but that moment was easily one of my favorites in all of life.

If I'd had a mic, I would have dropped it.

CHAPTER SEVEN

I found myself automatically looking for Alicia when I got to my office on Monday, and that put a little flutter in my stomach. It was the last day in March and I was crazy busy, but the first thing I did was look for her BMW in the lot. It wasn't there, so I did my best to shrug it off, actually parked in my parking spot, and got to work with my clients who had waited to file their taxes long enough to put a panicked fear in their eyes.

A few hours later, I had a short break and found myself glancing out the window to the sight of still no BMW. I wandered out into the reception area.

"Stretching your legs?" Mary asked.

I nodded, went out into the hall—the lingering scent of Chinese food was as obvious as if it had been visible—with Leo on my heels, and found myself stopping in front of the door to Just Wright. It was open and I could see Gisele and Pantone feeding themselves with chopsticks. Brandon was squinting at his computer screen. He barely gave me a glance, then went back to whatever it was he was scowling at. I turned to go, but Gisele looked up at exactly the same time Leo decided to run in and visit her, and then I was stuck.

"Hey, Lacey," Gisele said, her smile bright and kind, as always. She wore a vibrant yellow top, and her entire corner of the office seemed happy because of it. "What's new? Tax season's almost over. I bet you can't wait."

"Home stretch," I said with a nod, then made a show of looking around. "Hey, where's Alicia? I haven't seen her today."

"She and Justin are on a road trip to see a couple of new clients out toward Pittsburgh."

"Oh, wow," I said, honestly impressed. "I didn't know you guys worked with people that far away."

"We don't normally," Gisele explained. "But one guy is a friend of somebody Alicia knows well, and he's got other businessmen friends, I guess, so she's hitting a handful of them all at once. I don't think she's super optimistic about it, but—"

"She's crazy loyal," Brandon piped up, startling me. His eyes never left his screen.

"She is," Gisele agreed. "So, if she says she'll meet with somebody as a favor to a friend, she does it."

"I see." I wasn't surprised to hear that Alicia was loyal, but it was a nice tidbit to be told by others. "Okay, well, I was just wondering."

Gisele smiled at me, and it felt different than earlier, like it was more than just a simple smile.

But I was also busy and a little wired from too much caffeine. "I'll catch her when she gets back. Come on, Leo."

"Wednesday."

I glanced up at Gisele after I scooped Leo into my arms. "Sorry?"

"She'll be back in the office on Wednesday."

"Okay. Thanks."

"I'll let her know you were looking for her."

I opened my mouth to tell her that wasn't necessary, but then realized that I'd probably be placing even more of a spotlight on myself than I wanted. I mean, I wasn't *looking* for her. Was I? I was just… curious about where she was. She was usually in the office, but today she wasn't. So, I was curious. Being curious about where somebody is doesn't mean you're *looking* for them. Does it?

Yeah. I was totally looking for her.

I hurried back to my office, feeling a little silly. A little schoolgirlish. Also a little giddy, like a kid with a crush, but I did my best to shrug it off and focus on work.

Which I managed to do for two solid days, but we were into April, and I began to smile, to feel lighter, happier, because I could actually see that there was an end in sight.

Thank God.

Leanne used to laugh at me when we were together, and she still does. One year, she actually made a list, from January through April 15, and jotted down dates and how I was feeling. Then the next year, she called it up on her laptop and the duplication of it was almost eerie. And sort of amusing. And a little bit embarrassing, if I'm honest.

The fact that Alicia's car was parked in my spot that morning brought a tiny smile to my face—which didn't last long because I had to slam on my brakes to keep from getting sideswiped by Nascar Kyle, damn him. She was back, though, and something about that made things feel right again. I had no control over the way the corners of my mouth tugged back up a bit when I smelled the aroma of breakfast pizza in the hall.

I had a full schedule that day. Endless client meetings, which meant I'd be left with a ton of things to do after the last one, which meant I'd probably be in the office until well after nine. But still, it was April, light at the end of the tunnel and all that good stuff, and I was in a good mood. I pushed everything out of my head except my work.

The day flew by. That was the other thing about it finally being April. Time seemed to speed up, the days zipped past. It was like a reward for making it through the first three months of the year, as if the Universe said, "See? You did it. Nice work. Here you go," as it ripped the first two weeks of April right off the calendar.

My last client left my office at 6:45 p.m. I'd sent Mary home as soon as she'd announced him, so it was only Leo and me left. It was when I was ready to sit down and get some paperwork done, while eating the turkey sandwich I'd made myself last night, that I had a crystal-clear vision of that sandwich still sitting on my kitchen counter.

Where I'd left it this morning.

I was hungry. I had no qualms about staying and working for another hour or two, but I hadn't eaten since the Egg McMuffin I'd had for breakfast on my ride in, and my stomach was making sure I knew it. I was reaching a state of such immediate and desperate need for food that the thought of waiting twenty minutes for something to be delivered was out of the question, and twelve-hour-old breakfast pizza was actually sounding appealing. I knew somebody was still in the neighboring office, as the music had come back on, though at a reasonable level. "What do you think, Leo?"

He lifted his head from his bed and focused his sweet brown eyes at me, then yawned, his pink tongue unfurling like the red carpet at the Oscars.

"I mean, there are guys in that office. The chances of any pizza being left are probably slim, right?"

Leo blinked.

"Still. Worth a shot, don't you think? I'm starving." I stood up from my chair. Leo stayed put. "Plus, if there is any left, you get a bite of crust." That got his attention, and not for the first time, I wondered about how much dogs really understand. More than we think, I'm sure of it. He fell into step behind me as we headed out into the hall and stopped in front of the bright red door. A peek through the window told me Alicia was at her desk, black-rimmed glasses on, squinting at her computer monitor. I raised my hand to knock just as she looked up, and the smile that split across her face was radiant, even from a distance.

She's happy to see me.

Again with that thought. Seemed to be a recurring thing.

Alicia gestured for me to come in, so I pushed the door open and Leo—apparently with a spurt of new energy—sprinted across the room to see her. She was lavishing attention on him as I followed his path in, and she looked up when I got close.

"Hey." Still smiling and looking gorgeous in an emerald green top with three-quarter-length sleeves. She stood up, walked toward me, and wrapped me in a warm, gentle hug. My reaction was slightly delayed, as she'd surprised me a bit, but then I closed my arms around her, the subtle peaches-and-cream scent filling my head, and let myself subtly sink into her. Just a bit. She pulled back but kept hold of my upper arms as she studied my face. "You look tired," she said quietly.

"That might be because I'm tired," I replied, with a half grin. "And starving."

Her face lit up and she moved quickly toward the mini fridge. "I think we have some of that breakfast pizza left over. Would that help?"

I was torn between sadness over the loss of her closeness and excited relief to have food to put in my mouth. "It would help *a lot*. Thank you so much." I didn't tell her that was part of the reason I'd come over in the first place.

"No problem." She plopped a slice on a paper plate and tossed it into the microwave. Watching her was endlessly entertaining for me, and when she glanced back in my direction, I snapped my gaze to the wall, so as not to be caught staring.

"You have more work?" she asked, bending to pet Leo, who was doing a little dance around her feet.

"Yeah. Another hour or two."

"Same here."

"What are you working on? Stuff from your trip to Pittsburgh?"

Alicia's eyes caught mine. "Putting together a couple of proposals, yeah. How'd you know where I went?"

Oops. I guess Gisele forgot to tell Alicia I stopped by. "I, um, came to see you on Monday. Gisele told me you were traveling."

"You came to see me on Monday? How come?" The mischievous half grin she shot my way told me she knew exactly why I'd stopped by, and that little sheen of cockiness excited me even as I tried to play it cool. I wanted to say, *not because you kissed me. Nope. I certainly didn't hope you'd do it again. Absolutely not.* Instead, I said, "No reason," with a shrug, causing her to chuckle. The sound was throaty. Sexy.

"I see." The microwave beeped and she removed the plate. "Dinner is served," she said with a flourish as she held it out to me.

"You're saving me," I said as I took the plate, picked up the pizza, and took a bite that was too hot. I didn't care that I'd scorched the roof of my mouth. I was that hungry.

Alicia watched me eat for a few beats, her expression a mix of amusement and something I couldn't quite identify.

"I don't want to interrupt you anymore," I said, around a bite. "Thank you so much, though." I held up the half slice left in my hand. "I feel a million times better."

"I'm glad. And you're welcome." She stepped close to me, and for a split second, I was sure she was going to kiss me again. My head, of course, was shrieking no because I had a glob of half-masticated pizza stuffed in my face, but I didn't have to worry. Alicia squeezed my shoulder and then moved past me back to her desk. I called Leo and we went back to our own space, wondering why that whole exchange was both awesome and weird at the same time.

Working after that proved to be more difficult than usual. I had trouble focusing, keeping my mind on the returns in front of me instead of on the intriguing redhead I knew was working next door. She'd either turned the music down or turned it off completely, because the subtly beating bassline had disappeared, leaving me in an almost eerie silence as I worked. I have always enjoyed silence like that. No disruptions. No distractions. Just me and the numbers, the information. Facts.

That night, however, the numbers didn't comfort me. I was preoccupied by sunset red hair and ocean blue eyes and I found myself staring out the window on more than one occasion. When the rap on my door came, I was almost relieved to have an actual excuse not to focus.

"Come in," I called, just as the door opened and Alicia peeked her head in. Her green shirt, her presence in general, seemed to brighten up my entire office, as if she'd suddenly turned on a set of multicolored Christmas lights and strung them around.

"Hey. I'm gonna go out and grab something to eat. Come with me?"

"On a Wednesday?" I asked.

Alicia blinked at me. "Yes?" she said hesitantly. "Are you not allowed to eat on Wednesdays?"

"It's just…" I realized how lame I was about to sound, but said it anyway. "The middle of the week."

"Yes, it is," she said, with an undertone of amusement. "That's where Wednesday falls." Our gazes held for a beat before she said again, "Come with me?"

God, it was tempting. *So* tempting. The idea of sitting in a dimly lit restaurant with a good meal, a drink in my hand to loosen me up and a beautiful woman sitting next to me? Ridiculously tempting…

But there was work. And Leo. I had so much to do.

I wish I could. I've got way too much to get through here.

That's what I should have said.

"Okay. Just let me finish up this one thing," is what I actually said, and almost couldn't believe my own ears.

Her face softened into what I could only identify as happiness. "I'll be back in ten minutes." And just like that, she was gone, leaving me to wonder what had just happened.

❖

"Okay, can we just take a moment and admire the beauty of this cheeseburger?" Alicia was sitting across from me in a booth at Burger

Bar and gestured to her meal with her hand, like she was a spokesmodel on QVC and trying to entice me to buy it.

"I don't know," I said. "Mine might be more beautiful."

Alicia wrinkled her nose. "Um, no. Yours has that giant ring of onion. Deal breaker."

"Deal breaker?" I feigned horror. "On what planet? All burgers should have onions. I'm pretty sure it's a rule."

"No way."

"Well, you're just silly, then."

We sat there for a beat, each of us with goofy grins, each of us holding a burger dripping with greasy, cheesy, ketchup-y goodness. Then, by unspoken agreement, we each took a bite at the same time.

"Oh, my God," Alicia said, holding a hand in front of her mouth. "That's, like, a mouthgasm."

I choked on my laugh, stunned that she'd said the O word, sort of, but also finding it hilarious (and a little bit of turn-on, if I was being completely honest).

"If I ate here as often as I want to, I'd weigh five hundred pounds," she added, her eyes twinkling.

I nodded my agreement, my mouth still too full to form words.

"Thanks for coming with me." She glanced around the dining room, which was pretty much empty besides us and three teenage boys two aisles over. Two of them were watching something on a phone while the third used his straw to blow spitballs at them.

"Thanks for dragging me," I said, turning back to Alicia and taking a sip of my Diet Coke.

"Yeah, what is that?"

"What's what?" I asked.

Her furrowed brow told me she'd been wondering about this for a while now. "Why do you always need to be dragged? You never just say yes. You have to be…" She popped a French fry into her mouth and looked up at the ceiling as if the word she was looking for was written up there. "Coaxed."

"Hmm," I said, around a bite.

"How come? Is it me? Or is it you?"

Well, if that isn't a loaded question…

"It's me," I said. *And you*, I thought. "I've never been great at spontaneity. Even as a kid."

"How come?" Alicia's expression was enthralled, like I was telling her something she'd been waiting to hear for years.

I shrugged. "I don't know." Not a total lie, but not the whole truth. But I wasn't about to say *because I'm boring* or *because I've gotten too used to being alone*, both of which were true. "I guess I just…need the right incentive." *That* was the truth, and as soon as the words came out of my mouth, I wanted to snatch them out of the air and stuff them back in.

Alicia didn't pry, much to my surprise. Instead, she studied me with those intense blue eyes, one corner of her mouth tugged up the whole time. "See, now I'll have to make it my goal to provide worthy incentives in the future." She ducked her head a bit and raised an eyebrow at me before taking a large bite of her burger.

In that moment, I was pretty sure that allowing Alicia Wright to drag me to dinner with her after eight o'clock on a weekday was the smartest decision I'd ever made.

❖

Thursday blew by in a blur of clients, numbers, thumping bass through the wall, and the smell of I-don't-know-what kind of food coming from next door, but by Friday, I was beyond exhausted. Almost to the end or not, I was dangling by one hand at the end of my rope. The fifteenth was less than two weeks away, but I had to pep-talk myself regularly. I could do this. I. Could. Do. This.

When Leo and I pushed through the stairwell door into the second-floor hallway Friday morning, I was nearly beaned by a flying red rubber ball, like the ones we used to play dodgeball with in gym class at school. Thank God I have quick reflexes and managed to tip my head to the right just in time. The ball hit the door behind me and bounced to the floor, where Leo decided it was time to join in the fun.

Brandon and Pantone were in the hall, standing about fifty yards apart, Brandon near me, Pantone down past the door to Just Wright. Gisele was in front of Pantone, her knees bent slightly as if she were ready to spring. Justin mimicked her stance in front of Brandon, and I put together that they were two teams competing against each other in some form of soccer they'd made up. Of course, Leo had other plans and pushed the ball with his nose right down to Gisele, who was laughing so hard at his antics that she let him pass her. When he dribbled past Pantone, who was also doubled over with laughter, Justin threw his arms up in victory.

"Goooooooaaaaaaaaaal!"

He ran around, arms up like Rocky, and high-fived Brandon. Gisele swooped up Leo and gave him a kiss on his nose, then raised his little front paw up like a champion. It was a big, very loud celebration in the hallway at barely 9:00 a.m., and imagine my surprise when I felt myself chuckling lightly, despite my tiredness. I shook my head and turned into my office, knowing Leo would either follow me or Gisele would bring him in.

"Good morning," Mary said, chewing, in her hand some sort of empanada-looking thing with what seemed to be sausage spilling out of it.

"Hey," I said, and went straight to the coffee.

"How late did you stay last night?"

As if on cue, a yawn cranked my mouth wide open. "Midnight," I told her, though in actuality, it had been closer to 1:00 a.m.

"Did you sleep?"

"A little." That was the truth. I'd worked after dinner with Alicia, and I'd allowed myself to drink coffee too late into the night, forgetting to switch to the decaf Mary'd bought for me. By the time I lay down in my bed, I was wired. Sleep came sometime after three, and my alarm went off at six thirty.

"Sorry about that," Gisele said, as she appeared in the doorway holding Leo. My little terrier mix was looking far too pleased with himself. "Mr. Leonardo is just so much fun!" He licked her nose.

"He does love to play ball," Mary said, as Gisele set Leo on the floor. He marched right back into my office.

"I guess he's done with me," Gisele said, still smiling widely. "Thanks for letting us borrow him."

I gave a nod, hoping that meant the soccer game was over, but such was not the case. It simply moved into the office next door where cheers, clapping, and the occasional ball cracking against the wall served as my soundtrack for the next half hour. I even heard Alicia shout, "Foul," once or twice, and I found myself losing focus on my work so I could listen. A small part of me felt the urge to go join in.

The arrival of my first client put an end to that, and I did my best to tune my neighbors out. But the third time, she flinched in her chair when the ball hit the wall, and I knew I needed to put a stop to it, even though I dreaded having to be the party pooper yet again.

I excused myself for a minute and scooted quickly next door. They'd pushed the desks and tables to the walls so that the center of the office was wide open enough to serve as their playing field. When Alicia finally noticed me, she shot me one of her gorgeous smiles and I had a flash of her on the other side of the table last night, asking me a question and then focusing all her attention on me as I answered. My belly fluttered and I had to bite down on my lips to keep the wide grin from spreading across my face. I waved her over to me and she trotted—I swear she did—right to me.

"Hey," she said, and I noticed she was slightly out of breath. "Too loud?"

I squinched up my nose. "A little, yeah," I said quietly. "It's just... startling my client when the ball hits the wall."

"No problem. We'll ease up. Sorry about that." She winked at me, and since her back was to the others, I'm the only one who saw it. I claimed it as my own.

"Thanks. I'm sorry to be the Fun Killer."

Alicia shook her head, her waves bouncing. "Hey, it got you over here, didn't it?" When I squinted at her, she leaned in conspiratorially and whispered, "Incentive." With that, she gave my upper arm a squeeze and went back to the makeshift soccer field. "Okay, guys, we need to call this game for now." I heard a few groans, but she held up a hand. "Nope. This is an office building. We'll pick things up after hours."

She turned back to me and I gave her a little wave before heading back to my office and Mrs. Gates. That had gone way better than expected.

I had a couple of breaks in my schedule over the next few days. Luckily, while there were people who waited until the last minute to file their taxes, most people didn't. So even though I was pretty busy with panicked, oh-my-God-is-it-April-already clients, my appointment calendar also began to ease ever so slightly. That Friday, I had a three-hour block from one o'clock until after four where I was completely clear, and I was so happy about it, I caught myself giggling quietly more than once, Leo looking up at me from his bed like I'd possibly lost my mind.

My 12:30 client had left, and I was just settling into my comfy desk chair ready to knock off some work when I looked up to see Alicia standing in my doorway. She was wearing a bright yellow spring jacket that would've made me look like a walking lemon but made her look like summer sunshine, and her smile was radiant. Everything about her was warm and inviting.

"Come on," she said to me, and crossed my office to the small rack where my jacket hung, its earthy green color seemed so bland next to hers.

I blinked at her. "What?"

"I said, come on. You've got no clients for three hours. I checked. You're coming with me."

"I am?" I blinked some more, thoroughly confused, and I actually stood up and let her put one arm into my jacket sleeve before reason kicked in and I stopped her. "Wait. What are you doing? I can't leave."

"Sure you can. You're the boss." Alicia held my jacket so I could put my other arm in, which I did sort of automatically. "We've both been working too hard. We need a break. So we're taking one. Nothing wrong with that."

"But..." I looked down at my desk with what I was sure were fairly panicked eyes. I pointed at the papers scattered across it. "I have so much work—"

"And it will still be there when we get back. I need to decompress, and I think you do, too." Alicia slid her hand down my arm and grasped my hand. "Come on. Mary will watch Leonardo DiCaprio." Leo was watching from his bed as if he knew exactly what Alicia was saying, because he made no attempt to follow us. Alicia tugged me through the reception area. "I'll have her back by three," she said to Mary, who winked. *Winked!* Mary doesn't wink.

I was buckled into the passenger seat of Alicia's light blue BMW before I even realized it, my head still spinning. If I hadn't been tired, my protests might have been heartier. As it was, it seemed the best I could do was blink in bewilderment. "What is happening?" I finally asked.

Alicia steered us out of the parking lot and into the flow of traffic. "We've both been working like crazy," she said, her eyes on the road. "Too much, really. It's not good for either of us. When I feel like I'm all clogged up from too much work and not enough relaxation, I have a place I go and it helps me to just…" She seemed to take a moment looking for the right description before continuing with, "Breathe. It helps me to just breathe." She glanced at me then, and there was a combination on her face that I couldn't quite decipher. Tenderness. Worry. Hesitation. Turning back to the windshield, she said quietly, "I thought maybe you needed to breathe, too."

"I have so much to do," I said, as it was first and foremost in my mind. "April is crazy for me."

"All the more reason to give yourself a break. I promise it won't take long, and I also promise it will be worth it." She glanced at me. "Incentive."

While I was pretty sure I should be panicky and cranky—and in most cases, I would be—there was something about Alicia, some kind of pull. I protested, sure. But, in reality, I was happier than I cared to admit to be sitting in that seat next to her, zipping along on a gorgeous, sunny day.

It was so disconcertingly…*not me.*

We pulled into the lot of the Philadelphia Museum of Art—which simultaneously surprised me and didn't—and parked. The day was gorgeous, almost warm, sunny, and bright, the tan stone of the enormous, U-shaped building bouncing the rays back cheerfully. Tourists meandered everywhere and a short line of people stood waiting to have their picture taken with the larger-than-life statue of Rocky Balboa from the movies. It was the thing to do when you visited Philly, and even though I would normally roll my eyes at the predictability, I didn't. Instead, I found myself smiling as I walked past a young boy who had his arms thrown up over his head just like Rocky's were.

Inside, the museum was fairly populated, people milling around, on their phones, waiting for others, sitting to rest their feet. I allowed Alicia to lead me to the admissions area where she showed a membership card, then paid my twenty-dollar entrance fee before I could protest.

"It's fine," she said, holding up her hand, traffic cop style. "I dragged you here. The least I can do is pay." Again, she grasped my hand, and I tried not to focus on how much I enjoyed the way hers felt in mine. Warm and soft. Firm grip. The way her thumb rubbed over my knuckle. "There's an American Watercolor exhibit I'd like to see. That okay with you?"

"Confession: I don't know the first thing about art." I shrugged and half grimaced.

"I really don't either," she said as we followed the signs. "But there's something about watercolor that I find...I don't know. Calming? I don't know what it is. I like all kinds of art, all different mediums, but watercolors are my favorite."

I wished I had something to add, but instead I nodded and followed her obediently, looking forward to seeing something that seemed to move her, and putting the giant pile of work I'd left behind right out of my head for the time being.

The museum is huge, with more than three-quarters of a million people going through it each year, so it took us a while to find the first-floor exhibit. It was being shown for a limited time, so many people were strolling through, stopping in front of each painting. The signage told me it was "American Watercolor in the Age of Homer and Sargent," which meant absolutely nothing to me. But I figured that didn't mean I couldn't look. I can like art. I can appreciate talent.

I followed Alicia as she stopped in front of the first painting, which depicted a sailboat in rough waters. She tilted her head from one side to the other, studying.

"The colors are so serene," she said quietly. "Yet the subject is tense. I feel the tension of the sailors."

I nodded. She was right. While the shades of blue in the ocean were light and easy, the choppiness of the water made me nervous. We stood for a few moments, then moved on to the next painting.

I took the opportunity to look around, to observe the other patrons in the exhibit. Some stayed for only a moment or two in front of each piece, moving along fairly quickly. Some actually sat and stared for long periods of time. One man sat on a padded bench in front of a painting, an open sketchbook in his lap, his pencil making quiet scratching noises as he worked.

"I do that sometimes," Alicia whispered, her lips alarmingly close to my ear.

"Sketch?"

"No, but I can sit for a long time and just stare at a painting."

"Really?" I couldn't imagine it. I was sure it would only take a moment before my brain would drift off to all the other things I could be getting done as I sat and stared at a framed picture hanging on a wall.

She nodded and gave me that gentle smile as we moved on to the next painting.

We did this for the next four paintings. Moving. Stopping. Looking. Making a couple of comments. I was surprised how much I was enjoying myself. And Alicia had been right; I realized I felt much calmer than I had when we'd arrived.

We moved on to the next painting, titled *The Trysting Place*. It showed a woman in a long, flowing white dress embroidered with small blue flowers. She stood near a tree in the woods, the background of soft greens and browns, and I could almost hear the birdsong that must have surrounded her, the rustling of leaves in a gentle summer breeze. In her hand, a fan of red and white partially obscured her face, her chestnut hair pulled back in a chignon. She was expecting somebody, both the title of the painting and the expression on her face told me so.

As if reading my mind, Alicia whispered, "I wonder who she's waiting for."

A smile tugged one corner of my mouth up. "A boyfriend maybe?"

"A girlfriend?" Alicia raised her eyebrows when I looked at her. "This was painted in, what?" She squinted at the information. "Eighteen seventy-five. She'd definitely have to have a secret tryst to see a woman."

"I like that," I said, with a determined nod. "I'm going with that."

"Me too. I mean, look at her face. She's got both anticipation and worry going on. She's excited and also a little terrified."

"Then she's definitely waiting for a girl."

Alicia chuckled as she stood close to me; I could feel her body heat. I could smell the peaches-and-cream scent of her (Soap? Shampoo? Lotion?). Her fingertips lightly brushed the small of my back, the move gentle, yet slightly possessive. I liked it.

There were nine paintings altogether, so it didn't take long to see each of them, but we went around the room again. I was glad for that, as I wasn't quite ready to leave yet, the stack of work on my desk fading, finally, into the background in my mind as I let myself be calmed by the simple beauty of artwork. On our second pass, we noticed things in each painting that we hadn't the first time through, and we discussed each detail in quiet whispers, our heads tipped toward each other. Being so close to Alicia, feeling her breath on my face, seeing the tiny black flecks in the blue of her eyes, noticing the perfect arch of her auburn eyebrows…it was intoxicating. I felt a tingle in my thighs, and I tried to ignore it, as it was a sure sign of my arousal, and I wasn't ready to deal with that quite yet.

All told, we stayed for a little over an hour, wandering from painting to painting, letting the mood of each flow over us.

"What did you think?" Alicia asked on our way back to the car. Her tone contained a slight edge of…what was it? Trepidation? As though she was waiting for either my approval or my condemnation.

"I loved it," I said with a big grin, letting her off the hook. "Like I said, I don't know a thing about art, but…I've also never really *studied* paintings like that before."

"No?"

I shook my head. "Not like that, no. The way each one evoked a particular mood or feeling? It was amazing."

The smile that broke across Alicia's face just then made me want to find more things like that to say, just to keep her wearing that expression. She was radiantly beautiful. "And how do you feel now?"

I nodded. "You were right. I can admit that. I feel calm. Relaxed. Ready to get back to work and not at all stressed about it."

Alicia gave one nod of her head. "Excellent. My work here is done."

Once in the car and buckled into our seats, I reached over to lay a hand on her arm. I hesitated for just a split second—at that point, I was aware that any sort of touching of Alicia sent a zap of electricity through me—but I don't think she noticed. When her eyes locked with mine, I said simply, "Thank you."

I was pretty sure I saw a slight pinkening of her cheeks as she responded, "You're welcome."

I was back in my office by three, as promised, Mary giving me a knowing look as I entered. Leo was sitting in her lap, watching diligently as she pulled a chip from a pile in a container on her desk.

"Are those nachos?" I asked.

Mary nodded as she chewed. "They got Mexican next door."

I helped myself to one, then shook my head and pointed at her. "Don't give him any." Leo turned to look at me and I noticed a small glob of orange on his chin. Cheese. I shook my head again and went into my office.

The calm had been nice, that was for sure, and despite the work I now had in front of me, a big part of me was thankful for it. The more time I spent with Alicia, the more time I wanted to spend with her. I turned to gaze out my window, the sun still shining brightly, and it occurred to me that even though I'd had several occasions of time spent with her, I knew next to nothing about Alicia's personal life. She was very good at asking me questions and getting me talking, and I wondered if that was intentional.

Before I could analyze further, Mary intercommed me and sent a call through. With a sigh, I got to work, but a small part of me wondered when Alicia would show up again to spirit me away. Soon, I hoped.

CHAPTER EIGHT

I was in my office all day on Saturday. I had a lot to get done and three client meetings, so Leo and I were settled in, with coffee and a bagel I'd grabbed on the way, by nine. My first client was at eleven, and I worked diligently for two hours, part of my consciousness tuned to the office next door. I was surprised to hear no activity at all leaching through my wall.

The day went fairly quickly, and for that, I was grateful. I was having dinner that night with Leanne and a couple friends, and I was looking forward to it more than I realized. Leanne knows me well and tended to schedule such gatherings purposely to get me out into the land of the living, breathing people who did other things besides work.

My last client left me at 4:45, and I worked for another half hour before packing up my things and Leo and locking up the office. I couldn't help it; I wandered down the hallway and was surprised to find the space behind the Just Wright door dark. I was fairly certain it was the first Saturday since they'd moved in that nobody worked, and I tried—unsuccessfully—not to notice the disappointment I felt at Alicia's absence. Saturday or no Saturday, I'd hoped she was there.

"Oh, well," I said out loud with a shrug. "Come on, Leo. Let's get you some dinner."

At home, I filled Leo's dish, topped it with a sprinkle of Parmesan cheese (God, he was spoiled), and headed up to my bedroom to decide what to wear to dinner. I wasn't sure who else might be there besides Leanne and her friends, Martha and Lori, but I knew the restaurant. Angelica was contemporary Italian; some people showed up in jeans, others in evening wear. I could pretty much choose whatever I wanted.

I tended to dress more business than casual at work (a throwback from working with my old-fashioned father) and there were times when a pair of jeans was the only thing I wanted to put on. I'd ordered myself a new pair of very dark jeans a few weeks ago and had yet to wear them. I knew I could dress them up enough to wear to Angelica and not feel self-consciously casual. I paired them with a flowing white top and a lightweight scarf in a variety of greens. Slight heels helped with the "dressing up" aspect, and I donned some dangling silver earrings to top it off. With a nod of approval to the mirror, I spritzed on a body spray softly scented with vanilla and honey and headed downstairs.

Angelica was located in Olde City, which was a hopping neighborhood on a Saturday night, a blend of natives and tourists enjoying the early spring weather, wandering from Independence Mall and the Liberty Bell to restaurants or bars or clubs. Leanne, Martha, and Lori were all crowded around the bar when I arrived, and there was another woman with them, a tall brunette with large, dark eyes and the broad shoulders of a swimmer. Leanne saw me first and motioned to the bartender to get me a glass of white wine. As always, her brown eyes were smiling—Leanne was one of those people who put the group at ease with her laid-back attitude and approachable demeanor. She wrapped an arm around my shoulders and turned me to the rest of her crew.

"Lacey, you know Martha and Lori, right? You met them at the Christmas party."

I nodded in agreement. "I remember," I said, and smiled at the couple while shaking their hands. Martha had short, chestnut brown hair tucked behind her ears. Lori was a tall blonde with kind eyes and a gorgeous smile. "Nice to see you again."

"And this is Lori's cousin, Amy." Leanne indicated the brunette, who held out a hand.

"It's nice to meet you, Lacey. I've heard a lot about you." She smiled, and her words sent red flags up in my head.

This was a setup. I gave Leanne a sideways glance that she pretended not to see. "Nice to meet you, too," I said, and shook her hand, which was larger than mine and soft, her grip firm but not too much so.

My wine came and I had to make a conscious effort not to gulp it. Instead, I smiled and nodded along at different points in the conversation as we stood at the bar waiting for our table, and I plotted different horrific deaths for Leanne in my head. Tossing her off a cliff... Shoving her into oncoming traffic...Hiding pine nuts—which she's deathly allergic to—in the salad I serve her. When the hostess came to lead us to our seats, Leanne and I brought up the end of the line. I turned to her and ground out, "Why didn't you tell me you were setting me up?"

"Because I knew you wouldn't come." It was a simple answer. It was also correct, but it bothered me a little bit that I was so easy to read.

"I hate you."

"She's nice. Give her a chance."

"Fine," I said, a little flustered, and took another slug of my wine.

Our table was in a back corner, which was nice, as the restaurant was packed and humming with conversation. I took the chair against the wall, which I liked, as I could people watch as well as talk to my fellow diners. Leanne sat to my right, Amy to my left, Martha and Lori between them. We were given menus and a wine list and left to it.

"You enjoy wine?" Amy asked.

I nodded. "I do. You?"

"I do, though I don't know much about it."

We went through the menu and wine list together, and I helped her choose a robust Zinfandel to go with the strip steak she planned to order. I decided on the chicken piccata, so stuck to my Sauvignon Blanc.

"Leanne tells me you're an accountant?" Amy asked, leaning close enough for me to smell what had to be some very expensive perfume. It was nice, a little musky with just a hint of something floral.

"And a financial advisor, yes."

She shook her head. "Numbers make my brain hurt."

I grinned at that. "What do you do?"

"I teach high school English."

We talked about that for a bit. Amy was nice. She was pleasant. She seemed intelligent and well-spoken. What she *wasn't* was the gorgeous redhead who occupied the office next to mine. Though I kept trying to shove that thought back into its little box, it continued to pop the lid off and make itself known, like a tiny party reveler, waving its arms, tossing confetti, and blowing on a party horn. Still, I did my best to give her my full attention. She deserved that.

I couldn't speak for anybody else, but my dinner was excellent. My chicken was tender, the lemon juice and capers adding a lovely zing, the parsley fresh and bright green. I was just finishing my wine when the waiter set another glass in front of me.

"I didn't order that," I said, puzzled.

He smiled and pointed. "From the lady at the bar."

She was far enough away that, without the sunset red of her hair, I might not have been able to see who he meant. Alicia Wright held up her own glass in a toast to me and grinned as my entire table followed my gaze.

"Oh," I heard Leanne utter under her breath, drawing the word out.

"Who's that?" Amy asked, her tone a strange mix of intrigued and wary.

"A friend," I said. Not a lie. Not the entire truth either, really, though I'd be hard-pressed to explain it using actual words.

"She looks familiar," Martha commented as she furrowed her brow. "I can't place her, though."

"She runs an advertising company, I think," Leanne supplied, then turned to me. "Is that right?"

I nodded. "Close. Marketing and graphic design."

"Her office is next door to Lacey's," Leanne said in explanation, and a round of nods went around the table, as if that explained everything.

I was happy to leave it at that, but my eyes continued to be drawn back to the bar regularly. Each time, Alicia was still there. Once, she was chatting up the bartender. Once, it was the man next to her, and I absently wondered if he was trying to pick her up. My interest in Amy faded, no matter how hard I tried to force it, and I felt bad about that because I think she knew it.

Like I said, spontaneity isn't really my thing, and I felt a bit... off-kilter for the rest of dinner, as if my world had been tilted just enough for me to feel like I had to hold on to the table for balance. I tried—not very well—to keep my eyes and attention on the people at my table, but my gaze would wander to the bar, almost on its own, as if I had no control over myself.

"This must be a crazy busy time for you," Amy was saying, and

I blinked three times and ordered myself to focus on this nice woman sitting next to me. "Being so close to the tax deadline."

I turned my attention to her, literally shifting my body so I faced her. "It is. The last couple of weeks before April fifteenth, I usually put in twelve-, sometimes fourteen-hour days."

"Oh, my God. You must be exhausted!" Amy's dark eyes went wide and she laid a warm hand on my forearm. "I can't imagine."

"And she forgets to eat," Leanne said from the other side of me.

Amy gave me a gently disapproving look, raising her eyebrows and tilting her head just a bit.

I chuckled; I couldn't help it. "I know, I know. But Leanne shows up every now and then with food and then stares at me until I eat it."

"True story," Leanne said, with a nod.

"Well, it's nice to have people who care," Amy commented, and I smiled my agreement.

The waiter showed up to collect our empty plates, and I took the opportunity to glance at the bar, as at least five minutes had gone by, I was sure.

Alicia was gone.

Damn it!

I don't know why it upset me so much. I analyzed that as I quickly laid blame on Amy, on Leanne, before realizing how ridiculous I was being. I tried to grab onto logic. It wasn't like Alicia had come there with me. It wasn't as if she was supposed to stay and return my clandestine glances. She had obviously been there for some other reason, and I had no claim on her time or attention.

Still…

We settled up the bill, and the others discussed going out dancing. I don't dance, so that was a hard pass for me. I had an odd mix of guilt, and a little ego boost, when Amy was obvious in her disappointment.

"Do you think I could get your number?" she asked me quietly, as we trooped through the restaurant to the front door.

"Absolutely," I said. She pulled out her phone, and I rattled off my digits.

"Great." Amy slid her phone back into her purse, and her dark eyes settled on mine. They really were nice eyes. Richly brown, kind, expressive, outlined subtly and sporting thick, dark lashes. I liked her eyes. "I had a nice time tonight," she said with a gentle smile. "I'm glad we met."

"Me too," I replied, and it wasn't a lie. Despite my distraction, I really did enjoy Amy's company. It was nice to have somebody new to talk to, somebody who didn't already know a ton about me. Starting fresh and all that.

I guess it shouldn't have surprised me that, on my drive home, Alicia tiptoed back into my thoughts. Sending me a drink from across a crowded restaurant and then disappearing before I could properly thank her? Wasn't that what romantic movies were made of? Didn't that only happen in romance novels?

This train of thought stayed with me during my ride, the entire time I was loving up Leo (who apparently thought I'd been gone for days), and while I got ready for bed. I tried to shake it, but that red hair, that little salute, the mischievous grin—it all took up space in my head. Too much space.

I climbed into bed and clicked on the TV, did my best to lose myself in an episode of *Deadliest Catch*. In addition to being fascinated by the ins and outs of crab fishing, I found myself unable to stop thinking about how bad those boats must smell...the combination of cigarette smoke, fish, and unwashed men...gross. But even as one worker fell overboard in the midst of a horrific storm, he only had half my attention. I couldn't seem to help it.

I fell asleep and dreamed of working on the deck of a ship, pulling up a crab pot with the winch, and finding a beautiful redheaded mermaid inside, smiling at me with sex and mischief in her eyes.

CHAPTER NINE

Monday morning dawned bright and sunny and cheerful. My disposition was similar. Why? Because there were only eight more days until April 15, and I was psyched. Buried, completely underwater, in the weeds, all those clichés about having too much work to do, but I didn't care. Eight more days. I could do eight more days. I was going to survive another year.

As I said before, my work wouldn't suddenly stop after the fifteenth. Lots of my clients had extensions and there would still be much to do for several weeks after the deadline. But in my world, the fifteenth was cause for celebration. I am reasonably sure if you were to survey a plane full of people headed to a well-known vacation destination on April 16, a large majority of them would be in the finance industry.

I didn't have plans for a vacation; I'm not one of those people who needs to get away. Of course, a bad winter in Philly can make anybody wish for a beach and an umbrella drink. But the winter had been fairly mild, with less than a handful of notable storms, and I'd be happy just to work a regular, eight-hour day and do something fun with my Saturdays. Like sleep in, hit a movie, read a book, stay in my house. Getting my full weekends back was definitely something I looked forward to.

Mary was enjoying a Danish of some sort when I entered, so I lost Leo to her immediately. I shook my head, headed into my office, and began my day.

Eight more days...

My nine o'clock client, Mr. Callan, was a notorious pain in my ass. He'd been a pain in my father's ass for a decade before Dad retired.

Now he was a pain in mine. Each April (because he always waited until April), after the insane amount of time I spent organizing the things he needed itemized, we had a discussion about what he should be doing differently throughout the year to make this process easier on both of us. And by "both of us," I meant "me." Each April, Mr. Callan nodded sagely, squinted at me like he was paying very close attention. Sometimes, he asked questions. One year, he even took notes. And then the next April, he'd show up with a mess, just like always. Receipts that didn't apply. Missing receipts that should have applied. Things he'd remember at the last minute and blurt out just as I thought we'd finished. Irritation that I couldn't miraculously ensure he'd get a refund (he never did). He was ridiculous, and I considered more than once firing him as a client.

I never did. My dad wouldn't like that.

So, after spending three hours with Mr. Callan and not coming close to finishing, I had to send him on his way, because I knew we'd gone alarmingly far over his allotted time, and I had somebody waiting far beyond her scheduled appointment time. Mr. Callan continued to ask questions even as I ushered him through my door to the reception area.

I glanced at sweet Mrs. Sargent, who was sitting patiently in a plastic chair, and she smiled at me without so much as a mention that I was half an hour late for our appointment. Thank God. She was like the epitome of everybody's perfect grandma. Kind, gentle, serene. Just seeing her sitting there calmed my racing heart and boiling blood, and I took a moment to just breathe as Mr. Callan nodded to her and made his way out.

"Hi there, Mrs. Sargent," I finally said when I felt better. "I'm so sorry to keep you waiting."

Mrs. Sargent waved an eighty-five-year-old hand dismissively. "It's no bother," she said, as she got to her feet. "Mary gave me a very good cup of coffee and Leo kept me company." I hadn't noticed Leo at her feet, but he looked up at her then, with love in his brown eyes, and I chuckled. "My," she said, as she got closer. "You look more like your mother every time I see you."

I thanked her, held out an arm, and let her lead the way into my office.

The remainder of my day flew by, the rest of my clients being people I really enjoyed working for, people who reminded me why I loved my job, even at this crazy time of year. I loved the task of organizing and making sense of the chaos of people's financial year. It was exhilarating.

I waved as my last client of the day left my office. It was approaching eight, and Mary had left about an hour ago. Almost as if there was a camera in my office letting Brandon know I no longer had a client, the bassline of his music suddenly started up, loud and clear. I blew out a breath, but was a little taken aback to realize it didn't bother me so much. I had no idea why, but I sat there and listened as I watched a few comings and goings in the parking lot, my head bopping to the music. As I listened a bit longer, I figured it to be a Flo Rida song I liked, super catchy and fun. I crossed my office to get a new pad out of my little closet, did a little butt wiggle on my way, surprising myself, as I normally didn't dance. Then I was humming the tune. Leo glanced up at me from where he was napping in his bed and watched me critically as I put a few moves into action, dancing in the middle of my office.

"Come on, Leo," I said, pointing at him as I shimmied my shoulders. Nothing. He just stared at me, bored. "All right then. I'm gonna have to unlock these hips. Stand back." I moved my pelvis around in a circle, then back and forth, staying perfectly with the beat, letting my body move almost as if on its own. I threw my head back and closed my eyes, my arms over my head, and danced in a full circle as I sang. And when I finished my circle and opened my eyes, I stumbled to a halt, a little squeak of surprise escaping me—before the mortification hit.

Alicia stood in my doorway, arms crossed over her chest as she leaned against the frame. A huge, satisfied smile stretched across her face.

I was breathless now, and we stood, gazes locked, me breathing raggedly, her continuing to smile with glee.

"Hi," she said finally.

"Hey." I gave a lame wave.

"And thank you for making my entire week with that performance." Her expression was soft and friendly, and though she was teasing me, it felt gentle.

"Hey, once in a while, a girl's gotta cut loose. At least that's what everyone insists on telling me."

"I completely agree." She crossed the room to where my jacket hung and said, "That attitude will make things easier on me." She held my jacket out to me. "Come on. We're going out for a drink. I need one, and I bet you could use one as well."

I blinked at her, at a loss, as she stood before me in a shimmery silver top, sleek black dress pants, and heels, looking every bit the corporate entrepreneur, but with a generous helping of "extremely sexy" thrown in.

"I really shouldn't leave," I said. "I've got—"

"Work to do," Alicia interrupted and made a rolling gesture with her hand. "I know. You tell me that every time, so get it out and then we can go. I have work, too, but you know what we're doing? We're living in the moment. Right here, right now, Chamberlain. Life is too short. Trust me, I know." She shook my jacket. "Now let's go. Gisele is next door. Leo can hang with her. We won't be gone long, I promise. Just one drink." She paused a moment, made a thinking face, then amended, "Possibly two."

What was it about her?

Why did I find myself reaching for the jacket she handed me, despite my desire to resist? Flying by the seat of my pants makes me nervous and jerky. It makes me feel out of control, like I'm not calling the shots in my own life. Dramatic? Sure. I know this. But it's who I am, and I probably needed to make that clearer to Ms. Wright. I needed to put my foot down. I thought about doing so the entire time I followed her and Leo to the Just Wright office and left him there. I thought about it all the way down the stairs and out into the cool of the evening. I considered it even as Alicia grasped my wrist and pulled me away from the parking lot and down the sidewalk instead. For the entire five-minute walk to Boomer's, I shuffled through wording, phrases, the best way to tell Alicia that I didn't appreciate her ordering me around.

But you know what I realized? I kind of did.

Not the ordering around part, necessarily, but the part of Alicia that stood up to me and my protests and said, "I understand, but let's do this anyway." I was starting to understand that I needed that in my life.

Two bar stools stood vacant at the end of the bar, and I was led to them. It didn't escape my notice how many heads turned to get a good eyeful of Alicia as we passed.

Once on our stools, the bartender came right over, and his eyes might as well have been his hands the way they roamed over Alicia's body. I squinted at him. He didn't notice.

"What can I get you ladies?" he asked. He was fairly handsome, with sandy hair and sparkling blue eyes, and I probably would've liked him immediately if I hadn't been able to read his thoughts regarding what he'd like to do with the redheaded customer before him. Conversely, my hair could have been on fire and I don't think he'd have given me a second glance.

"What's your house red?" Alicia asked.

The bartender reached for a bottle and held it up for Alicia's inspection. She gave a nod and held up two fingers.

When the bartender went in search of a corkscrew, Alicia turned to me. "Long day?"

"Yes, and it'll be longer now that you've dragged me down here," I said, feigning a curmudgeon attitude, even as I half hid a smile.

Clearly, she didn't catch it. She twirled a finger in the ends of my hair and gave a gentle tug. "You need to ease up, Lace. You're wound so damn tight."

I furrowed my brow at her. "Um, rude. Didn't your parents teach you any manners?"

Something passed across her face, a shadow, so quickly I almost missed it, and she waved me off with a hand as the bartender set our wine in front of us. "Relax. I didn't mean it like that." She held her glass toward me.

"How did you mean it, then?" I asked, forcing myself to take a breath and not overreact in the middle of a bar. Even if I thought it was warranted. I touched my glass to hers. We both sipped.

"It's just that you work so hard for so long. I'm afraid you're not getting enough…recreation time. That's all."

The concern in her voice seemed genuine to me. "It's like this every spring. I don't work like this all year long, you know. But I'm an accountant. It's tax time."

"No, I get that. I just…" Alicia let her words trail off, and I got the impression she wanted to say more but thought better of it. "I worry. A little. And I thought you could use a break. I didn't mean to stomp in like a bull in a china shop." She sipped her wine and caught my eye, a glint in hers. "Though it was totally worth it to see you going all *So You Think You Can Dance*."

"Shut up," I said, and we both laughed even as I felt my cheeks heat up. "And thank you for worrying about me, warranted or not." I paused before saying quietly, "It's nice."

"I'm often guilty of putting my job before everything else in life," Alicia said, her voice so quiet I had to lean close to hear. "So I tend to step in when I see somebody I care about doing it. You've got to be present. Live in—"

"The moment," I interrupted, with a smile prompted by her admission of caring about me. "So you've said."

"Words to live by." She shrugged, then sipped. After a beat, she said, "How was your dinner the other night?"

The mention of Saturday tossed me a quick flash of Amy. She'd texted me on Sunday and I'd responded, keeping things friendly. She'd been nice. I liked her. "Delicious. I'd never been there before. Had you?"

Alicia nodded. "A few times. I take clients there a lot. It's classy, quiet enough to carry on a conversation, but not so quiet that it feels too romantic, you know?"

I did. "Were you there alone?" It was the closest I could get to asking if she'd had a date without actually asking if she'd had a date. Which was none of my business.

"I was definitely doing some wooing, but not a date. A potential client."

"And?"

She inhaled a big breath and let it out. "Not sure. I think he's still wavering."

I bobbed my head up and down once. "I've never really had to woo a client. That's got to be hard."

Alicia tipped her head one way, then the other. "It can be. Depends on the client and what they're expecting." She sipped her wine as she seemed to search for the best way to explain herself. "If they're just looking for the best marketing strategy or logo design, I can win them easily. I'm excellent at what I do, and so is my entire staff." The way she said it wasn't at all egotistical, but simply confident and sure. "But if they're looking to pit my price quote against a bunch of other firms because they're only interested in the cheapest one, I don't always win that."

"You like your job?"

"I love it."

"Tell me why." I really wanted to know. Leaving my office hadn't been on my schedule. But now that we were here, just the two of us, I realized it was a great opportunity to learn as much as I could about this woman who'd kissed me unexpectedly in a hallway and hadn't mentioned it since.

Alicia seemed to take a moment to think, and when she turned to look at me, her eyes held that spark I'd seen the first time I met her. Excitement. Anticipation. Energy. "It's the creativity. The brainstorming. I love that part the best, the discovery of the right path for any given company. When a client comes to me and tells me what he or she hopes to accomplish with a new marketing strategy, and then I and my staff throw dozens of things at the wall to see what sticks, and we find that awesome idea that *does* stick, it's..." She'd been talking with her hands, waving them around animatedly as she gazed off at the air. Her focus came back and those eyes grabbed mine. "It's the best feeling in the world. It's exhilarating. The sense of accomplishment, of certainty. It's like a rush. A high. I live for it."

"Wow," I said, with a big grin. Listening to her explain her love for her job was like watching a film. A film I wanted to play again and again.

"Another round for you ladies?" The bartender popped the little bubble of intimacy we'd been sharing.

Alicia looked at me and raised her eyebrows in expectation.

What the hell. I was already there. "Sure. One more," I said, and the smile that split across Alicia's face told me I'd made the right decision. I pointed at her anyway and joked, "You are a very bad influence."

"I will take that as a compliment," Alicia said, with an incline of her head. The bartender refilled our glasses and laughed as well, like he desperately wanted to be a part of our fun. I still prickled at the way his gaze lingered on Alicia, but hey, she was with me, not him, which puffed my chest a bit. Not to mention, I couldn't blame him. Another customer summoned him, and once he was gone, those blue eyes snagged my brown ones and held them. "What about you? Do you like your job?" She sipped her wine, set the glass down, then propped an elbow on the bar and her chin in her hand, projecting the epitome of *I am interested in every word you have to say*. It gave me a little flutter in my gut.

"I do," I said. "Very much."

Alicia waved her hand in a rolling motion, telling me to elaborate.

"I've always loved numbers," I said. "Ever since I was a little kid in elementary school. Numbers were comfortable to me. They never lie. They're always definitive, not subjective. I did fine in school, but with something like an essay, your grade really depends on the teacher and how they view what you write. With math and numbers? There's no room for opinion."

"You like to be right," Alicia said, tilting her glass in my direction.

"Who doesn't?"

"Good point."

"I used to sit in my father's lap and watch him do returns. He didn't have a computer at first, so he did everything with an adding machine. He was so fast!"

Alicia's grin was soft. "I can see little tiny Lacey sitting in his lap, her pigtails tied with ribbons, trying to take in all the numbers flying by."

"That's actually pretty accurate," I admitted, with a chuckle.

"Did you always know you were going to take over your dad's business?"

"I don't know that I'd say I always knew, but I did know I'd work with numbers in some way, whether it was for a big company or a small one. Owning my own, even my father's, didn't really occur to me until after college."

"How come?"

I thought about it for a beat as I sipped my wine. "Because when you're young, you don't really think about your parents getting older and retiring. You know? I think I just assumed my dad would always run his business and that I'd help him during tax season but do something else the rest of the year. It wasn't until he asked me how I felt about working for him full-time that I started to look down the road and see the possibilities."

"How did it feel the very first day you owned the place and were there without him? Like, when you realized you were the sole proprietor?"

It was so weird to have her ask me that, as I actually had that exact day etched in my brain. "I was a walking dichotomy that first day. I was filled with opposing feelings. I was ecstatic and terrified. I was happy and sad. I was anxious, but relieved. It took several months for all of those feelings to ease up and let me just…settle in."

"That makes total sense. Does your dad pop in? Check up on you?"

I chuckled. "He did for a while, but I think it got to be hard on both of us. He wanted to tell me what to do and how to do it, and I wanted him to leave me alone and let me make changes and do things my way. It got a little testy a couple of times, but my mom finally stepped in."

"You're close with your parents," Alicia said and it wasn't a question. It was a statement, and I couldn't quite gauge the emotion that zipped across her face.

"I'm closer with my mom. My dad is tight with my brother, whom you know. Which is weird, because I'm the one who followed in Dad's footsteps." I shrugged, then sipped my wine, not wanting to get on the subject of Scott but knowing I opened the door.

Alicia waltzed right through. "Scott. He's going to be a good client for me, I can tell."

"Well, good."

As if sensing my trepidation around him, she observed, "He's a little bit full of himself."

A laugh burst out of me before I could catch it. "You think?"

Alicia joined me. "Seriously. The boy thinks he's God's gift."

"He always has. Try growing up with that. And with a father who kind of agrees."

Alicia shook her head and said quietly, "Fathers and their sons."

"I told him we kissed." I blurted it out before I lost my nerve. I thought she deserved to know.

"Oh, I know. He mentioned it." Alicia hid her grin behind the rim of her glass as she arched one red eyebrow.

"What?" I was stunned. "He did?"

My tone must have been amusing or something because a little laugh escaped Alicia. Then she leaned in close to me and whispered, "I don't think he believed you."

I scoffed. "Well, that figures."

"I was actually a little bit insulted for you. So I set him straight—so to speak." Her face radiated mischief, and I found myself wishing I'd had a friend like Alicia during high school when I was known as a quiet, nerdy math geek who couldn't possibly be related to that gorgeous, football-playing, perfect specimen of a man she claims is her brother.

I cocked my head a bit and squinted at her. "How?"

"I gave him details."

I blinked at her, which she must have found hilarious, because she almost choked on her sip of wine as she laughed. "I'm kidding. But I did tell him it was true. He was hitting on me—attempting to prove his point about you lying, I guess—and I just told him the truth: that I don't play on his team, and in addition, I happen to find his sister wildly attractive."

I stared at her, unable to make words for some reason, and she smiled as she laid a warm hand over mine.

"Don't worry. I was gentle with him." That twinkle of mischief came back as she lowered her voice and said, "I don't want to lose his business."

I couldn't help but grin at that. "Understandably. His company is big."

Alicia nodded and finished off her wine.

I followed suit, then glanced at my watch and did my best not to look horrified. I was unsuccessful.

"Okay, I recognize that look—I've kept you long enough." Alicia stood and slipped her arm into her jacket. "Let's get you back to your office before you turn into a pumpkin. Or turn *me* into a pillar of salt." She paid the bill, brushing me off when I offered to contribute. "Nope. My treat. You get it the next time."

I tried to stifle the idiotic grin that came with the idea of there being a next time. Again: unsuccessful.

Back in the office, I hung up my jacket and looked at the work on my desk, a silent groan sounding in my head.

I shouldn't have let her talk me into leaving.

There's so much work to do.

I should've fought her harder, damn it.

Those thoughts only made me roll my eyes. I took a seat and Alicia came in carrying a very sleepy Leo.

"He was out cold on Gisele's lap," she said, scratching him under his chin where he loved it. He yawned and swiped at her cheek with his tongue. Alicia crossed the office and set him in his bed where he turned in a circle three times and settled in. "I'll see you tomorrow."

"Alicia?" I said, as she was headed toward the door. She turned to look at me, and I couldn't help the flood of arousal that washed through me as I looked at her. The sudden desire I had to stand up, walk across the room, and kiss her like there was no tomorrow was almost too much to fight off, but I managed. Because I knew if I started, I wouldn't stop. Instead, I shot her a quirky half grin. "Thanks for pulling me out of here."

Her smiled widened. "Thanks for letting me pull you out of here."

"I'll see you tomorrow."

She pointed a finger at me. "Don't work too late."

I saluted her and she was gone. Strangely, it felt like she'd taken all the color with her. The rest of my night felt bland, like a washed-out, black-and-white photograph.

CHAPTER TEN

I didn't see Alicia at all on Tuesday, which meant I was in the office working until all hours that night. Maybe that's why I woke up Wednesday morning with a screaming headache that felt like somebody running a jackhammer into the sides of my skull. The weather was gray and rainy—typical for spring but completely unhelpful for trying to allay a pounding head.

I'd only managed about three and a half hours of sleep the night before. I find when I work late, there's a point on the clock—usually around midnight—that, when surpassed, allows my second wind to breeze in. I become awake, wired, and weirdly energetic. Getting to sleep takes a good, long time. I remembered seeing the clock at some time around 3:45 a.m. before I finally nodded off. My alarm woke me back up at 6:30, and I hit the snooze, rather viciously, four times—a very rare occurrence for me.

A super-large cup of coffee and a handful of Motrin got me into my car and headed to the office. Even Leo was low-key, and I wondered if he was as tired as I was. Did dogs get headaches? I was pondering that question when Nascar Kyle missed T-boning me by mere inches, his brakes squealing loud enough to make me squeeze my eyes shut in pain. I looked to my right, out the passenger-side window, and he smiled, shrugged as if to say, "oops, my bad!" and gave me a wave.

If I hadn't been buckled into my seat, I'd have gone for the little bastard. That had been too damn close.

I noticed the absence of the baby blue BMW right away but tried not to dwell. There was still another car in my spot. A little Hyundai sports car of some kind, and I absently wondered if it was Brandon's. He seemed like a guy who needed to compensate for some weakness by driving a hot car. Didn't matter. Nobody could compare in hotness to Alicia in her Beemer, Ray-Bans on, top down, wind gently ruffling that auburn hair…

I shook my head (a mistake which brought a groan with it). No time for fantasy. Plus, it had occurred to me last night, as I sat at my desk zoning out, that since our hallway kiss, there'd been nothing more. On the one hand, Alicia did say in the bar that she found me…what was it? Oh yes, *wildly attractive*. On the other hand, she'd made no moves at all to act on that observation for…it had been a couple weeks now, hadn't it?

I wondered, on my way up the stairs, why *I* hadn't made a move on *her*. Maybe that's what she was waiting for. I hadn't really thought about that, as doing so lay just outside my comfort zone…

"Good morning," Mary said to Leo and me as we entered. She had a slice of breakfast pizza in her hand and the smell threatened to make me throw up all the coffee in my stomach at the moment. "Alicia brought over some breakfast before she left for a meeting." Mary bestowed a smile that basically said, *that woman is a goddess; we should keep her.* "She put a slice on your desk for you."

My stomach roiled a bit, and I could do nothing other than nod and head in, losing Leo to Mary and her food.

Sure enough, a paper plate sat on my desk with a large slice of breakfast pizza on it. Scrambled eggs, diced ham, crumbled bacon, melted cheese… I swallowed down a little bile that had crept up my throat, picked up the plate, and took it all the way out to Mary.

"I can't," I said simply. "I don't feel well this morning." I left before she could ask questions, then closed the door between us, leaving it slightly ajar in case Leo wanted in. It was only when I sat down at my desk that I noticed the note that must have been under the plate.

Most important meal of the day. How do you expect to crunch those numbers with no fuel in your body? Didn't you take health class in school? Eat!

Below the words were two primitive stick figures. One was seated at a desk wearing a big smile, various numbers flying above her. The other had *X*'s for eyes and a squiggly mouth that made it look ill. A small arrow pointed at the first one and labeled it *You and numbers*. The second was labeled *Me and numbers*. I grinned widely, forgetting my throbbing head for a few seconds.

But only a few seconds. The pounding returned and I glanced at my watch to see how much longer I had to wait before I could take another pile of ibuprofen.

Too long.

With a heavy sigh, I sat down and got to work.

I managed to live through two client meetings and file more than a dozen returns by early afternoon, but my headache had barely eased. As I was slamming another handful of Motrin, downing it with nauseatingly cold coffee, a quick rap sounded on my door and Scott peeked his head in.

So much for getting rid of my headache.

"Hey there, Lace-Face. How's it going?" He looked immaculate in a tan suit with a white shirt underneath and a navy blue tie. He sauntered in and took a seat across from me, uninvited and in no hurry.

"It's going fine," I said, but avoided any detail.

"You look like hell," he observed, tilting his head as he studied me.

"I feel like hell."

He chuckled. "You're exhausted, huh?"

"Is it April?" I made a show of glancing at the old-fashioned calendar on the wall behind me, the one with puppies and kittens that made me feel warm and fuzzy when I needed to. "Oh, it is. Then yes, I'm tired."

"Want some help?"

That was a loaded question and I knew it. Help from Scott often came with strings. "Nope. I'm good."

"You sure? Looks like you could use it."

"Why are you here, Scott?" It was blunt, but I didn't care. My head felt like it was in a vise and the twelve-year-old inside me was peeking her head out in worry, fully expecting her big brother to make her feel incompetent and silly.

He studied me for a long moment. When he finally spoke, his voice was surprisingly gentle. "Look, Lace-Face, I know you. I know you've got your entire world under control. I do, believe me. But you know how Dad is. He expects me to look out for my little sister and he expects a full report from me. Cut me a little slack, okay?"

I sat back in my chair, surprised by his words and also touched by them. How could I have not realized that this was why Scott always stopped by? It felt like my world had shifted. "Okay. I'm sorry. Please tell Dad I very much appreciated your offer, but I'm okay."

He took a couple seconds before saying, "You know what? I'll tell him you're doing great. How about that?"

A beat went by and our gazes held. Yeah, girl-crush stealing aside, having a big brother could be pretty awesome. "What else are you up to?" I asked, after we'd realized we were suddenly uncomfortable gazing lovingly at each other.

"I had a meeting next door," he said, and shifted in his seat like that was some sort of accomplishment to be proud of. "Alicia had some things to go over with me."

I didn't realize she was back. I glanced out the window and saw the BMW parked next to my car. Something about seeing it that close to mine gave me a little, sort of evil, spurt of energy and I said, "You didn't take her to some romantic restaurant to go over stuff? I'm surprised." I smothered my grin, but I'm sure my face projected a bit of playful, if a bit gleeful, self-satisfaction.

He chuckled. "No, Lace-Face, she's all yours. I will be a gentleman and bow out gracefully."

I snorted a laugh at him. "Like you have a choice."

He gave a good-natured chuckle back. Then he stood up and took a couple steps toward me. I saw him take stock of my desk strewn with papers, the piles on my floor. "Yeah, you got this." Then he leaned over, kissed the top of my head, and said, "I'll catch you at the 'rents' on Sunday."

"See ya." I watched as he sauntered out the door—that's how he walked everywhere. He sauntered. I heard Mary giggle girlishly, so I knew he probably complimented her in some way, flirted a little bit. Not many women were immune to my brother's charms.

Alicia was, though.

I let that thought, and the unexpected insight into my big brother's motives, keep me warm throughout the rest of my day.

❖

It was as if my headache was in control and chose its own schedule. It hung around until well into Wednesday evening, then left me alone all day Thursday so I could actually get work done without feeling like I had a fifty-pound anvil on my shoulders. But when I opened my eyes at the sound of my alarm on Friday morning, that sucker was back, full force.

"Goddamn it," I muttered, throwing a hand over my eyes as I lay in bed and was subjected to the morning kiss routine from Leo. I didn't need this. I had five days left of work, including today, and a boatload to get done. Weirdly energized by the new, still kind of shocking, insight that my big brother-slash-former-arch-nemesis actually *believed* in me, I made a pact with myself that I was going to beat this headache. I felt strong and competent and I'd had enough.

With a groan, I threw off the covers and got going on my morning routine, beginning with my trusty handful of ibuprofen, determined it would work better this time than it had on Wednesday.

Five more days. Five more days.

I actually had a great morning. No kickball in the hallway. No overpowering smell of Chinese food or some such thing permeating the air (though Mary was eating a bagel when I arrived). I was even able to park adjacent to my own, beloved former parking spot. No BMW, but I didn't really have time to dwell on that anyway. I left Leo eyeing Mary's bagel with utter expectation, went into my office, and worked straight through until almost noon.

I heard the buzz of conversation in the reception area, but I'd shut my door so I could concentrate on work. I recognized my father's voice only a split second before he knocked loudly on my door and then came on in without waiting for a response from me.

"Hey there," he said, his voice gruff, as usual.

"Hi, Dad," I said, trying not to look as wary as I felt. "What brings you by? You and Mom going to lunch at that little café you like?" *Please say yes.*

He shook his head but didn't look at me. Instead, his focus was on the various forms and files I had strewn around the office. "Talked to your brother yesterday."

I knew it.

"Oh, yeah?" I asked, feigning ignorance. "He was here

Wednesday. Just stopped by for a couple minutes after his meeting with the marketing firm next door."

Dad was nodding now, and he picked up a file folder from my desk, part of the pile I was slowly transferring to the computer system. "Said you looked busy."

"I am busy. It's almost the fifteenth. I'd be worried if I wasn't busy."

"He said I shouldn't worry. That you had things under control."

So Scott *hadn't* thrown me under the bus. "I do."

"Mrs. Stenglein," he muttered as he looked through the folder. "She never remembers to—"

"Include her donations for the year," I finished for him. "I know, Dad. I've got it."

He picked up another folder and another and I just watched him.

"I don't know this guy," he mumbled under his breath.

"Referral," I said.

He grunted and reached for another folder. I considered stopping him, but instead, let him continue to sift through them.

After a few moments, he looked at me. "Lotta new clients."

I nodded. "I've gotten a lot of referrals from old clients and I've been part of a networking group—remember I told you about that? Got several new clients from that."

He nodded and let the folders drop back down to my desk. Then he glanced around, gave a curt nod, and headed for the door. "Okay then."

My dad isn't a demonstrative man. He's not emotional. He's factual and practical and logical. He loves me, I know he does, and I got an extra-clear view of it right then. But he'd much sooner show it by buying me a new adding machine than saying the actual words. It's just how he is. So, his "okay then" felt like the warmest of warm fuzzies.

"I'm glad you stopped in." And I was.

At the door, he turned back and pointed at me. "Make sure you eat," he said, back to gruff. "You can't live on coffee this month. Eat."

"I will," I said, biting back a smile. "Thanks, Dad."

He shut the door behind him and I let out a huge breath that had been stuck in my lungs. I hadn't expected that to be a fun meeting, but it had ended up surprisingly pleasant and revealed something to me that

I didn't know until that very moment I'd been uncertain of: my father was proud of me.

I sat back in my chair and allowed myself to revel in that for a few minutes. It was a nice feeling. Then, ready to get back to work, I took some more Motrin and downed it with my coffee just as my cell phone pinged an incoming text. A quick glance told me it was Amy.

New Mediterranean place in Olde City. Stavros. Great reviews. Wanna go?

I sighed. I had no energy to finesse an answer. *Too busy with work. Maybe in a couple weeks?*

The reply came back quickly. *Sure.* No emojis. No elaboration. I felt bad, but I just couldn't deal with it right now.

Mary paged me on the intercom with a phone call to remind me how busy I was. I grabbed the handset.

"Lacey Chamberlain. How can I help you?"

The day went on, and I was able to get myself back into a rhythm. E-filing made things so much easier for everybody involved. Mary would bring me the mail, and I'd go through the forms that people had signed, giving me permission to send them via email, a click, and it was done. On to the next. My headache had eased considerably, and I even opened Pandora and put on some soft, unobtrusive jazz to be my soundtrack for the remainder of the evening.

At seven thirty, I sent Mary home. I gave myself fifteen minutes to play tennis ball with Leo, who fetched four throws and then was done. As he curled up in his bed, I shook my head affectionately. "You're like a little old man in a young dog body, you know that?"

He gave me a look that unmistakably said I was boring him, then picked up the Nylabone near his paws and gnawed on it lazily.

I got back to work, humming to the sounds of Diana Krall, and was in the zone when my door burst open, startling both me and Leo, as we both gave a little yelp.

"Come with me," Alicia said, her face glowing. "I'm starving." She radiated energy, and the bright blue button-down top she wore made her eyes pop in the best of ways.

"I can't," I said, regretfully. I could *not* let her pull me away again, even though the idea of spending time with her was so much more appealing than just about anything else. I was too close to the end now. I needed to stay nose-to-the-grindstone and push through.

"Come on," Alicia prodded, as she crossed the room and plopped herself into a chair. Leo hopped right up into her lap. Of course. "I haven't eaten since a late breakfast and I have more work to do, but I'm going to faint from hunger."

I looked at her with as much apology in my eyes as I could muster and shook my head. "I—" I waved a hand over my very messy desk.

"Please?"

Oh, God, don't beg me. You cannot beg me. I felt myself caving.

"We'll be super quick. I promise. Seriously, Lacey, doesn't a big salad sound perfect right about now?"

"You're killing me," I said to her, trying to glare, but failing.

"No, I'm saving you. From starvation."

I had to admit that, given how awful I'd felt all day, a salad was probably exactly what I needed. "Half an hour. Not one second longer. And I'm not kidding or playing around here, Alicia. My deadline is really looming."

She clapped her hands together and popped up from her chair like it was spring-loaded. "Okay, deal. Let's go."

I locked Leo up in the office, and in less than ten minutes, we were sitting in the café portion of the grocery store down the block. I dug into my Greek salad like I hadn't eaten in days. For a solid five minutes, there was no sound at our table but the crunching of greens. Even when we did start talking, it was sporadic, like each of us was just too tired to put forth the energy it would take to have an in-depth conversation. We finished up and were back in our office parking lot with almost a full minute to spare.

"You okay tonight?" Alicia turned the car off and looked at me as I sat in the passenger seat.

I inhaled very slowly, filled my lungs to capacity before slowly letting it out. "It's been a weird day. I've had a killer headache on and off for the past couple days, and today, my father decided to show up and make it clear that he thinks I'm actually doing a good job."

"Seriously?"

"I think so. I'm pretty sure. But it was uncomfortable for a bit."

"What do you mean?" Alicia pulled on her door handle and exited the car.

I followed and we headed into the building and up the stairs. "He pretended he was visiting, but the whole time, he was looking around, picking things up and putting them down, judging."

"Judging? Are you sure you weren't overreacting because you were tired?"

"I mean, maybe I was. But come on, how would you like it if your father came strolling into your office one day, checked out your whiteboard, looked at your ideas and pitches, and found them all lacking?"

I couldn't identify the expression that settled on her face in that moment. The only word I could think of was "closed." It was as if she suddenly closed up like a clam. I had the vision of those bars that shops pull down to cover their storefronts when they close for the night. I was no longer allowed in. She was quiet for so long, I started to think she wasn't going to respond at all. Finally, she did, looking down at her feet, her voice low but steely. "I would love it if my father would stroll into my office, Lacey. I'd love it." Then, instead of going back to her office, she walked toward me, touched my shoulder softly, then passed me to the stairwell we'd just come up. Her hand flat on the door, she didn't look at me as she spoke. "Thank you for going with me. I hope you feel better."

She pushed her way through and was gone.

I stood in the hallway for I don't know how long, wondering what the hell had just happened.

CHAPTER ELEVEN

It's amusing to me how easily total exhaustion can be overshadowed and put on a back burner when excited anticipation shows up. I woke up Tuesday morning feeling groggy and headachy yet again from not enough sleep. The sleep I did get had been fitful, as it had since my evening with Alicia and the weird way it ended. I hit the snooze on my phone and buried my face in my pillow in the hopes that ten more minutes of rest would make a world of difference. It didn't. But when my alarm went off again and I groaned and reached for it, that changed. I hit the off button and then noticed the date emblazoned across the screen of my phone.

Tuesday, April 15.

A happy little gasp escaped my lips, and I sat up quickly enough to startle Leo, who also wasn't getting enough sleep, judging by the fact that he had barely moved with each alarm. His morning routine was totally off; no morning love fest for me for the past week.

"Leo," I said quietly, ruffling the overgrown hair on his head. He really needed an appointment with the groomer. He made a snuffling sound, lifted his head to blink at me, and yawned widely. "It's today, buddy. It's today. It's the fifteenth! We made it!" I scooped him up and proceeded with a morning love fest role reversal, kissing all over his face and head, then tipping him back in my arms like a baby so I could skritch that little belly. To his credit, he allowed all of it. I think he liked it.

The weather was bland. Not warm. Not cold. No sun, but no rain. Overcast and gray, but it didn't matter to me, because today was April

15, and the torture was over for another year. It would be a long day, but that was all right. I'd learned in the first couple of years working with my father that blocking out the fifteenth so there were no appointments was the way to go. I'd met with my very last client before the deadline last night at eight. Today would be dedicated to e-filing the remaining tax returns I had left on my computer and making sure Mary got to the post office to mail out any other things that needed to be postmarked before they closed at seven. It sounded like a lot, but I didn't care. I couldn't stop grinning.

As I did every year, I stopped on my way in to get some flowers for Mary for putting up with me for the past three months. I also grabbed a dozen donuts, smiling the whole time, being endlessly cheerful. I think the girl behind the counter thought I was a little bit insane.

In the parking lot, I heard a loud blast of a horn and saw the man driving a Chevy roll down his window and display his middle finger to Nascar Kyle as the yellow muscle car cut him off.

"Ugh," I said, shaking my head. "Better him than us, though, right, Leo?"

Leo glanced at me in agreement.

I glided my car gently into the spot next to Alicia's BMW. I got a little thrill at the sight, though I did my best to tamp it back down. She'd been out of the office, so I hadn't seen her since that inexplicably uncomfortable end to our conversation in the hallway, and I really wanted to talk to her about it, make sure she was okay. Make sure *we* were okay.

I managed to get a grip on my bag, the donuts, the flowers, and Leo's leash—albeit a little precariously—and we headed inside.

Gisele was just leaving my office as we opened the stairwell door. "Hey there," she said cheerfully and squatted to be on Leo's level. I let go of his leash and he trotted over to her, lavishing her with kisses and love. She was wearing jeans and a bright orange top that looked fantastic against her dark skin.

I stopped when I reached her and said hello as she glanced up at me.

"I just dropped a bagel off to Mary," she told me.

"Well, I've got donuts if you guys get hungry," I responded, holding up the box.

"Those are pretty," she said, eyeing the flowers as she stood up.

I shrugged. "Mary puts up with my tax season grumpiness for a long time. She deserves more than flowers, but…"

"You're a good boss, Lacey." Gisele gave Leo one more pat, then said, "Gotta get back to work."

Leo and I went inside the office just as Mary was taking a very large bite of a bagel slathered with cream cheese. I lost Leo immediately.

"Today's the day," she said happily. "We made it another year."

"We did. For you, m'lady," I said, with a flourish as I gave Mary a bow and handed her the flowers. "Thank you for all your hard work and for keeping me from killing myself or others during tax season."

Her face lit up, her smile wide as she took the flowers from me and put her nose in them. "I think I'd be hard-pressed to find a better job, so keeping you from jumping out the window is actually a little bit of a selfish move on my part."

"Well, thank you anyway."

"You're welcome."

We held one another's gazes for a beat or two. We did this every year. It was like a silent acknowledgment of what we meant to each other. Mary may have worked for my father for much longer than she'll ever work for me, but she made the transition from one boss to another seamlessly. She was one of the few people who never, ever tried to tell me how to do my job. If I asked her opinion, she'd give it, and she didn't always agree with me, but that was okay. We both knew it and accepted it.

For the first time in more weeks than I could count, I felt like I could breathe freely. Easily. Normally. The pressure was off. Yes, this exact thing happened every year on the fifteenth, but every year, I forgot how poignant it all was. I had a lot to do, but doing it actually felt good, productive, and reminded me how much I loved my job. I worked diligently throughout the morning, but there was a shift in the air, and I felt zero pressure. I'd get it all done. I had no doubt. Even the bassline from music next door didn't bother me. I cocked my head as I listened—Bruno Mars, I was pretty sure—and bopped along to the beat.

Around eleven, my bladder let me know that it could only hold so much coffee, so I went out to reception only to find the nail for the bathroom key empty. I pointed to it and raised my eyebrows in silent question at Mary.

She gave me a silent answer by pointing to her left in the direction of Just Wright. I nodded. *All right. I guess now's as good a time as any to humble myself.* I'd use the bathroom key as an excuse to see Alicia.

I'd been right about Bruno Mars. He was just finishing up when I arrived in the doorway, the door wide open, the Just Wright staff buzzing around like worker bees. Gisele was squinting at her computer monitor, as was Justin. Pantone Patrick was pacing in front of the whiteboard. He'd stop and doodle with a green marker for a few seconds, then pace some more. Alicia's desk was deserted, and I didn't see her anywhere in the room. Brandon must have been down the hall because he startled me as he entered the office behind me.

"Hey," I said, working hard to inject friendliness into my voice.

"Hey," he said with a grunt and didn't look up as he tossed the bathroom key onto the food table as he passed.

Gisele looked up from her computer and smiled at me as she gave a little wave. I picked up the key and said, "I just came for this."

Gisele shook her head with half a grimace. "I'm so sorry. Alicia's been in constant contact with maintenance about our bathroom. We really thought we'd have it up and running by now. They said next week for sure."

"It's no problem." With a small wave of my own, I pocketed the key and hit the restroom, a little bit bummed that Alicia hadn't been around. I missed her face. And that thought, that simple fact, brought a smile of my own.

The afternoon was very much like the morning: relaxed. Busy, but relaxed. I fielded a few last-minute questions from clients. I e-filed nearly forty returns. My pile for the post office was ready by five thirty, so I gave it to Mary and sent her on her way, knowing there'd be a line and she'd probably be there for a bit. But I told her to go home after that. She'd been working overtime for nearly a month, and she deserved a break.

Just before seven, I called Jules at ChopStix and placed an order. I would be there until midnight, but I wasn't frantic, so I wouldn't look up at ten and realize I hadn't eaten all day. It was another perk to seeing that light at the end of the tunnel: I went back to taking better care of myself.

The knock on the door startled a little yelp from Leo.

"Relax," I told him. "It's just dinner." I called for the person to come in. But when the door opened, it wasn't dinner.

It was Alicia.

Alicia, with a very large bouquet of flowers in one hand and the strings for what had to be at least eight balloons in an array of bright colors floating above her head in the other.

"It's April fifteenth," she said, as she closed the door behind her with a foot and stood there with her back to it.

I blinked at her. "Oh, my God," I said quietly, so touched that I had trouble finding words. "Are those for me?"

Alicia cocked her head a bit. "Well, if I was going to bring something for Leo, it wouldn't be flowers and balloons. It would be made of meat." She gave a gentle laugh. "Yes, they're for you."

"I…I don't know what to say." And I didn't. Nobody had ever done that for me before. Most people didn't get how significant this date was to somebody in my line of work. My gaze moved from the rainbow of balloons to Alicia. She wore tan slacks and a navy blue top. It was a subtle color for her, but it made her eyes and hair pop, and the added display of color from the balloons and flowers only served to accent just how gorgeous her face was. She was smiling, and I swear to God, I'd never seen anything so beautiful in my entire life.

I pushed my chair back and walked toward her with determined steps. I had no idea what I was going to do until I was inches from her. Then I grabbed her face in both hands and kissed her.

Like, a lot.

Like, *really* a lot. Like, enough to make her drop the flowers (I heard them fall near my feet) and let go of the balloons (they softly hit the ceiling above us). I felt her hands on me then, one at the small of my back, pulling me closer to her; the other sliding into my hair at the back of my head.

This kiss was so different from the last one. Much less tentative. Much less trepidatious. More intense. *Much* more intense. It's hard to accurately describe a really good kiss, to put a really good kiss into words, and this was definitely one of them: *a really good kiss.* Alicia's mouth was crazy soft, and she tasted amazing. Intoxicating. I had no idea why, and I actually pulled back and whispered, "God, why do you taste so good?"

She smiled and kissed me again. I leaned into her and she let out a soft grunt as her back hit the door. I pressed the length of my body against hers and did my best to get more. That was the only word in my head for long, long moments: more. There was so much I wanted then. I wanted to slowly remove her clothes and touch every single millimeter of her body. With my hands. With my lips. With my tongue. At the same time, I wanted to kiss her forever, because my God, she was the best kisser I'd ever had the pleasure of kissing. If there'd been a Best Kisser trophy, I'd have happily handed it over. If there'd been a Best Kisser list, she'd have been at the top. I was pretty sure I could just stand there and make out with her. For hours.

It felt like that's exactly what we did. I had no idea how much time had passed when we finally broke apart, ragged breathing the only sound in the room for a stretch. We stayed close together, our foreheads touching as we each tried to catch our breath. Alicia's hand at the back of my neck toyed with my hair, sending thrilling shivers across my shoulders and down my back. My arms were wrapped around her neck and I had no intention of letting go just yet. Her other hand had made its way under my shirt and was softly playing across the skin of my lower back. More shivers.

"So *that's* what it takes to get you to kiss me," she said, humor in her tone. "Finally. I've seriously been wondering if you'd ever make a move." She pulled her head back far enough to meet my eyes, and hers were sparkling with happiness. "If I'd only known, I'd have brought gifts much sooner."

"What can I say? Apparently, balloons get me hot."

"Who knew?" And then she was kissing me again, but this time, I was certain I could not do this for hours because that word was back: more.

I moved my hand to her face, cupped the side of it for a few more blissful seconds before wrenching my mouth away. My vision felt blurry, hazy, as though I was trying to focus through a fog, and I ran my thumb across her swollen lips. Once. Twice. Trying to orient myself and stop the blood that was rushing hotly through my body. "We have to stop," I managed to breathe out. "Or we're going to end up naked on this floor, and I don't think this carpet would be kind to bare skin."

The knock that sounded on the door against Alicia's back made us both jump apart, tandem gasps escaping our lips, as if we were teenagers about to be discovered by our parents. I squinted at her in confusion and she mirrored my expression until I realized who it was.

"Dinner," I mouthed.

"Oh," she mouthed back and took a step toward me. With a quick reach, she flicked her finger along the corner of my mouth, then stepped back again and gave me a nod of approval.

I shook out my arms like a boxer preparing to spar, and then opened the door to my usual delivery guy. I signed and tipped him, he handed over the food, and I thanked him and shut the door. A huge sigh left my lungs as I turned around and saw Alicia sitting on the floor next to Leo's bed, petting him as he looked up adoringly at her. She, in turn, looked up at me, and I felt a rush of combined affection and arousal.

"God, you're beautiful," I said quietly, before I had time to think about it.

She responded by blushing, her smile almost shy, which seemed really unlike her.

I held up my bags. "Care to join me? There's always way too much for just me."

"I like that idea." She stood and pulled a chair closer to the desk as I cleared it off. I took my seat and pulled an extra set of chopsticks and a plastic spork from a drawer. I offered her both; she took the spork. Then I opened all the containers and spread them across the surface of my desk.

We ate in companionable silence for long moments. I couldn't speak for her, but I can say that I was stupidly happy just being in the same room with her, eating dinner and getting to look at her the whole time. I never realized just how easy to please I actually was.

A gentle rustling sound had us both looking up as the balloons softly drifted their way across the ceiling. I grinned. "That was the coolest," I said to Alicia. "I love getting stuff like that, and I rarely do. So thank you."

"I don't know if I believe that," she said, tossing a glance at the bouquet of flowers still on the floor.

I gasped. "Oh, my God. I forgot about those." I jumped up from my chair as she laughed and said she was only teasing me. "No, seriously. How ungrateful could I be?" I was slightly mortified as I picked up the bouquet and straightened them, making sure no stems had broken. Then I felt a wave of mischief wash through me, looked at her, and said, "And *I'm* not the one who dropped them on the floor."

Alicia lifted her chin as she chewed some rice. "Well, *somebody* caught me off guard and distracted me in a major way. Not my fault."

"Okay. I'll cop to that."

Our gazes held for a moment, and I felt captured by those blue eyes of hers. Once I somehow managed to break free, I found a vase on a bookshelf, filled it with water from my afternoon water bottle, and arranged the flowers in it. I could feel Alicia's eyes on me the whole time until I sat back down and continued eating. Leo had decided to get his lazy butt up from his bed now that food was involved, and he parked himself at my feet.

"So," Alicia said, switching to a spring roll. "Tonight's your last late night? Is that how it works?"

I nodded as I chewed. "Pretty much. I mean, the work isn't over. Extensions and so forth. And I do other things besides taxes. Financial advising. Help with investments. Retirement guidance. So work isn't over, but yeah, the crazy hours are. I've got more to do tonight—I'll probably be here until midnight—but after that, I can breathe. The rest of the week should be much easier." Saying that out loud was even better than knowing it in my head.

"Good. That means you can have dinner with me Saturday night then, right?"

It was my turn to snag her gaze and I did, held it for a beat or two, then nodded. "I can. Yes."

"There's a new place over near Olde City that specializes in contemporary Mediterranean…"

"Stavros?" I asked, remembering Amy's text not long ago.

"Yes!" Alicia pointed her spork at me. "Interested?"

I gave an enthusiastic nod. "Very."

"Excellent. I'll get us reservations."

"You think it'll be that easy? You're talking a new, popular restaurant on a Saturday night with not a lot of notice."

Alicia grinned at me like a Cheshire cat. "I did their marketing. They'll fit us in. Meet me there Saturday night at seven?"

"Perfect."

She took one last bite of her food, then gathered up her litter and tossed it in the trash. She came around my desk and stood next to me. "I'm going to let you get back to work. I know how cranky you get when your routine is messed with." She softened the words with a playful tug on my hair.

"Ha ha," I said, knowing she was right.

Her tug turned into a gentle pull until my head was back and I was looking up at her. She brought her lips to mine and kissed me. Softly. Languorously. Besides her hand in my hair, we didn't touch each other. I kept my hands on my desk. Her other hand was at her side. Only our mouths connected and it was indescribably sensual. I'd never been so turned on by a simple kiss in all of my thirty-three years of life. Her mouth was magic.

When Alicia finally pulled away, she stood looking down at me for a moment. Her face was flushed. Her lips were swollen, and she looked slightly disoriented. She smiled, cleared her throat, and rubbed her lips together. "Okay," she said, on a sigh. "Well, that was…ridiculously hot, and I need to get out of here before I can't stop myself."

God, she made me feel sexy.

"I'll see you later," I said.

"You will." Alicia bent over and scratched Leo's little head. "Bye, buddy," she whispered, then headed for the door.

"Alicia?" My voice stopped her and she turned back to me. "Thanks for the flowers and the balloons. That was really sweet of you."

"You're welcome, Lacey. Bye."

The door clicked shut and she was gone.

I fell back against my chair, feeling like I'd been completely tensed up and my muscles all decided to relax at the same time. "Holy crap," I muttered, bringing my fingers up to lips that I was sure were puffy and very pink. I could still taste Alicia on them, on my tongue, a surprisingly sexy combination of her strawberry lip gloss and the food she'd shared with me.

I allowed myself to stay lost in sense memory for several minutes before literally shaking my head and pulling my brain back to the present. "Okay, Leo. Enough. I can't be daydreaming like this. I have work to get done. Don't let me get preoccupied again, all right? I'm counting on you."

My dog gave me his signature party-horn yawn and curled up in his bed.

"Yeah, you're a huge help," I said, and cleaned up my dinner mess. Once my work was back on the desk where it belonged, I did my best to focus. And I succeeded. Because there was dinner this weekend to look forward to. A grin spread across my face as I worked.

I have a date.

Chapter Twelve

It was the first Saturday in nearly two months that I didn't go in to work. I was home and I planned on staying there all day, getting things done that had been neglected while I worked toward the fifteenth. Things like laundry and cleaning, especially. My plan not to leave the house altered immediately after I opened my refrigerator and was greeted with not much more than two sticks of butter, a bottle of ketchup, three yogurts way past their expiration dates, and something brown and squishy that I thought may have been a cucumber at one time. All I was sure of was that it was gross and smelled awful. I added "clean fridge" to my to-do list.

I was dusting what seemed like six inches of build-up off my living room furniture when my cell rang. I saw it was Leanne, and I put it on speaker so I could continue to clean.

"Happy end of tax season," she said, her voice cheerful. "You survived another one."

"I did," I said, running my dust cloth over a picture frame.

"How was it? Everything go okay? No last-minute catastrophes?"

"Nope. It went great. I got everything in on time. No stragglers this year."

"Amazing."

"Right? And," I added, putting extra emphasis on the word, "I got flowers and balloons."

"You did? From who?"

"Alicia."

"The hottie next door?" Leanne's tone was a fun mix of surprise and excitement.

GEORGIA BEERS

"That very one."

"I told you she was into you. The drink at the restaurant. Now flowers and balloons. Why don't you ever listen to me?" She was teasing me, I knew. She was also right.

"I listen to you," I claimed lamely. Leanne's response was a snort, which made me laugh. "I do!"

"You don't and you know it. You're stubborn, so you don't really listen to anybody. And a lot of the time, we're right."

I was nodding, even though she couldn't see me. "I know," I said grudgingly. "You're right."

"I'm sorry, what was that?"

My smile widened. "I said you're right. Now shut up."

"Music to my ears, those two little words."

"Ha ha."

Leanne laughed, then shifted gears slightly. "So, I guess I now know why you've been ignoring Amy's texts."

I wrinkled my nose and made another face that Leanne couldn't see. "I'm not ignoring her. I've tried to respond a bit here and there. I mean, she's nice enough…"

"But you've got Alicia on your mind."

I sighed in response.

"I get it," Leanne said. "Actually, I suspected as much."

"Has Lori been giving you a hard time about it?" It hadn't occurred to me that Amy might say something to Lori, who might say something to Leanne.

"Not a hard time, no. She just asked me about it. I guess Amy's a little bummed. She really liked you."

I wasn't really sure what to say to that. I mean, really. What could I say to that? There wasn't a good answer.

"No worries," Leanne said before I could interject something, anything. "I just wanted to check on you, make sure you hadn't thrown yourself from your office window."

"Since I'm only on the second floor, that'd get me nothing but a couple of broken legs. Unless Nascar Kyle then runs me over, which isn't out of the realm of possibility."

Leanne laughed. I thanked her for calling and we hung up.

I felt bad about Amy. A check of my phone showed me that her last text had come three days ago and I hadn't responded. It was a

• 138 •

simple *Hope you're doing okay. I know it's a rough time of year for you.* I could feel the corners of my mouth pull down. Amy was being nice. She deserved better than I'd given her. I quickly typed out a text.

Doing much better now that the 15th has passed. Thanks for checking on me!

I punctuated it with a smile emoji and hit Send.

"There," I said to Leo, who was lounging on the floor in a square of sunlight beaming in through the window. "That's better. Now I'm less of an asshole."

I set the phone down and had barely turned away from it before it beeped, letting me know there was a text.

"Damn it," I muttered, and picked it up. Sure enough, a text from Amy.

I'm so glad! Got time for dinner or drinks tonight? Or both? And then about twelve smile emojis.

"No good deed, Leo. No good deed." I stared at the phone for a long moment, trying to figure out the best response. Finally, I typed, *I'm so sorry. I have plans. Another time?* I hit Send and braced myself.

Sure. And then twelve not-quite-frown emojis.

Feeling a little guilty but also reasonably sure another response was not required, I set my phone down and went back to dusting. The guilt didn't last long, though, because really, Amy and I didn't owe each other anything. We'd never gone on a single date. Not to mention, my thoughts turned fully to the gorgeous redhead I was going to dine with that night. As I cleaned, I mentally went through my closet, wondering if I had something that would stop Alicia in her tracks for a moment.

This could be fun.

❖

My full-length mirror had been given a workout, as had Leo, with me constantly changing outfits and asking for his opinion every time. He was obvious in his boredom, stretched out on my bed like a prince, barely taking the time to even *look* at my outfit before turning away to wait for the next one. The mirror, however, was a huge help, and together, we decided on the little black dress I'd purchased for an evening wedding last fall that I ended up not going to, thanks to a sneak attack of the stomach flu. It had been hanging in my closet for more than six months, price tag still dangling, just waiting for the right occasion.

This was it.

The butterflies started as I stood there, turning to one side, then the other.

The dress was made of a snug, stretchy fabric and hit just above my knees, and while I wished I had a bit more of a tan, it didn't look bad. I had my mother's legs, and that was a good thing—one of my better features, I knew. The sleeves were long, and that was also a good thing. The temperature was predicted to be in the low sixties but would drop a bit through the evening, and with these sleeves, I could get away with no jacket. A small blessing, as I didn't have one that would go. The neckline wasn't exactly plunging, but it was low and showed much more cleavage than was normal for me. Strangely, I felt a little self-conscious and a little sexy at the same time. The fact that—based on the dip of the neckline and the shortness of the dress's hem—I knew my father would hate the dress only made me think Alicia would love it. I hoped she did. It was important to me, I realized in that moment. I wanted her to see me and be struck speechless for a moment. Was that weird? I hoped not…

I fastened a simple silver necklace around my neck to fill in the expanse of skin left by the dress. Matching earrings and some silver bangle bracelets completed the accessorizing, and I slipped my feet into what I referred to as my Special Occasion Heels. I hated wearing them, hated walking in them even more, but damn if they didn't look terrific with my dress. One more glance in the mirror to inspect my makeup and my hair and I was pretty sure I was good to go.

Leo hopped off the bed and followed me down the stairs into the kitchen. I got a cookie out of his treat jar, bent to kiss the top of his head, and gave it to him. "Okay, pal. I'm off. Wish me luck." I grabbed my black clutch and my keys. "Be a good boy. Hold the fort. No parties, no strippers," I instructed my dog, as I exited my house and locked the door behind me.

The butterflies kicked into high gear.

Stavros was packed, just as I suspected. I walked into the lobby and up to the hostess station, which was unoccupied. I squinted into the restaurant and didn't see Alicia anywhere in my view, but I did see a petite blond woman carrying menus, two people following her. I took in my surroundings as I waited, noting the way the restaurant seemed upper class and welcoming at the same time. *Hard to pull off*, I thought. A large bar with a brass foot rail and brown leather stools ran along the wall to my left, the bartender dressed in a white oxford and black tie and shaking what might have been a martini. Mirrors lined the wall behind the bottles, making the place seem much more spacious. The tables were round and covered with chocolate brown linen tablecloths, and the lighting was as dim as I'd expect from a nice restaurant. I was scanning the patrons when the hostess returned and asked if she could help me.

"Yes," I said. "I'm here to meet someone, and I believe she made a reservation. Under Wright?"

The hostess smiled, showing me a mouthful of very white teeth. "Oh, you're with Alicia." She said it like they were old friends. Maybe they were. "She's not here yet, but I'll seat you. Follow me."

The hostess led me on a maze, weaving around and between tables until we were at the very back corner of the restaurant. Private without being completely removed. I wondered if Alicia had specifically asked for this table. The idea put a flutter in my stomach. The good kind.

I sat and the hostess handed me a menu and a wine list. "I'll send Alicia back as soon as she arrives."

I thanked her and watched her go, then scanned the tables around me. To my left, I could see mostly couples, along with two families of four, a family of three, and one table of five women, which made me smile at the thought of Girls' Night Out. I could see some of the bar, and before I could scan the tables to my right, my eye was snagged by a spot of bright blue.

Alicia.

She was walking toward me, and I swear to God, she walked in slow motion. She waved to the bartender, who waved back, causing the two men sitting at the bar to turn and look. They continued to look as she walked past them, as did the table of four men dressed in suits and a couple of the women at the Girls' Night Out table. And who could blame them? Alicia was absolutely stunning. Her royal blue dress had capped sleeves and a V-neck, and it hugged her hips like it was sewn specifically to do so. She smiled at a waiter, then her eyes found mine and locked, and the rest of her approach was just for me. Her hair sparkled in the dim lighting, and I did my best not to look her up and down like some creeper, but I almost couldn't help myself. She reached the table and suddenly a waiter was there, materializing out of nowhere to pull her chair out for her. She sat and thanked him.

"Wow." It was all I could manage in the moment.

Her smiled made it worth it. "I was about to say the same thing. I can only see half of you, but you look gorgeous."

"And you…" I picked up my water glass and took a sip. "The guys at the bar got whiplash. You're beautiful."

She blushed prettily and we sat there, holding one another's gaze for a long beat.

"Hi," she said quietly and propped her chin in her hand.

"Hey, you."

And then there was a lot of quiet looking at one another.

Our waiter broke the spell by introducing himself—he was Mark—and asking if we'd like to start with a cocktail. Alicia ordered us a bottle of Merlot without ever opening the wine list, and once Mark had left, I raised my eyebrows at her.

"Impressive."

"Yeah? Good. That was my plan. I actually have no idea what I ordered." She unrolled her napkin as I laughed. "How was your day? You didn't work in your office, I noticed. Good for you."

"The first Saturday I didn't in about six weeks."

"What'd you do?"

"I cleaned," I said with a chuckle. "I did laundry. I got groceries. I took Leo for a walk. All the things that get put on the back burner during tax season, I catch up on in April. It's all very glamorous."

"And it was a gorgeous day. That had to help."

"It did. Sunshine always puts me in a good mood."

Mark arrived with our wine, showed the label to Alicia, and opened it with his wine key. He poured her a taste, she approved it, and he filled our glasses, recited the specials, and left us to our decision-making.

"What did you do today?" I asked as I opened my menu. Alicia didn't open hers. She simply continued to look at me. To the point where I almost squirmed in my seat. "What?" I asked, my voice quiet.

"Nothing," she said, shaking her head, her chin propped in her hand again. "I'm just enjoying the view."

I felt my face heat up, a combination of being self-conscious and being flattered, and I smiled my gratitude as I twirled my hair around a finger.

"That means you're nervous," she said, as she picked up her menu.

"What does?"

"When you twirl your hair like that. You do it when you're nervous."

"I do not." But I could feel my own half grin, because I knew she was right. "Fine. I've done it since I was in kindergarten," I admitted, feigning annoyance.

Alicia laughed lightly. "Well, I like it. And your hair looks fantastic like that, all wavy and…" She cleared her throat then, almost as if she'd said more than she meant to, and turned her focus to her menu.

For the next few minutes, we both pretended to be engrossed in the dinner selections, and when Mark returned, I ordered the pecan-crusted salmon. Alicia went with chicken Florentine and ordered us an appetizer of spanakopita. Mark topped off our wineglasses and was off.

"You didn't tell me what you did today," I pointed out.

Alicia dabbed at her mouth with her napkin. "I worked. My life is riveting."

"You know, you give me a hard time for working too much, but you're no better."

She nodded, didn't argue. "I know."

"I think I'm going to have to start paying attention to your hours now," I teased.

"I'm totally okay with that," she said, and she looked happy enough that I was pretty sure she was telling the truth. "How's my boyfriend, Leo?"

"He's good, but his life is hard. He spent most of today sleeping in the sunshine. Then he acted as my fashion consultant as I tried to decide what to wear tonight."

Alicia picked up her glass and let her eyes wander to my cleavage. Again, I was hit with a small zap of self-consciousness, but this time, it was followed by a large wave of arousal. "Stop it," I whispered.

"Stop what?" she whispered back.

"Looking at me like that."

"I can't. Sorry."

"No, you're not." My blush deepened.

"No, I'm not."

I'd never been in this situation before. I realized it in that moment. Sure, I'd dated. I had a relationship with Leanne. I had one before her. I didn't know Alicia that well, but what I did know, I liked very much. I wanted to know more. But I was having trouble getting past the crazy-hot levels of arousal she created in me, and I wasn't sure what to do about that. It was beyond distracting.

And oh so sexy.

"What did you work on today?" I tried again. I gave her my best pleading look, and she seemed to get it.

"We have a new potential client. A big one. So, I spent the day brainstorming some ideas, doing some online research on the company to see what they've done in the past."

"Alone?"

She nodded as Mark brought our appetizer, set it in the middle of the table, and left. Alicia took a bite of the spanakopita and made a humming sound of approval that made my stomach flutter. "While I love having a staff, and brainstorming with them is always beneficial, sometimes I like to work by myself. I can focus a bit more without having other people's ideas distracting me. You know?"

I nodded as I took a bite of the little puff pastry.

"I could've used Leo, though. Just having him in the office is oddly helpful. I have no idea why."

"He wears many hats, that boy of mine."

"He's got some depth, that's for sure." Alicia stabbed another pastry. "Also, how good are these?"

"God," I said, chewing. "*So* good."

"You have a house?" Alicia asked me.

I nodded. "Small, but cute. You?"

"Town house. New, though. It's nice. You should come see it." She held my gaze and I knew exactly what she was saying.

"I'd like that."

"Maybe tonight."

"Maybe tomorrow." I arched an eyebrow at her teasingly.

"Oh. Hard to get. I see." Her smile was wide and the glint in her blue eyes was completely, utterly sexy. "Okay. I can handle that."

"I have no doubt."

A staff member removed our empty appetizer plate as Alicia and

I sat there, making direct, intense eye contact with each other. I swear to God, I'd never been so turned on in my entire life, and I almost told her so. Instead, I used my wine to keep from talking. I couldn't let her know how much power she had over me.

Our dinners arrived, and our conversation went back to safer topics. Thank God, because I didn't think I could even touch on anything sexual again without crawling across the table and kissing Alicia senseless.

"Are you from Philly?" I asked, in an attempt to tamp down my raging libido.

Alicia nodded. "Wyncote."

"Your parents still there?"

"No, they're both gone now."

It took me a minute to realize she meant they were dead. "Oh, Alicia. I'm so sorry."

She shrugged. "What about you? You from here?"

"Flourtown. My parents still live there."

"And is there just you and Scott?" Alicia cut her chicken and took a bite.

"Just the two of us, yup."

"I've gleaned a little about your relationship now," she said with a wry smile, "but did you get along growing up?"

I chewed a piece of salmon, loving the texture of the pecans, while I looked for the right words. "Well, you've met him. You got a good dose of his personality. He hasn't changed much since we were younger. I mean, he can be kind of a dick, but he's my big brother. He's a pain in my ass, but he's always there if I need him. You know?"

Alicia nodded and a shadow zipped across her face, but it was gone so quickly, I wondered if I'd imagined it. "What do you like to do when you're not working?" she asked.

"Oh, a topic shift," I said with a grin, trying to lighten a mood that felt like it had gotten a little heavy somehow. "Okay. Let's see. I like reading, though I haven't done much of that lately. I like walking. A lot. I'm kind of a wanderer. Leo and I go all over the place. And I love Spruce Street Harbor Park, but it's closed until next month. One of my favorite things to do is take a book and find an open hammock in the park—they're all over the place, as I'm sure you know. Then I just swing and read and people watch and breathe in the fresh air."

"That sounds awesome. Maybe we should go when it opens."

"Maybe we should." I smiled softly at her across the table and whatever had been weighing her down was obviously gone. The smile she returned to me was nothing short of radiant. "God, you're beautiful," I whispered, not meaning to say it out loud, but glad I had when her cheeks turned pink.

We finished up our dinners in the midst of conversation about mundane things because—and I'm only speaking for myself here, but I was pretty sure Alicia was in the same boat—we couldn't seem to focus on anything deeper. Our brains were very, very preoccupied.

Alicia wouldn't let me pay for my dinner. "No, *I* invited *you*. I pay. Those are the rules."

"Whose rules?"

"My rules."

I laughed. "Oh, I see."

"Good. I don't want to have to explain them again."

There was that eye contact again. We sat at the table and said nothing for what seemed like hours. Just held one another's gaze. I loved her eyes. They were big and expressive; I was sure I could figure out everything she was thinking just by staring into those eyes. And the color. Like when the ocean is the deepest blue it can be. That shade of blue.

Mark returned with the check for Alicia to sign and thanked us both. She signed quickly and we stood. She held an arm out, indicating I go first, but I could feel her fingertips on the small of my back, not so much guiding me…more like staying tethered to me. It made me feel warm and mushy inside. The same men were at the bar, and the same men turned to regard us as we passed them. The bartender waved again and I heard Alicia say, "Bye, Jeff."

My car was closer, and Alicia walked me to it, where we stood quietly, nervously—at least on my part. The air had gotten chilly and I saw goose bumps break out on Alicia's bare arms.

"Aren't you cold?" I asked.

She nodded with a gentle laugh. "I am. But I don't have a wrap that goes with this dress."

"I'm very fond of that dress," I said, and my voice had a husky quality to it that surprised us both.

"I was hoping you would be. I could say the same for yours…

RIGHT HERE, RIGHT NOW

though 'fond' isn't the right word. I'm not 'fond' of that dress, I'm ridiculously turned on by that dress."

A throbbing began in my lower body. "Yeah?"

"Oh, yeah."

"Good."

Alicia leaned forward then and kissed me and it wasn't gentle. We were way past gentle. Her tongue pushed into my mouth immediately, and I pushed back with mine, my hands grabbing her waist and pulling her closer. I wanted her to feel my body heat against her, wanted to warm her up in the best of ways.

We might have kissed for a year. It might have been thirty seconds. I had no idea, but when we wrenched apart, we were both breathing heavily, and we stood there looking at each other, my hands on her hips, hers in my hair, both of us all swollen lips and dilated pupils and flushed faces.

"Come home with me," Alicia whispered.

"I can't. I have Leo."

"Right. Okay. I'll go home with you."

There was a split second of consideration, I admit it. But then logic slid in and reminded me that this was not planned. In my head, I was scanning my house, thinking about the dirty dishes I'd left in the sink, the piles of discarded clothing on the floor of my bedroom—the outfits that didn't make the cut for tonight's dinner, had I made my bed...?

Alicia's hands slid down my arms, grasped my hands. She ducked her head to catch my eye as she coaxed, "Come on, Lacey. Live in the moment. Don't think about it. Don't weigh the pros and cons. Just be right here, right now. With me." She bounced a little bit as she pleaded and I found myself agreeing before I even realized it. But she was so happy with my decision that it was almost not stressful for me. Almost. "Fantastic! I don't want you out of my sight, so I'm just going to ride with you. Can you bring me back to get my car tomorrow?"

I nodded and hit my key fob, the locks clicking open as our gazes held.

She looked giddy, and that helped me to push aside my dislike of spontaneity. After a quick kiss on the mouth, Alicia zipped around the front of the car and got in. We buckled up, I started the car, and we pulled out of the parking lot.

And so began the sexiest drive home I've ever experienced.

Alicia let her hands wander, but the car was dark, so I never knew where they were until they landed on my body. The back of my neck first where she dug her fingers into my hair and scratched my scalp. I almost drove us off the road right then. Then down the back of my dress a bit, fingertips dancing along the skin between my shoulder blades. Alicia's face was close to mine; she nuzzled her nose against my neck, flicked my earlobe with her tongue.

I swallowed hard, whispered her name. "I don't want to wreck us," I pointed out, my voice weak and shaky.

"Then I guess you'd better concentrate on the road," she replied, causing a little whimper to escape me. She trailed one finger around my neck, down my throat, and traced the plunging neckline of my dress. "This, by the way? So, so sexy." Her finger dipped down between my breasts and I could feel my nipples tighten.

Suddenly, getting us back to my house, her house, whatever, it didn't matter, just a house of any kind—was the only thing I wanted to do. I pushed a bit harder on the gas pedal and heard her chuckle.

"Is somebody anxious to get home?"

My knuckles were white as I gripped the steering wheel, forcing myself not to look down as I felt Alicia's hand skim teasingly over the outside of my bare thigh, around my knee. It moved up and over, her fingers now brushing the inside and tugging subtly, forcing my legs to part just a bit.

"Alicia…" I said, trying to make it sound like a warning, but instead sounding like I was begging.

"Lacey…" she whispered, then sucked my earlobe into her mouth and ran her tongue around it.

Oh, my God, I thought, as I felt a surge of wetness from my body. Somehow, I managed to pry the fingers of my right hand off the steering wheel, plant my palm against Alicia's sternum, and push her several inches back into her own seat. "Alicia, I swear to God if you don't stop, I'm going to drive us into a tree. You have to…I need you to…you're just…*stay there*. Stay right there. Please. We're almost home." I gave my head a slight shake to clear it. "God."

She didn't say anything, so I ventured a glance her way. Her grin, the glint in her eyes visible even in the dimness of the car, the warmth of her hand as it wrapped around my wrist. Yeah, she was far too satisfied with herself in that moment. Her sexiness, my intense arousal for her, they were almost alarming.

Alicia kept her hands to herself for the remaining five minutes of our ride, and actually held herself in check until we got through the front door. I closed it and hit the deadbolt as she wandered through my small home, into the living room.

"This is so cute," she said with a smile as Leo came bounding down the stairs to say hello.

"Thanks." I called Leo, opened the back door and let him out, then turned and made the three steps it took me to get to Alicia. I said nothing, simply grabbed her waist with one hand, her head with the other, and brought her mouth down to mine as I backed her into the couch, where she fell into a sitting position. I broke our kiss only long enough to hike up my dress so I could straddle her lap. Then I grabbed her face with both hands and crushed my mouth to hers once again.

She moaned against my lips, and I felt her hands rubbing up and down the sides of my bare thighs causing goose bumps that had nothing at all to do with the temperature to erupt across my skin.

I couldn't recall a time in my life when I'd ever been so completely aroused. Or so assertive. She'd turned me on to such a high degree during that ride that there was only one way I was coming down. I pulled away and looked into Alicia's eyes. Those gorgeous blue eyes that were nearly all black now, which only served to intensify my desire.

Absently, I heard Leo scratching at the door, and I pushed myself off Alicia's lap to get him, smiling at the gentle whimper of loss she let out.

I was determined. This was my show now. I let Leo in, gave him a treat, then held my hand out to Alicia. She took it, I pulled her to her feet—taking a moment to let my eyes roam over her entire body—then tugged her to the stairs and up to my bedroom.

She stood in the middle of the room, looking around, taking it all in, I assumed, as I turned on a small lamp, kicked piles of clothes out of the way and chose some music on my phone. Something soft and sexy, the volume low. I turned back to her and caught my breath. The sight of her standing there in that beautiful blue dress, her hair tousled, her face flushed a lovely pink, her lips dark and parted slightly, her gaze intent upon mine…it did things to me. Erotic, sensual things. I crossed the room in four quick steps and we were kissing again. Deep, passionate kissing that had the rest of the world falling away. There was nothing in that moment for me but Alicia. Her mouth on mine. Her hands exploring my body. The heat from her skin. It was almost too much. If I'd simply imploded right then, left nothing but a pile of ash on my bedroom floor, I really wouldn't have been all that surprised.

I maneuvered us to the bed where we both sat, still kissing. I loved the way her face felt in my hands. I held her tenderly but also firmly, and when I dug my fingers into the sunset hair at the back of her head, gave it a tug so my tongue could have easy access to her throat, the little gasp she released caused a tingle low in my body that steadily grew in intensity. The gasp morphed into a moan when I closed my hand over her breast and squeezed gently. Her hands came up to my face and she kissed me harder.

Without realizing we were doing it, we slid our bodies up and back so we ended up lying on my bed, our mouths never parting. While I was sure I could make out with Alicia for hours on end, I also felt like we'd done that and it was time for more. Her hand was in my hair as I leaned over her body, her fingers digging in, and it was blissful. Shivers of arousal ran all across my body every time she scratched at my scalp. I moved a hand to her knee, then up the side of her thigh to her hip where I stroked absently as I explored her mouth with mine.

I felt hurried, but not. I felt desperate, but not. I felt overwhelmed by sensation, yet perfectly content to just touch her. My hand was still on her hip when my fingers sent information to my brain, and I pulled my mouth from hers just far enough to speak.

"Are you going commando?" I asked, in aroused disbelief.

A super-sexy grin broke across her face. "Have you seen how tight this dress is?" was her response.

I nodded. "As a matter of fact, I have."

"Then you understand."

"It's a good thing I didn't know that little factoid during dinner." I kissed her again while my fingers found the hem of her dress and slipped beneath it.

Alicia took a turn pulling her mouth away. "Yeah? Why? What would you have done?"

I held her gaze as my heart rate kicked up yet another notch and I said, "I would've sat much closer to you, and I would've put my hand here." I slid my fingers around to the inside of her thigh, and I felt the hitch in her breath. "And then—and I'd have been very subtle because there were other people around us—I would've done this." I slid my hand a little higher, very slowly, drawing it out as I held that blue-eyed gaze with my own. I could feel the heat. And then I could feel the wetness on the insides of her thighs, causing me to moan quietly. "You're so wet," I whispered, and I could hear the wonder in my own voice.

"I've been like this since I saw you at the table."

I continued to look in her eyes as my thumb skimmed over her center and she gasped. I kept my touch feather-light, just barely brushing her skin, watching her face and feeling an unfamiliar sense of luck. Of being blessed, if there was such a thing. Of being special enough to be allowed to put my hands on this woman, to kiss her, to be this close to her. I pushed a little harder and Alicia gasped again, and even though I wanted to go slow, I also wanted to make her feel amazing. I kissed her as I continued to stroke her, and soon her hips picked up the rhythm and we moved together, gently, up and down. Without missing a beat, I slid inside her, and that was all it took. A long moan pushed its way up from her throat, wrenching her mouth from mine and forcing her head back, exposing a long, elegant column of throat that I wanted to devour with my mouth as she came...but I couldn't pull my eyes away. Alicia was so beautiful in that moment. Sexy, erotic, sensual, vulnerable, strong, all of it mixed together to form this one, blindingly stunning image just for me.

I felt so incredibly honored that tears welled up in my eyes.

I could feel Alicia everywhere. One hand gripping my hair, the other's fingers digging into the small of my back, her breasts pressed against my body, her leg wrapped around mine, the warmth of her center holding my fingers inside her. It was as if we were a single entity, melded together in one intimate moment. And I never wanted it to end.

It did, of course, but it was seared into my memory forever.

Alicia's eyes were closed. Her hand slid off my back and dropped to the bed like a dead tree branch as she whispered, "Oh, my God," over and over again and I smiled down at her.

I kissed her mouth and rolled myself off her so I wouldn't squish her completely. When I did that and glanced at the two of us, I started to chuckle.

Alicia opened her eyes, narrowed them as she mock-scolded me. "Laughter is not something a girl wants to hear in the heat of the moment, Lacey."

"I know," I said in amusement. "But look at us. Notice anything?"

Alicia lifted her head and then she chuckled as well. "We're both still dressed."

"Completely. With the exception of shoes, we are both completely dressed."

Dropping her head back to the pillow, Alicia said, "I don't think I've ever had that intense an orgasm with all my clothes still on." She turned those blue eyes on me, and her expression grew tender as she reached out a hand and stroked my cheek, ran her fingertips across my lips. Her voice dropped to a whisper. "That was *amazing*."

I couldn't control the grin the broke out across my face. "It was."

"I could use some water."

"You got it." I slid off the bed. "I'll be right back."

I padded down the stairs to the kitchen, which was lit only by moonlight. As I filled a glass with water, my brain tossed me flashes of what had just happened, and it occurred to me that this was the first time I'd gone off-script as far as my planning went, the first time I'd gone with "live in the moment," and I didn't regret it.

Interesting.

I headed back upstairs and into my room. And stopped dead in my tracks.

Alicia was still on the bed, but she was reclined on her right hip, facing me, her right arm bracing, holding her up.

Her eyes were bright.

Her smile was sexy.

Her body was naked.

She was lounging on my bed, in all her naked glory. Her skin looked smooth and creamy, flawless, tiny freckles dotting her bare shoulders. Her breasts were beautiful, porcelain white with dark pink nipples enticing me simply by existing. I swear to God, she looked like a painting. A gorgeous, unbelievably sexy painting that was for my eyes only.

"We're not done," she said, her voice quiet as she crooked a finger at me.

As I set the water glass on the nightstand, I was overcome with what I can only describe as a totally unfamiliar sense of courage. I stood there for a moment and held Alicia's gaze. Without letting it go, I reached down to the edge of my dress, but she stopped me.

"No. Come here."

I did as I was asked and walked to the bed as she sat up. Her fingers grasped the hem of my dress and tugged me closer as she got up onto her knees on the mattress. That alone was enough to kick my breathing into high gear, and I did the best I could to keep myself under control, a little bit shocked that she'd ratcheted me up again so quickly...and also not shocked at all.

"The undressing is part of it for me," she said quietly, as her hands skimmed along my hips, my sides. Then she pulled the dress up and over my head and dropped it to the floor. I watched as Alicia's lips parted slightly and she let out a very, very soft "Oh" that she drew out as her eyes raked over me, so sensually, I was sure I could feel them. Like the caress of her hands on my skin. And then her hands *were* on my skin, her fingertips brushing up the sides of my legs, then to my hips, then to my waist where she grabbed on and pulled me toward her, covering my mouth with her own.

I tried to pay attention to everything that happened. I did my best to feel exactly where her hands were, her fingers, her tongue, but being with Alicia Wright went way beyond simple touch. It was so much more. It was sensation. Endless, overwhelming sensation. She made love to me in a way that was both desperate and controlled, both raw and tender, like it might be the last thing we ever did on this earth and she wanted me to remember. And when the orgasm finally ripped through my body, tightening my muscles, lifting my hips off the bed, colors exploding in my head, I could do nothing but hold on to her for dear life, whispering her name as if I was unsure she was still there, uncertain she was even real, fearing the possibility of waking up only to discover my entire evening with her had been a dream.

But she was real. She was so very real. When my heart stopped feeling like it was going to detonate in my chest, when my breathing calmed down from "panting dog" to "I just jogged a tiny bit," when I could uncurl my fingers from the death grip they had on the pillow under my head, Alicia was still there.

She smiled down at me, her eyes filled with tenderness as she brushed my hair off my forehead. "Wow," she said quietly.

I swallowed, then cleared my throat before I responded hoarsely, "I think I'm supposed to say that."

We stayed in that position for what felt like a long time, but I was biding my time while I regained my strength. Because, to quote Alicia, we weren't done yet.

CHAPTER THIRTEEN

I don't think the morning after the first time is easy for anybody. You're stone cold sober. You go over everything you said in the heat of the moment the night before and, inevitably, you remember things that make you cringe. *Oh, God, did I really say that? Did I actually do that? Did I really make that sound?* Each moment—hell, each second—is subject to scrutiny and criticism because, in the morning, you have a clear head.

Or at least, I did until Alicia started moving. Touching. Exploring.

It was barely the crack of dawn, judging by the purplish crimson color of the horizon I could see out my window. Leo would have to go out soon, but I could hear the little snuffly-snoring sounds coming from the vicinity of his bed, so I allowed myself to drift a bit. Alicia's soft, warm body was tucked up against my back; she took on the role of Big Spoon, her knees in the crook of mine, her arm tossed over my side, her fingertips grazing my stomach. And then she started moving.

I am not a morning person. Remember when I mentioned that? The only thing I want to do at oh-dark-thirty is burrow more deeply into my pillow and under my covers and continue sleeping.

Turns out, Alicia *is* a morning person.

When her fingers shifted from grazing my stomach to brushing across my nipple, my breath caught, a zap of arousal sizzling down my spine to sit low in my body. Alicia slid her other arm under my neck, and I wasn't sure why until she switched hands, and that one began toying with my breasts. She nuzzled my ear, quietly, gently, as her fingers played. My mind wanted to scream at her that it was too early, it was time for sleeping, so just let me do that, please, it's *morning*.

But my body betrayed me. In a big, big way. Alicia's other hand trailed down over my hip, my thigh, and back up. Her fingernails left a path of goose bumps along my back, my shoulders, and I was embarrassed to feel myself squirm under her touch.

Alicia never made a sound the whole time she tortured my body. Neither did I until she used a hand to lift up my knee and tuck her own between my legs, which gave her better access to that part of me that had become so wet, so fast I was kind of stunned at my body's reaction, especially when I let out a little moan that had nothing to do with wanting to sleep.

She took her time, which I think made it more frustratingly delicious. Sensation oozed through me like warm water, slowly filling me. The only movements in the bed were her fingernail gently scratching across my hardened nipple, sending tiny electric jolts down to my center, and the fingers of her other hand as she slid them between my legs and into the hot wetness she'd created in an alarmingly short time. She sighed in my ear as I began subtly moving my hips to the slow and easy rhythm of her hand, and when she whispered, "Come on," so very quietly, I had no choice but to obey. I brought my arm up to grasp the back of her neck and hold her tightly to me as my body trembled in climax. There was no sound. Only the two of us, melded together, breathing as one. When I came down and my body relaxed, Alicia simply kissed my temple, tightened her arms around me, and snuggled back in. She fell back to sleep in minutes, her deep, even breathing a comfort behind me. I followed her soon after.

❖

The next couple of weeks were a whirlwind for me. I'd never been with anybody who was simultaneously so opposite from me and such a ridiculous turn-on that I could barely look at her without picturing her naked.

Working in adjacent offices proved to be interesting. By unspoken agreement, we'd been keeping our relationship under wraps. I can only speak for myself when I say that I had no idea where things were going, so I was hesitant to share details with others until I had a better handle on it all. Alicia seemed okay with that, as she never mentioned it in any detail. Still, I think people had their suspicions. And why wouldn't they? I don't think we were exactly subtle about it.

Alicia would come over under the pretense of bringing a treat for Leo; that's what she'd tell Mary. Then, more often than not, she'd come into my inner office, shut the door behind her, cross the room to me, grab my face, and kiss me until I could barely focus. I'm sure Mary noticed more than once when Alicia left with a self-satisfied smile on her face and I had trouble forming words for the next five or ten minutes.

I couldn't do the same thing to her, as her office was completely open, but that didn't mean I didn't stop by. I'd pretend to want a slice of the god-awful Hawaiian pizza the staff had apparently fallen in love with. I'd go looking for my bathroom key, which Alicia would purposely keep so I'd have to come get it, even though her own bathroom was now functional. I'd bring Leo over so he could help the staff brainstorm. Each time, all I wanted was a few minutes to look at her, to feast my eyes on her body, to take in the day's outfit, to gaze at her face, her hair, that mouth. I stared at her hands all the time—once, I'm sure Gisele caught me, and she gave me a conspiratorial smile that I wasn't sure how to respond to.

We didn't spend all our time together. We were both busy. Alicia did a lot of schmoozing of potential new clients, which meant she was often busy for happy hour or dinner or both. I hadn't been to her place, but she came to mine two or three times a week, and when she did… My God. The sex. There were no words to accurately describe the sex.

I can honestly say that I've never been so completely attracted to, so sexually satisfied with, or so endlessly turned on by a person in my entire life. Everything Alicia did to my body, every touch, every kiss, every position…it all worked amazingly well. In fact, it almost frightened me a little bit just how perfect we were in bed. I realized it was probably a good thing we didn't spend every night together. We'd never sleep.

It was the last day in April, a Wednesday, and we were in my kitchen, Alicia standing behind me, her chin on my shoulder while I stirred the risotto.

"Pretty labor intensive," she observed.

"Totally worth it," I replied, ladling another scoop of broth into the rice. I turned to meet her eyes. "Promise." I meant the kiss to be a quick peck, but Alicia's fingers captured my chin and held it while she deepened things easily. I finally pulled away with a quiet chuckle. "Stop it. You're going to make me burn dinner." The pork was resting on the counter behind us. As soon as I finished with the risotto, we could eat.

"Sorry," she said with a kiss to my temple, then went back to her previous position, arms wrapped around my middle, chin on my shoulder. "Oh, I wanted to mention something."

Her lips were very close to my ear, and her voice sent a pleasant shudder down my spine. "What?"

She pressed her body tighter against mine, her front to my back. "That thing you did with your mouth the other night? Yeah, I'm gonna need you to do that again in the very near future."

My spoon went still in the pot, and I was pretty sure I stopped breathing for a beat or two. I swallowed hard, audibly, as I recalled the moment she referred to. A couple nights ago. The orgasm I brought her to had been…vocal. Very vocal. Which was unlike her and also awesome. I turned to meet her gaze. "I think that could be arranged."

"Yeah? That is fantastic news." Alicia kissed me again, but this time, it *was* a peck. "Should I open the wine now?"

"Yes, please," I said, relieved to see my risotto hadn't stuck to the pot and also relieved to have her body away from me for a little bit. Well, not *relieved*, because I'd have loved to have her body right next to me twenty-four hours a day. But in that moment, if she'd stayed that close to me any longer, dinner would've fallen by the wayside as other things took over my attention.

A few minutes later, we sat down to eat. Leo was perched politely at Alicia's feet, obviously understanding where his chances for scraps were better. We touched our wineglasses together in a toast, then dug in.

"Hey, have you ever seen *Wicked*?" I asked, then took a bite of my outstanding (if I did say so myself) risotto.

"The show? Onstage? Nope." Alicia shook her head.

"Good. Because it's awesome, and I have tickets."

"Oh?"

I sipped my wine, then said, "Yeah, I have season tickets at the Academy. I have for a couple years, so I see a lot of shows. Sometimes I take my mom. Sometimes Leanne and I go. I've let my brother take a date here and there. But this time, I want to take you." I gave her a tender smile across the table.

"When?"

"It's not for a couple weeks. I thought we could get an early dinner, maybe at Stavros again." My smile grew, as I thought of Stavros as "our place." "Then we could hit the show, maybe go to your place after? What do you think?"

I admit I'd been hoping for enthusiasm. A little excitement. Maybe some flattery at having been asked. Instead, Alicia chewed her pork and looked out the window for several beats. "Maybe," she said finally.

Maybe? I tried not to let my disappointment show too obviously. "Oh. Okay. Well, let me know." I wasn't sure what to say on the whole subject, and when Alicia asked me about a particular client I'd had that day, I realized she didn't want me to say anything.

That night was the first night we spent together and didn't have sex. I think I surprised Alicia a little bit when I told her my stomach felt off and asked if she could just hold me. She agreed easily and even smiled as she held out her left arm and I tucked myself into her neck, got comfortable on her shoulder. She smelled amazing, as always. Today it was coconut and a hint of the tang of lime. I inhaled deeply and she pressed a kiss to my head, then tightened her grip, and just like that, I felt better. I told myself I was being silly. *Maybe she just doesn't like the theatre and doesn't want to hurt my feelings by saying so.* A distinct possibility, I knew, so I inhaled another deep breath, let it out slowly, and felt myself relax.

There was nothing to worry about. Nothing at all.

❖

May has always been my favorite month. The sun finally decides to show up on a regular basis. Early spring flowers start to bloom. The muddy brown of the entire world begins to recede, and green slowly takes its place. It's the promise of warmth and beauty, I think, that draws me to that month.

Friday that week was gorgeous. Sunny, sky the color of an Easter egg, temperatures in the low seventies. The absolute perfect kind of day for me. My mood matched the weather, as it so often does, and I entered my office floating on a cloud. The cloying scent of sausage wafting down the stairwell didn't bother me. Neither did almost getting brained by a kickball that I dodged smoothly at the last second. It hit the wall behind me with a loud smack and bounced back to Pantone, who gave me a little wave and muttered a sheepish apology. I waved back as Leo and I went into the office.

Leo split his time between me and Mary. The second time he sauntered back into my office to curl up on his bed, he had a dab of peanut butter on his nose. I just smiled and shook my head.

I had a new client in the morning, a man in his forties who'd changed jobs recently and wanted to roll his 401(k) into something worthwhile. In the afternoon, I had an old client, a couple who had worked with my dad for years and were in need of some estate planning. This was the kind of workday I loved. Not packed full, but steady. When no clients were sitting across from my desk, I had forms to fill out, phone calls and emails to return, and articles to read, as keeping up with the changing tax laws and the ins and outs of the finance world were paramount to my remaining competitive at my job.

I was lost in one such article when a knock sounded on my door, and I looked up to see Mary with her windbreaker on, purse in hand. I glanced at the clock just as she said, "I'm heading out."

"Holy cucumbers, it's five already?" I asked in disbelief. The day had flown.

Mary's dainty laugh pealed out of her. "Holy cucumbers? That's a new one."

"Well, I really wanted to say holy shit, but I didn't want to offend your virgin ears."

Mary's scoff was exactly what I'd expected. "Please. My ears weren't virgins when your ears were born."

With a chuckle, I said, "Have a great weekend, Mare. See you Monday."

Mary closed the outer door behind her, leaving Leo and me to ourselves. I reached above my head and stretched, my back having tightened up from sitting in my desk chair for so long. A glance out the window showed me Alicia's baby blue BMW parked in my spot, of course, and I realized I hadn't seen her all day.

"Come on, Leo," I said, as I stood. "Let's go see our girlfriend." I said it quietly because we still weren't official, and I didn't want anybody hearing me call Alicia that. It was true that I tended to think of her that way but, in reality, it had only been a few weeks, and I knew I needed to be careful establishing any kind of permanence too soon. There was no better way to scare somebody off, or so my big brother had told me ages ago.

I wandered down the hall and to the red door of Just Wright. The whole staff was sitting in front of the whiteboard as Alicia stood, dressed in a sexy gray pantsuit and heels, pointing at the notes on it, and it amazed me that she could make even the color gray seem vibrant. Leo, unsurprisingly, sprinted across the room to the group and jumped up into Gisele's lap, forcing a laugh from her. Alicia looked my way, our eyes locked, and my legs grew weak. This seemed to be my standard response now.

She gave me a little wave from where she stood, but turned back to her staff. I didn't want to interrupt her flow, so I moved as quietly as I could toward Gisele, scooped up Leo, and gave Alicia a smile as we headed back to the door.

Since I had no way of knowing how late the Just Wright staff planned to work that night, I gathered my things, and Leo and I headed home. It was Friday night, and I hoped to see Alicia, so I sent her a text telling her so. It was nearly ten o'clock by the time I'd given up on her. Leo and I were cuddled on the couch watching *Dateline* when my doorbell rang. I hadn't heard back from Alicia at all—which bothered me a bit—so I was a little shocked to find her standing at my door.

I didn't get to say a word. She stepped inside, grabbed my face and kissed me. Hard. Possessively. I heard her kick the door shut with her foot. Then her purse and bag hit the floor. But the whole time, her mouth was fused to mine, her tongue owning me, her hands all over me before I could even comprehend what was happening. My body overrode my brain, though (not a surprise), and soon I was grabbing at her just as desperately as she was grabbing at me. Finding and navigating the stairs seemed like way too difficult a prospect, and within ten minutes, we were on the couch, my sweats were in a ball on the floor, and Alicia was kneeling between my spread legs.

I covered my eyes with both hands and let out a small cry as her mouth closed over me. I felt her hand on my leg, pushing it up and over her shoulder to give her better access. Which it did, judging by the much louder cry *that* pulled from my throat. Her warm hands slid up my body, over my stomach to capture my breasts. She kneaded them gently at first, then with a bit more firmness as she pushed her tongue into me and I lifted my hips, searching for more. She gave it.

It was mere minutes before my orgasm tore through my body, forced my head back, had me grappling for a pillow, an afghan, a shirt, anything I could clench in my fist. Alicia grasped my hips, held me tight, stopped moving her tongue, but kept her mouth fastened over me the whole time until I slowly lowered myself back down. Then she took her mouth away, pressed a gentle kiss to my center, and finally looked up at me.

Our eyes met over my rapidly rising and falling chest, and she gave me a smug smile. "That's just what I was hoping for." Her voice was quiet as she raised herself to a sitting position. I'd managed to get her jacket off her, but other than that, she was still fully clothed. Rumpled and flushed, but fully clothed.

"That was..." I shook my head, and stayed lying down. "My legs are numb."

Alicia's chuckle was amused. "I'll take that as a compliment."

We were quiet for a long moment, just enjoying being together. When feeling returned to my limbs, I pushed myself to a sitting position, then stretched to grab my pants. "I didn't hear back from you," I said, as I pushed a leg in. "So you surprised me."

"I know. I'm sorry." She rubbed her forehead, then reached down to scoop Leo off the floor where he'd curled up. "Today was crazy. Way too much going on."

I nodded as she talked about three different pitches she was working on, two different designs she and Pantone were creating from scratch, and meetings she had scheduled next week. I listened, nodded or commented when something warranted it, but there was something in Alicia's eyes tonight. Something...far away. I couldn't think of a better way to describe it. I reached my hand toward her, brushed her hair away. "You okay?"

She turned to me and nodded, gave me a smile that didn't quite reach her eyes. "Just tired."

"Come upstairs with me. I'll rub your back." I stood up and held out a hand.

Her shoulders fell a bit. "I can't stay," she said. "I've got some traveling to do tomorrow. Need to get an early start."

"You do? I thought we could spend some time together. It's the weekend." It was harder to hide this time, as disappointment draped over me like a sheet over old furniture.

"I'm sorry," she said, and stood without taking my hand, then set Leo on the couch. Her jacket was in a heap on the floor, and she retrieved it, pushed her arm in.

"Well, can you come to dinner at my parents' on Sunday?" I hadn't planned on blurting it out like that, but I was feeling young. Inexperienced. Desperate. I realized I probably shouldn't have mentioned meeting my family when she went perfectly still for a beat.

"I won't be back until Sunday night," she said and finished putting on her jacket.

"Oh. Where are you going?"

"I've just got some things to take care of." Alicia didn't meet my eyes at all, and I swallowed hard, a weird, uncomfortable pit forming in my stomach.

"Oh," I said again. *Lame, Lacey. So very lame.*

Alicia turned to me, gave me a very small smile, like she had to force it onto her face. Then she kissed me quickly and started toward the door.

There was so much I wanted to say right then. So much I should've said. Instead, I followed her like an obedient puppy and held the door as she walked to the driveway and got into her car. She gave me a little wave, and I waved back as she drove away.

"What just happened, Leo?" I asked my dog, my voice low, slightly confused, a little stung. Surprisingly, he had no answers for me.

I did my best to push the concern away. It was true that it had only been a couple weeks. We'd only been together a handful of times, and I couldn't say that I knew Alicia, because I didn't. I didn't really have the right to feel entitled to all the details of her life.

Which didn't mean my feelings weren't hurt.

I thought about texting her. I even thought about calling her. I was fairly certain she wouldn't respond to either, though, and the chances of my saying something needy, stupid, childish, or all three were pretty high, so I chose to take a breath, relax, and let it all sit until tomorrow.

"Come on, Leonardo da Vinci," I said, as I clicked off the living room lamp, then the TV. "Let's go to bed." As we headed up the stairs, I tried my best to ignore the gentle throbbing still happening between my legs.

Chapter Fourteen

My mom was frying chicken for Sunday dinner, and that realization—which hit the second I entered the side door and smelled it—brightened my mood. Not a lot, but at least a little bit. There really is nothing like favorite foods from your childhood to make you feel the tiniest bit better.

"Hi, Mom." I kissed her cheek as Leo jumped at her leg.

She laughed at my dog's antics. "Well, hello there, Mr. Leo. How are you today?" She scooped him up, and he kissed her as expected, even as I saw him looking toward the chicken out of the corner of his eye. "I saved you the giblets, don't you worry."

I shook my head with affection, loving that my parents loved my dog and understood what he meant to me. In the living room, my dad was in his usual spot watching his usual thing, but I was surprised to see my brother on the couch.

"Hey," I said. "What are you doing here?"

Scott turned to look at me. "What are *you* doing here?"

"I'm here for Sunday dinner. Duh."

"Me too. Duh." He tossed a wink at me and I grinned.

"Hi, Dad."

"Hi, honey. How's life after the fifteenth treating you?" My dad asked the question without looking at me, but I was used to that.

"Blissfully." Back in the kitchen, I asked my mom if I could help and she put me on salad duty, which I loved. The labor of chopping, dicing, peeling…it gave me a sense of accomplishment. Plus, standing in the kitchen with my mother as we both worked on dinner for our family felt perfect. Some might find it horrendously sexist that my dad and brother sat on their asses while the women did all the work—and to be honest, I had days where I thought that exact thing *and* said so— but for the most part, I looked at it as time with my mother. That was something to be treasured as far as I was concerned.

As if reading my mind, my mother said, "Do you remember that one Thanksgiving when you got all over Scott for not helping?"

I grinned. "I do. I believe my angle was 'He ate three times as much as I did. Why do I have to wash his dishes?' Something like that."

"That was it. You were, oh, twelve or so." Her smile was wistful. "And he did end up doing the dishes."

"Yeah, that went in my win column."

"I just wish you kids didn't have win columns," Mom said, softening it with a wink.

"They're shrinking," I told her.

"I'm so glad." The look on her face, the mixture of relief and happiness, did something to me then. Something inside me...eased. I don't really know how to explain it other than to say I felt like, in that moment, I finally understood that constantly competing with my brother was just...unnecessary. Don't get me wrong, I'd never stop ribbing him about the Alicia thing...but other than that...

We sat down to eat about twenty minutes later and it was great, as always. I didn't say it out loud, but it was always best when Scott was there, too.

Maybe I should say it out loud. I'd work on that.

There was a part of me, though, that harbored a sadness, a disappointment that Alicia wasn't sitting in a fifth chair we would've brought up from the basement. While I still believed that asking her to meet my family had probably been premature, it didn't keep me from being bummed out that she'd said no, that her work—or whatever she was doing—was more important. And yes, I did realize I was being slightly irrational and more than a little whiny about it, but that didn't change the way I felt. I adored Alicia. I just wanted her here because of that.

Scott bit into a drumstick, wiped his chin, then chewed. "So, Lace-Face," he said, as though privy to my thoughts. "You seeing Alicia now?"

His question came out of nowhere, but because of my train of thought, didn't really feel that way. Still, I gave him a look as my mother said, "Wait. What?"

I narrowed my gaze at Scott. "Why do you ask that?"

"Because I ran into Leanne the other day, and she said she thinks you are."

I made a mental note to kill Leanne next time I saw her. Or at least maim. I blew out a breath. "I guess *seeing* is the right word."

Scott's brow furrowed. "As opposed to?"

I shrugged. "I don't know. Dating? Girlfriends? Commitment?"

Scott nodded like he knew what I meant. I was pretty sure he had a clue, as it was rare for him to get past "seeing" anybody. It had only happened twice in his life, and the second time, he'd gotten his heart broken. Although the expression on his face was…different somehow, like he had thoughts on his mind he wasn't expressing. I'd have to ask him about it later.

"This is the girl from the office next door?" my mother asked, all ears and curiosity. "The one you said you were kissing last time we had dinner?"

I nodded slowly. "Yes. That one."

"You should bring her to dinner."

"You should," Scott agreed and shot me a wink, his face back to its normal, annoying self.

"Maybe." I shoved a bunch of salad in my face so I could stop talking about it. It was funny, though. I was sure that Scott thought bringing Alicia to Sunday dinner with Mom and Dad would be the last thing in the world I'd want to do. Which was why he brought it up: to mess with me. Stupid brothers. What he didn't know was how much I'd love to bring her. She and my dad could talk business. My mom would love her manners and sense of humor. My brother would love her— never mind about that. My point was, I could totally see her sitting there with us and completely fitting in, like she was meant to be there.

Of course, I kept all of this to myself and almost wept with relief when my father changed the subject to the Phillies.

Thank God for the Phillies!

❖

By Sunday evening, I had to admit that Alicia's sporadic contact was starting to weigh on me. I didn't hear from her at all on Saturday—and that troubled me. So I occupied myself. I took Leo for a walk, started a new novel I'd been wanting to read since Christmas, I even went to a movie by myself. And when I was home, I kept my phone away from wherever I was sitting, finding that if it wasn't within easy reach, I checked it much less often.

By the time I got home from my parents' house on Sunday, I decided I'd exercised enough care so as not to be considered pushy, and I typed out a text.

I've missed you this weekend. Get done what you needed to?

I sent it off, set the phone down, and tried hard—and unsuccessfully—to turn my mind to other things. The reply didn't come for nearly an hour.

Hi. Things are fine. On my way home.

Okay. A less than personal response, sort of…heavy, but I was all right.

Wanna stop by? I can feed you. My finger hovered over the Send button as I analyzed whether that sounded too needy. Deciding it wasn't, I sent it.

Another ten minutes went by.

Tired. Just need to sleep. Thanks, though.

The utter lack of emojis also bothered me, as Alicia was good at announcing the mood of her texts with faces so there'd be no confusion. In this exchange, there were none. No smileys. No frowns. Not even the sleepy face with the little *Z*'s. Just words. And not many. Not very personal, not at all.

I sent my own smiley and left it at that. There was so much more I wanted to text, to say, and I actually dialed the first three numbers before instinct warned me that calling would be a mistake—assuming she'd even answer, which I doubted. In the end, I put the phone on the kitchen counter, curled up on the couch with Leo, and cleared a couple of shows off my DVR. I didn't look at the phone again until nearly eleven, when Leo and I headed up to bed.

Didn't matter anyway, as there was nothing on it.

❖

I failed to anticipate one issue that came with my workload easing up as May strolled slowly along: the fact that, with less work to occupy my days and my mind, I had lots and lots of time to dwell. To wonder. To overanalyze, which I excelled at. I had barely heard from Alicia on Monday and Tuesday. I'd texted her a good morning. I got a good morning back about two hours later, but nothing more. I'd texted her good night just before I turned out my light and tossed and turned for a few hours. It wasn't until the next morning that I'd seen her responses, both very generic good nights, both at ridiculous hours of the morning—one at 1:37 a.m., the other at 3:17 a.m. Alicia obviously wasn't sleeping any better than I was.

On Wednesday, I took a different tack, simply doing my best to focus on work. When Alicia was ready to talk to me, she would. The thumping bass beating through my wall didn't help my chill, though, and I was seriously considering stomping next door to give Brandon a piece of my mind when a knock on my door caused a surge of hope to swell through my chest. I knew Alicia wasn't in—a quick glance out my window showed me the continued lack of baby blue BMWs in the parking lot—but I felt that hope anyway, which just made me feel worse. I blew out a breath.

"Come in."

"Hey, Lace-Face."

I tried to hide my surprise as Scott came in and shut the door behind him. Leo lifted his head from his spot in a sunbeam, and his little nub of a tail wagged three times before he apparently decided he was too comfortable to get up and say hello. Instead, Scott squatted down to scratch his head, which was also a bit out of character for him.

"It's too late for lunch and too early to go home," I said, watching him as he took a seat. "What are you doing wandering around?" Then I remembered he was a client of Alicia's. "Oh. Got a meeting next door?"

"Not a scheduled one," he said, but didn't meet my eyes. "No."

I waited for him to elaborate. He didn't. He looked out the window. He picked up the apple-shaped stress ball I had on my desk and squeezed it in his big hand a couple times, then set it back down. His attention moved to a framed photo of me and my mother, which he'd seen a million times, but still picked up, looked at, set down.

I couldn't take it anymore. "What's going on, Scott?"

He looked up at me as if I'd surprised him, and I was pretty sure he was about to tell me nothing was going on. Instead, *he* surprised *me* by chewing on the inside of his cheek and looking out the window again. It hit me in that moment. The lack of eye contact. The fidgeting. The nibbling. He was nervous.

"What's up, big bro? Talk to me," I said, softening my tone.

I saw his Adam's apple move as he swallowed, but I waited him out. One thing I knew about my brother: when he was feeling vulnerable—and he was; that much was obvious to me—you couldn't rush him. He'd talk when he was ready. And he must have wanted to, otherwise, why come see me like this?

"I like somebody," he said, then stopped, as if that explained everything.

I waited a couple beats before saying, "Okay," and drawing the word out.

He met my gaze then, and I could see that vulnerability in his eyes. It startled me a bit. Even though I was expecting it, it was still a very unusual emotion for my big brother. Seeing him uncertain about himself in any way was almost foreign to me.

"I mean, really like her."

I nodded. "Does she know?" I knew better than to blurt out the question of who the object of his affection might be. In the back of my mind, I prayed it wasn't Alicia.

His sandy brow furrowed above those killer eyes of his. "I'm not sure. Maybe?"

"So, you haven't told her? You haven't asked her out or anything?"

He shook his head and grimaced.

"Do you think she likes you, too?"

He inhaled and let it out slowly, apparently giving the question some deep thought. "I think it's possible."

I folded my hands on the desk in front of me as I leaned forward and squinted at him. "Scott. You date all the time. You're a master at the art of seduction. Why does this have you in such a—" I stopped, the information sinking in even though he'd already said it. "Oh," I said, in a long, slow exhalation. "You *like* like her."

"That's what I said."

"Well, I know, but…you say that a lot." I gave him a smile so he wouldn't think I was mocking him. I gave him credit for reining in his exasperation with me, instead focusing on the matter at hand.

He sat forward on the edge of his seat. "This girl…" His face went all dreamy in that moment, and I widened my eyes at him.

"Oh, my God, who are you?"

His smile was weak as he shook his head. "I know, Lacey. I know. That's why I'm here. I don't know what to do."

"Can you tell me who it is?"

"It's Gisele. Next door."

He caught me off guard by being so forthcoming, but I recovered quickly. "Oh, Scott. She's awesome." I had a mix of emotions but tried to stay positive. I liked Gisele. A lot. And I knew my brother. I didn't want either of them to get hurt.

"I know, right? She's been in on most of the meetings I've had with Alicia and she's just…" His face lit up then and he started talking about her and I just watched. In awe. He talked about her smile and her intelligence and her eyes and her style and her creativity and he just went on and on until I finally held up a hand.

"Okay, okay, I get it. She makes the world go 'round. She's the sun and the moon and the stars. She's chocolate ice cream with sprinkles. She's a Ferrari."

He nodded his agreement, his expression telling me he was dead serious.

Once I saw that, I gave him the simple, obvious advice, the only advice I had. "So ask her out."

"Just like that?"

"Just like that."

"Okay."

We stared at each other, and I chuckled internally at the weirdness of this entire conversation. After a few beats, I said, "That's it? That's what you needed? Me to tell you to do the thing you already wanted to do anyway?"

He shrugged, his eyes wide with the lack of reasoning. "I guess so."

We looked at each other some more before we both burst into laughter, which started light and then worked its way into full-on belly laughs. Leo looked up at us in apparent confusion, which only made us laugh harder. Finally, Scott stood and I followed suit.

"Okay," he said, finger-combing his hair. "I'm gonna do this."

I walked around the desk, reached up, and straightened his red tie. "Well, you've got the power tie going, so I'd say your chances are pretty good."

"You think?"

"I do."

"Thanks, Lacey." The room hung heavy with the unsaid.

Then again, I understood it all without it being said. Words? Unnecessary. This was my *brother*. I gave him a nod. "You're welcome."

He kissed my forehead, and I watched him go. He was seriously good-looking in his navy suit, all broad shoulders and commanding posture, and he radiated confidence, even though I knew better. Scott and I, we had our issues—it was true. Lots of them. Some of them pretty significant. I could count on one hand the number of times he'd sought advice from me…and I'd use about three fingers. But in that moment, I was feeling so much about him: worry, affection, exhilaration, excitement, love, even a little bit of envy. He glanced back at me, and I gave him a thumbs-up as he shut the door.

Scott and Gisele.

"God, they'd make beautiful babies, Leo." My dog lifted his head to look at me, and I was sure he agreed. "Right?"

I sat back down at my desk, glancing out the window again to look for Alicia's car, which was still absent, but then I forced myself to put her out of my mind for the time being. Instead, I focused on sending good thoughts to the office next door.

Gisele would make a stellar sister-in-law…

CHAPTER FIFTEEN

By Thursday, I was frustrated beyond belief. I'd gotten a total of six texts from Alicia all week. Not one of them was longer than five words. Not one of them felt the least bit personal. Not one of them contained any sort of explanation or apology for her basically dropping off the face of the earth. She hadn't shown up to the office at all, as far as I could tell. I even entertained the idea of driving to her house to demand that she tell me what the hell was going on when the horrifying realization that I'd never been to her house, and had no idea where it was, hit me full force and made me feel that much crappier.

I'd sent her a text last night that was a bit more than just a good night. Instead of focusing on how much I missed her—and telling her as much—I went in a different direction. I'd told her that I was worried about her. Was she okay? Could I do something to help? It was all true. My feelings were everywhere. I missed her. I knew she didn't owe me an explanation. She didn't owe me anything. But I was worried. It had been over a week since her late-night, unannounced appearance at my door. Over a week since she'd made love to me on my own couch and left with barely a word. Had that been good-bye? I was genuinely concerned, so I texted to tell her so.

This morning, there was nothing. No response at all.

I sat on my bed and cried.

Just before noon, I took Leo for a walk at the Schuylkill Banks and even managed to keep him from getting too muddy. The day was gorgeous—sunny and warm with a gentle breeze, and I simply wanted some fresh air, some time outdoors to keep me from imploding while I sat in my office. My office that butted up next to the office of the woman I cared way too much about (a fairly recent realization) and who was making it pretty clear she didn't feel the same. I mean, I could be wrong, but the fact was, she seemed to be avoiding me like the plague. Honestly, what was I supposed to think at this point?

When Leo and I returned from our walk, however, my feelings of being refreshed and maybe a bit more at ease evaporated in an instant when I entered my reception area and couldn't see Mary over the stack of boxes.

I stood and blinked at them.

"It's okay," I heard Mary say, and she was right. Having recently told UPS it was fine to deliver packages here if Just Wright was locked, I had no reason to be upset. "They're coming to get this stuff in a few minutes."

I shook my head with a sigh and let it go. Yes, the chaos grated on me. But the chaos paled in comparison to simply doing something nice for Alicia and her business. I unclipped Leo from his leash and he wove his way around the boxes to Mary, probably hoping for some of her lunch. Something Mexican, judging from the smell.

"Mary, I mean it this time. Don't give him any," I warned her as I went into my office.

I did my best to throw myself into my work. I had a couple new articles I needed to read and a two o'clock phone call with a client, and I did pretty well until the music started next door. I'd almost gotten used to the occasional basslines thumping through the shared wall, but this seemed much louder than usual. Alicia's car was still nowhere to be seen, so I figured Brandon was taking advantage of the boss being gone to really crank it up.

I tried to ignore it.

I did.

I even turned on my own music in the hopes of drowning out his, but that only made my brain work harder as I tried to listen to my stuff while simultaneously trying to figure out what he was playing from hearing just the bass. After nearly twenty minutes, I threw the pen in my hand across the room and growled.

Coffee. Maybe coffee would help.

You know what didn't help? The mountain range of boxes *still* taking up my entire reception area.

"Goddamnit," I muttered, as I stalked out the door and down the hall. It was all coming to a head. I knew it. I could feel it, and I tried to stop it. Every little thing that had anything at all to do with Alicia—the boxes, the music, the kickball, the sickening smells of whatever food they ordered, Alicia's utter disappearance with no explanation, no text, no call, no nothing—it all boiled over in my chest until I couldn't keep it contained any longer. The door to Just Wright was open, and once I did a quick sweep with my eyes to be sure there were no clients around, nobody other than Alicia's employees, I closed it. I didn't slam it, but it must have been pretty close, as Gisele, Pantone, Justin, and Brandon all swiveled their heads to look at me, having heard it above the music.

"Enough," I said loudly. "I have had so much more than enough." The four of them exchanged glances, apparently looking to one another for direction. "There is a mountain of boxes in my reception area. Your boxes. *Again*. My bathroom key is nowhere to be found. *Again*. The window to the stairwell door has a crack in it now, and I'd bet good money it came from a kickball." I shot a look to Brandon. "And seriously, with the music? Seriously? This is a goddamn place of business, for crying out loud. You're not the only business here." I lifted my arms in a gesture of *what the hell*? They looked like the proverbial deer in headlights. Well, all except Brandon, whose expression darkened as he reached for his computer and turned the music down. "Where is Alicia?"

Nobody said anything. Again, they looked to one another, then back at me.

"I've been texting her for a week. When she texts back, it's a word or two, which seems very unlike her. I need to talk to her." To my own horror, I heard my voice crack the tiniest bit, and I hoped nobody else noticed. When still no answer came, I raised my voice. "Where is Alicia?"

"Who do you think you are?" Brandon said to me, and the growl in his voice very much matched the anger that suddenly clouded his face.

"I'm sorry?" I asked, surprised by his tone.

"Brandon," Gisele said, and it sounded like a warning.

"We don't work for you. You are not our landlord." Brandon took a step closer to me, but stopped several yards away. "We don't answer to you. We have a boss. And just because she's banging you, that doesn't mean you suddenly get to demand information from us.

You think you're special? You don't know anything about her." He turned away. Then, as if having an additional thought, turned back. His eyes narrowed at me, the most eye contact I'd ever gotten from him. "Maybe she doesn't want to talk to you. Maybe she's over you and is just waiting for you to take the hint. Ever think of that?"

"*Brandon.*" Gisele stood from her desk, her expression very serious.

"What?" he snapped, his anger obvious in everything from his facial expression to his tone of voice to his body language. He dropped into the chair at his desk and turned the music up again.

I stood there, blinking rapidly, in shock. I couldn't move. My face burned with that toxic combination of fury and shame. My clammy hands trembled. I couldn't move. I wanted to—God, *so* desperately. But I couldn't.

Gisele was suddenly by my side. "Come with me," she ordered, her voice soft but her grip on my arm firm as she steered me to the door.

I let her lead me, still stunned by Brandon's vitriol, by the things he'd said.

At the door to my office, we stopped and Gisele peeked her head in. "Hey, Mary? I'm taking Lacey for an off-site meeting. You got Leo?"

"We're good," Mary said. She stood up from her desk so we could see her over the boxes, Leo in her arms. He had cheese on his chin, I noted absently.

I continued to let Gisele lead me. Neither of us spoke until we were on bar stools at Boomer's and the bartender waited for our drink order. The last time I was there, I was with Alicia, so the irony was not lost on me.

"We'll each have a glass of Pinot Grigio, please," Gisele told him, and then went silent again until our glasses were set in front of us. She slid mine closer to me and held hers up, waiting for me to touch my glass to it.

I blew out a breath and clinked, then took much too large a gulp, wincing as it went down.

I could feel Gisele's eyes on me. "You all right?" she asked, her hand on my arm.

"I can't believe that just happened," I said, in total honesty. "Oh, my God, I was such an asshole." I took another gulp of wine.

"Well…but, Brandon can…lack finesse," Gisele said, her tone telling me that I wasn't wrong about my own behavior.

"Doesn't matter. I was totally out of line. He was right. No wonder he hates me. He's hated me since day one."

"That's true."

I snapped my head around to face her.

She laughed. "What? You said it. I'm just confirming it."

"Why, though? Why? I mean, I'm not Google, but I'm a nice person!"

Gisele sipped her wine, much more sophisticated about it than me. "Look, I'm not disagreeing with you. But he has his reasons, silly and high school as they are."

When she didn't elaborate, I widened my eyes and held my hands out, palms up. "Care to share?"

Gisele debated.

I watched it happen.

She really was beautiful, her complexion smooth and dusky, her hair swooping to the left, the rust-orange-colored top she wore making her seem approachable and friendly. Finally, she made eye contact with me, hers deep, rich brown and soft. "He's very protective of Alicia. Always has been. They've known each other since they were teenagers. Brandon and Alicia's brother Ryan grew up together."

"Alicia has a brother?" She'd never mentioned one, even after I went on and on about mine.

Gisele inhaled, let it out slowly. "Yeah, I figured she hadn't mentioned that. Alicia *had* a brother. He died."

"Oh, God." I covered my mouth with a hand. "No, she never said."

"She wouldn't. She just…doesn't." Another sip of wine. I started to think it was serving as liquid courage for Gisele. "So, Brandon is protective of Alicia."

"But why does he feel the need to protect her from me? I mean, from the minute I met him, he hasn't liked me. And he's made it pretty obvious."

"Brandon doesn't like anybody at first. It's just how he is. But once it became clear that Alicia *did* like you, he went into protection mode."

I furrowed my brow. "I'm not following."

"Once Alicia likes you, you have the potential to hurt her. At least that's how Brandon looks at it. Brandon knows her well, and I'm sure he saw it right away. I know I did."

"Saw what?" I was so confused. I felt completely out of the loop, like I was standing outside a house and looking in the window while all the people inside carried on conversations I couldn't hear.

"Saw that she was attracted to you," Gisele said, a hint of frustration in her voice.

"Oh. Oooohhhhh." I finally got it, finally followed. I needed a beat, sipped my wine and we were quiet for a moment. Finally, I said, "Well, I don't think it matters at this point. She's sort of...gone." My eyes welled up, much to my own mortification, and I tried to hide it behind my glass.

Gisele closed a hand over mine, then motioned to the bartender for refills. "You don't know everything," she said gently.

"Yeah, as Brandon made clear to me."

Gisele wet her lips and she looked suddenly nervous. No, not nervous. That was too strong a description. Uncertain was better. She looked uncertain, and I got the impression she was weighing pros and cons of telling me...something.

Our refills came, and she took what seemed like a fortifying mouthful of hers. Then she turned on her stool so she fully faced me, her knees bumping my thigh. "May is a hard month for Alicia."

I waited, sensing big stuff coming.

I wasn't wrong.

Gisele blew out a big breath and I knew somehow in that moment, she was trusting me with sensitive information. "When Alicia was thirty-five—so about three years ago—her father passed away from cancer. Pancreatic. He went very quickly. Almost too quickly, before the family had much chance to prepare."

I swallowed hard. "That's awful."

Gisele nodded and went on. "Ryan was five years younger than her and had always had trouble. He was just one of those guys who couldn't seem to find the right path, you know? He barely graduated from high school. He never went to college, didn't really learn a trade. He tried lots of different jobs, but nothing stuck. And then he found drugs. He was a mess for a long time. I can't even tell you how many times Alicia had to go looking for him in terrible parts of Philly, bail him out of jail, how often she tried to help him. Their parents were heartbroken, watching their son struggle so much and not be able to pull himself out of the muck. But on his thirtieth birthday, Ryan somehow made the decision to put his whole being into recovery. Nobody knows what happened to change his mind, but he was determined."

I sat riveted, on the edge of my stool, picturing all of this in my head.

"He was doing great. Alicia and her parents were right there by his side, which…I give them a lot of credit for, because he'd been trouble for years. He caused their parents so much worry and stress, said horrible things, stole from them. But he made massive changes and they supported him, especially their dad. He went to meetings with Ryan, helped him find a job. They became closer than ever."

I saw where this was going and my heart broke a little bit in my chest for this man I never met, this man with the same genes as Alicia. "And then their dad got sick?"

Gisele nodded sadly. "And then their dad got sick." She paused like she needed a moment to collect herself. A sip of wine, and she continued. "Like I said, he went really fast. I think he'd put off going to the doctor because he was so focused on helping Ryan get better. But it was barely six months from diagnosis to his death, and Ryan…" She grimaced, drank more wine. "He didn't handle it well."

"I don't imagine he did."

"He went into a major downward spiral," Gisele said, not surprising me at all. "Fell off the wagon in a huge way." She paused, blew out a big breath. "He overdosed on heroin. Alicia found him."

"Oh, God. Oh, no." My eyes filled with tears of sorrow, tears of sympathy. Despite the number of times I'd wanted to kill my brother, I couldn't imagine finding Scott's dead body, how horrific that would be. How scarring. How traumatic. How life altering. "Poor Alicia." A tear slipped down my cheek. I didn't bother wiping it away.

"Almost exactly a year after that, Alicia's mother had a massive heart attack at work and died."

This time, no words came out of my mouth. I just sat there, mouth open in disbelief, throat clogged with sorrow. I shook my head very slowly.

Gisele nodded. "I know," she said, and we sat quietly for long moments.

"So," I finally said when I felt like I could talk without bursting into tears. "Alicia lost her entire family, all within a year of each other."

"All in May," Gisele confirmed with a nod. "Her dad, then Ryan a couple weeks later, then her mother the following year."

"God, no wonder she hates this month."

"Right?"

We sat quietly again before I finally asked, "Where is she?"

Gisele shrugged. "She tends to go off the grid for a few weeks during early May. She'll be back."

I turned to look at Gisele, held her gaze for a long beat before summoning the nerve to ask my question. "Do you know her address?"

We continued looking at one another, and I could see the internal debate going on inside her. Finally, she gave one nod, pulled out her phone, and asked for my number. Then my phone beeped. "I texted it to you."

I pulled out my own phone and glanced at it. When I returned my gaze to Gisele, she was still looking at me. "Why?" I asked, startling myself with the question. "Why give it to me?"

Gisele turned to her wine, turned the glass in her fingers for a moment before speaking. "Because, despite what Brandon said up there, you *are* special. Alicia cares about you, I can tell. And you obviously care about her. So…" She shrugged as if running out of words.

"Thank you." My voice was barely above a whisper.

"You're welcome. Just…tread lightly, okay? It's only been two years since her mom died, and she's still…raw."

"I promise."

We sat there, the two of us, side by side. Gisele had turned back around and now we each had our forearms on the bar, sitting like twins, lost in our own thoughts. My heart was crushed for Alicia. I couldn't believe one person had to endure so much loss. No wonder she barely talked about her own life, instead keeping me occupied by asking endless questions about mine. It was a good strategy.

At the same time, we each slid off our stools, knowing we needed to get back to our offices, at least for a little bit before the end of the day. It was Thursday afternoon and the crowd in the bar was growing, anticipation of Boomer's famous Thursday happy hour wafting through the air. I paid the tab, waving Gisele off.

"You did me a big favor today," I told her. "And I'm grateful." I signed the receipt and turned to her. "I'm going to go over there tonight. I'll see if Mary can take Leo home with her."

"I'd offer to take that little love muffin, but…" Gisele nodded her thanks at the big man holding the door for us. "I have a date," she whispered.

"Wouldn't be with a tall, handsome man who has the same last name as me, would it?" It felt good to lighten the mood even just for a minute.

"It would."

I grinned at her. "I have so many things I want to say, but I'm not going to say anything except, enjoy yourself." We hit the stairs to our office building. "And report back to me!"

Gisele laughed, her eyes dancing, and a thought hit me: she was excited. She was looking forward to a date with my brother. I was really happy. For both of them. I made a mental note to check in at some point soon and see how it had gone.

For now, though, I had other things on my mind…

CHAPTER SIXTEEN

Alicia's town house complex was nice, newly built and modern. I remembered when it was still in the construction stages not more than a year or so ago. The buildings were all sided in either a pleasant slate blue or a beachy sandy beige, bright white trim on all the windows and balconies. Alicia was in number seventeen, and once I located it and parked, I saw it was an end unit.

And then I sat in my car and stared at her white front door.

I was parked right next to Alicia's Beemer, so I was reasonably sure she was home. A pepperoni pizza sat on the seat next to me, because I assumed she probably wasn't eating, given all the emotional turmoil I expected she was experiencing. Or wasn't eating much. Of course, this was all utter conjecture on my part. For all I knew, she could've been having a party in there.

"Only one way to find out," I muttered into my empty car. I got out, went around and grabbed the pizza, then walked up the walk, slowly.

At the door, I stood for a beat. Two. I focused on my breathing, did my best to calm my racing heart. Alicia might not even let me in. Despite Gisele's assurance that Alicia did find me "special," she could be mistaken. Right? She could be totally off base, and I could've been right in my assumption that Alicia was done with me.

"Only one way to find out," I muttered again, and pushed the doorbell.

There was a peephole, so Alicia would open the door knowing it was me. I schooled my expression to be open and friendly, not too cheery and not too morose. It wasn't easy.

I was debating ringing the bell again when the door opened slowly and Alicia stood there looking tired and weary and very, very sad.

"Hi," I said softly.

"Hey," she replied and leaned her head against the edge of the door.

"I thought maybe you could use some dinner." I held up the pizza box and gave her sort of a half shrug.

She stood aside and held out an arm, waving me in.

I tried to hide my surprise and entered her house wordlessly.

The foyer was narrow, and a small table stood sentry against the wall where a black-framed mirror hung above it. Alicia's keys were there on its surface, but there were no knickknacks. Aside from the mirror, the walls were bare. A doorway to my right led into the kitchen, and I followed Alicia in so I could set the pizza down. The room was small but functional, all modern appliances in stainless steel, the cabinets a deep, beautiful mahogany, the countertops dark and speckled. I wasn't sure if they were granite or soapstone or what. All I knew was that they were not laminate and they were not cheap.

Alicia pulled plates from an upper cabinet, saying nothing as she found a spatula and dished out a slice of pizza to each plate. I watched her, watched her eyes, her hands. Next, she retrieved a wineglass and filled it from the open bottle of Merlot on the counter. She handed it to me, took one of the plates, and walked through the second door in the kitchen that, I assumed, led to the living room. I picked up my plate and followed her.

The town house gave off a weird vibe, and it was immediately obvious to me why. I mean, it was gorgeous. Super modern, lots of bells and whistles. The hardwood floors were beautiful and rich. The gas fireplace in the corner was inviting, even in spring. The enormous French doors that opened onto what seemed to be a significant backyard area were elegant. But the place felt...stark. Unlived in. I noticed a stack of boxes in a corner. There were built-in shelves on one wall, and aside from a good-sized flat screen TV, they were bare. There were no photographs, no collectibles, nothing that would tell me a single thing about the woman who lived here. The couch was gray with a couple of red throw pillows and a red afghan in a heap, making it obvious that somebody had taken up residence there recently. The TV was off and

I wondered, sadly, if Alicia had simply been lying there, staring into space.

She sat on the couch and set her plate on the coffee table next to a wineglass that was half empty. I took a seat next to her and we ate in silence, which was both weird and totally not. I sipped my wine, which was velvety on my tongue, and finished my pizza, then watched as Alicia ate the last bite of hers. I was grateful for that, at least…that she'd eaten. Her face was drawn and it seemed she'd lost weight since the last time I'd seen her, which didn't seem possible but *looked* like it was fact.

I pushed my plate away, picked up my wineglass, and adjusted my position on the couch so I had one leg crossed beneath me and faced Alicia rather than the TV.

"Are you okay?" I finally asked gently. They were the first words spoken by either of us since I'd entered Alicia's space.

She lifted one shoulder, then sipped her wine.

"Gisele told me what happened. I'm so sorry, Alicia." I reached to touch her arm, but she flinched away from me, which felt a bit like a stab to my heart. I tried a different tack. "Why didn't you tell me? I've been worried about you." I made sure to keep any accusation out of my voice, to be as supportive and nonjudgmental as I could. I studied her, took in her gray sweats and oversized burgundy sweatshirt that looked like it might have been older than me. The cuffs were frayed, as was the neckline, and it hung off one shoulder in a way that I would've found devastatingly sexy in any other circumstances. She wore no makeup, and she was beautiful despite the obvious pain in her eyes.

Alicia was silent for so long, I became fairly certain she wasn't going to answer. But then she did. "It's not really something I talk about. To anyone." Her voice was hoarse, and it occurred to me that she might not have spoken to anybody in days. She sipped her wine, not looking at me.

"Maybe it would help. To talk about it."

She shrugged.

"Well, I'm right here if you want to." I sank farther into the cushions as I watched her face.

She gave one nod and went back to her wine.

"More pizza?" I asked after a while. I didn't wait for an answer, just took her plate and mine and went back into the kitchen. Once there, I braced my hands on the edge of the counter and let my head drop between my shoulders as I blew out a breath. I had no idea how to proceed here. I was totally winging it, and as somebody who plans out her life, winging it was so far from comfortable for me, it was laughable. But all I wanted was to be there for Alicia. If she wanted to talk, I was here. If she wanted silence, I could do that. I reminded myself that the most important thing was to simply *be there*. I swallowed down my emotion and dished out more pizza.

Back in the living room, I reclaimed my seat and set the plates on the coffee table. I'd brought the wine as well and set the bottle down. Long moments of silence went by, and I let my eyes roam the room, again surprised by how barren it looked.

"How long have you lived here?" I asked, before I could analyze whether I should.

"Fifteen months, I think." Alicia was looking out the French doors.

"Oh," I said, trying to hide my surprise and doing a terrible job of it. I swallowed, a sudden lightbulb going off in my brain. "This is where your whole live-in-the-moment attitude comes from, isn't it?"

She turned to me and, again, I felt her anger, her frustration with the situation, with me, with life in general. "Nothing is permanent, Lacey. Nothing. Planning for the future is stupid and naïve. Anything can be taken at any time."

"Of course it can," I said, keeping my voice level. "That's what life is. For everybody." I waited for her to unload on me, but she just got sadder, which I didn't think was possible.

"It's worse for some of us than for others."

I nodded quickly. "It is. That's true. That's also life."

Alicia took a beat, glanced at me and then away. "Life can be horrible."

"It can."

"And so unfair."

"Yes."

"It can break your heart. Into a million little pieces so you're sure you won't ever be able to recover." Her eyes filled with tears, which made mine follow suit.

"I know," I whispered. "I'm so sorry."

She looked at me again, and there was so much in her face then. In her eyes. Sorrow, need, pain, confusion. "Would you just hold me?" she asked, and her voice was so small that I almost didn't hear her at all.

"Oh, my God, of course I will. Of *course* I will. Come here." I opened my arms and she moved closer. I leaned back a bit so we could both stretch our legs out. She was on the inside of the couch, tucked snugly between my body and the back. She positioned her head just under my chin, tossed a leg over mine, and draped an arm across my midsection. I wrapped my arms around her, held her as close as I could, pressed my lips to her forehead. We lay that way for a long time—or at least it felt like a long time. Maybe it wasn't. I squeezed her shoulder with my hand and that's when I felt the very subtle trembling. I held her tighter and the trembling got stronger. I pressed my mouth, my nose into her hair and shifted us a bit so I had a better grip and she let out a little whimper.

"It's okay, Alicia. I'm right here." I dug my fingers into her hair. "I'm right here. Let it out. It's okay. Just let it go."

And then her breath hitched, and she didn't try to hide it any more. The first sob came out of her like it was ripped from her lungs against her will, like she'd been trying to hold it in and simply couldn't any longer. She closed her fingers around my shirt, squeezing a handful in her fist, and turned her face into my chest. My eyes filled, and I felt my own tears well up and spill over, but I did my best to stay quiet. This was her moment, her anguish, and I didn't want to steal any of it from her. It tore me to shreds to see her in such pain. To *feel* her in such pain.

She cried against my neck, and I held her to me and allowed her to do so.

For as long as she needed to.

Forever, if she needed to.

"I've got you," I told her with all the tenderness I had in my heart. "It's okay. I've got you."

I said things like that for what felt like the remainder of the evening. Alicia cried like she'd been holding it all in for years. Maybe she had. There was nothing I could do but hold her and tell her it was all right, that I was here, that I would hold her as long as she wanted me to, that I had her.

"I love you," I heard myself whisper at one point. If she heard me, she had no reaction, and I decided that was probably for the best. It wasn't really the right time to be spilling my own stuff to her, so I didn't say it again. But holding her while she cried, wanting to do nothing more than be there for her, be whatever she needed at whatever time, that's exactly what I felt. I loved this woman. I loved her.

I had no idea what time we drifted off. Or what time I drifted off. I knew when Alicia did, as I felt her body slacken, her breathing even out. I lay there in the dark living room, uneaten pizza on the coffee table and a woman with a broken heart in my arms, and there was no place else I would rather have been.

It seems kind of weird and crazy to say it was perfect, but in that very moment, somehow it was.

❖

While I wasn't at all uncomfortable the next morning, it was very apparent that Alicia was. I think she tried to climb off me without waking me up, but when that proved impossible and I opened my eyes and greeted her, she couldn't look at me.

"Hey," she said, her eyes puffy from a night of sobbing. "I, um, have an appointment this morning, so I need to get in the shower."

I nodded, surprised she was going in at all after yesterday. "Okay. I can get out of your way." She gave one nod back to me, then headed up the stairs.

I took the plates into the kitchen, found the wine's cork and plugged it, did my best to clean up without going through her cabinets to find things like plastic wrap. I put the plates and the wineglasses in the dishwasher, then heard the shower turn on above me.

For long moments, I stood in the kitchen, leaning back against the counter, trying to decide if I had a good reason to hang. There really wasn't one at this point. Alicia was embarrassed. It was obvious. Coming to the conclusion that I didn't want to exacerbate that feeling for her, I decided I'd just go, give her some space and some time, and then maybe pop in to her office later to see how she was doing.

That seemed like a good plan.

I went back into the living room, folded the afghan, fluffed the pillows, and took a last look around. It really was a very beautiful room with tons of potential…potential that Alicia didn't tap into even a little bit. It looked like she'd moved in last week.

Nothing's permanent, Lacey. Nothing.

Her words echoed in my head.

Anything can be taken at any time.

I was suddenly hit with a wave of sadness so heavy it doubled me over. I stood with my hands on my knees like I'd just sprinted the hundred-yard dash. The depth of Alicia's sadness had also colored her outlook on life—which I wasn't really surprised by, but still. I shook my head in sorrow for this woman I cared way too much about, as I gathered my things and closed her front door behind me.

I took my time at home, brewed myself some coffee, stood in the kitchen taking small sips as I replayed the previous night in my head. I'd never seen anybody in that much pain before, and it had obviously affected me. I was sure it was all amplified by my feelings for Alicia, but wow. Her pain and sorrow were practically tangible. It almost felt like I could've reached into the air above where we lay on the couch and grabbed it in my hand, turned it and examined it from different angles. It was that big, that strong, that solid.

It wasn't lost on me that we had mirror families, that despite Scott being older than me and Ryan being younger than Alicia, we had similar home lives. Two siblings, two parents who loved us. I still had all of mine and Alicia had none of hers. It was heartbreakingly unfair, and for a quick moment, I felt guilty.

I showered and dressed and gathered my things. It occurred to me on my way out the door that having my entire morning focused on Alicia made me almost forget that Leo wasn't there. Almost. I threw a scoop of his food into a Ziploc baggie and stuck that in my bag, though I was pretty sure Mary was filling him full of anything and everything. He probably had a donut for breakfast.

Alicia's car was nowhere to be seen, but then I remembered she hadn't said she had to go to work in those exact words. She'd said she had a meeting, which could very easily have been off-site. I chose to go with that and headed upstairs.

The boxes were gone. Mary was at her desk, typing away on her keyboard, Leo sitting at her feet. When he came running to me, my spirits lifted. Seriously, is there anything better than a dog who's ecstatic to see you? I scooped him up, and Leo wiggled happily in my arms.

"Were you good for Aunt Mary? Hmm?"

"Of course he was," Mary said. "He was a perfect little angel, as always."

"He ate his dinner with no problem?" It wasn't uncommon for Mary to take Leo home on occasion or dog-sit him for me, so I'd given her a bag of his kibble to keep at her house.

"No problem at all. He loves my beef stew."

I shook my head in mock disapproval, but my grin gave me away. I loved that Mary loved my dog as much as I did. And her beef stew was the best I'd ever had in my life, so I couldn't really blame Leo.

"Thanks so much for taking him."

"Any time at all. He's good company." Mary's gaze grew serious. "Everything okay?"

I nodded. I wasn't about to share Alicia's personal tragedy with anyone, nor did I want to dredge up the unpleasantness with Brandon that had happened yesterday. Instead, I smiled at Mary. "Totally okay." Leo and I headed into my office.

Try as I might, I could not manage to keep myself from glancing out the window at the parking lot below every five minutes to see if a baby blue BMW convertible had magically appeared. *She's fine*, I told myself. *It's a rough time for her. Just relax.* But I had an alarmingly hard time heeding the advice from my own brain. Which is always a bit worrisome.

Lunchtime came and went, but I wasn't hungry. I forced myself to eat a granola bar I found in my desk drawer, but thinking about anything more made me slightly nauseous. As I sat there staring at my computer screen, but not actually seeing anything on it, I was suddenly hit with the realization that Scott and Gisele had gone out the night before. I stood up, deciding to go find out how it went.

I left Leo with Mary and headed down the hall. It wasn't until I got to the cheery red door of Just Wright that I stopped and remembered that Brandon was probably there. I decided I'd just take the high road. I gave a quick rap on the door frame, then headed into the office and took quick steps in the direction of Gisele's desk, seeing Brandon out of the corner of my eye.

"Hey, Brandon," I said as I passed him. He didn't respond, but I was okay with that. It wasn't really an olive branch—more like a twig—but I'd keep at it.

Gisele sat looking what I could only describe as "dreamily" out the window to her right, chin propped in a hand. Her top today was sunshine yellow, and I was once again envious of how amazing she looked in bright colors. She looked up just as I approached.

"Hey," she said, and her tone told me she was happy to see me. Or maybe just happy in general. "How are you?"

"I'm fine," I said, taking a seat in the orange plastic chair at the end of her desk. "But the important question is, how are *you*? How did it go last night?" I raised my eyebrows expectantly.

Her smile grew, crinkling the skin at the corners of her eyes. "It went great. I had a terrific time. He's so nice."

I squinted at her. "He is? Are we talking about the same guy? Scott Chamberlain? The one who used to give me noogies and tried to convince me our parents found me in a ditch and only took me home because they felt sorry for me? *That* guy? *That* guy's nice?"

"Well, I can't speak for the noogies or your apparent adoption, but he was wonderful to me. I had so much fun. We're going out again tonight."

"Another date? Already?"

"It is Friday, Lacey."

"Good point. Wow. That's great." She was floating, and it was a sight that made me happy for her. I made a mental note to give Scott a serious talking-to because I really liked Gisele, and despite the discussion he and I'd already had, I wanted to reiterate a few things.

"Tell me more about him," Gisele asked, again propping her chin in her hand and settling in like a child waiting for story time.

I chuckled at the image. "Like what?"

"Tell me something most people wouldn't know."

I pursed my lips and stared off into space as I thought. "Okay. He's terrified of mice. Like, freaks out when he sees one, complete with girly squeals of terror."

Gisele laughed. "Mice? I mean, I don't enjoy mice, but—"

"*Terrified.*"

"Noted. What else?"

"He's a pretty excellent cook."

"No."

"Oh, yes. Ask him to make you his chicken parmesan some time. He's famous for it."

"Seriously?"

"I kid you not. Whenever I do him a favor, that's what I want as payment: a big pan of his chicken parm."

"I am so filing that away."

This was kind of fun, I realized.

Once our quiet laughter died down, Gisele's expression grew serious. She lowered her voice and asked, "Did you go last night?"

I nodded and picked up a stray paper clip from her desk. "I did."

"And?"

I gazed out the window as I toyed with the clip. "It was...tough." A quick glance at Brandon told me he didn't seem to be paying any attention to us, thankfully, so I went on. "She was...in a pretty bad place." I didn't go into detail. I didn't want to betray any perceived confidence there might have been around the time I spent there, and I also assumed Gisele had a pretty good handle on what I'd been walking into without me giving her a play-by-play, having known Alicia for much longer than I had. But I gave her an expression that I hoped projected what it had been like. "I actually stayed overnight."

"You did?" Gisele's eyes widened. "Really?"

"Well." I shook my head and lifted one shoulder. "Not in any capacity other than friend." My brain tossed me a flashback of Alicia, broken and sobbing in my arms. "I just...held her. We fell asleep on her couch."

Gisele was quiet for a long moment before she finally spoke. "That's kind of big," she said, covering my hand with hers so I'd make eye contact. When I did, she nodded. "She doesn't often let anybody get that close."

"Oh," I said. "I was just trying to help her."

"Sounds like you did."

"I don't know. She was...different this morning. Back to her walled-off self."

Gisele sat back with a nod. "Yeah, that's not surprising. That girl's a tough one to crack. But it sounds like you made some progress."

"Maybe." I set the now-straight paper clip back on the desk, feeling a small spark of hope at Gisele's words. I stood. "Okay, gotta get back to work. I hope you have a blast tonight."

"I've got a good feeling."

I pointed at her. "Remember. Chicken parm."

"Got it."

As I crossed the office, I was stopped in my tracks when Alicia came through the door. For a moment, we each stood still, seeing each other, but also glancing away, as if too much eye contact was forbidden or something.

"Hey," I said quietly, painfully aware that Brandon was only a few yards behind me.

"Hi," Alicia said. She set down the bag she was carrying, as well as her purse. Just put them right on the floor inside the doorway. "Can I talk to you for a minute?" Her voice was quiet and her eyes darted around.

"Sure," I said, waiting as an odd sense of dread seeped into my blood like ice water.

"Out here?" She backed into the hall as she waved for me to follow.

"Sure," I said again, and trailed her out into the hallway and a couple feet down the wall, keeping my eyes on her elegant charcoal gray suit and matching heels rather than looking at her face. Something told me I wouldn't like what was in her eyes, so the four-year-old in me decided if I simply didn't look, whatever bad thing it was didn't exist.

Silly.

"Listen," Alicia said, her voice barely above a whisper as she scraped at the molding on the wall with a fingernail. "I'm really grateful for what you did last night, but…"

Her sentence dangled while I entertained responses. *What did I do last night? But what? Why are we in the hallway and whispering? Why won't you look at me?* I settled on, "You're welcome. I was glad I was there."

"I like you, Lacey." That was a surprise, even though she kept her eyes on the wall.

"Good. I like you, too."

"No, you don't understand." She swallowed audibly, and I waited for what felt like much longer than it actually was until I couldn't stand her silence any longer.

"What don't I understand, Alicia?"

"I don't...I can't have a relationship with you."

I squinted at her. "Because..." My turn to let my sentence trail off, forcing her to elaborate.

"Because I can't." Her voice was firmer this time and she actually looked at me. I was right: I didn't like what was in her eyes. They weren't the inviting, sparkling blue I was used to. They were hard. Cold. Icy. "Because I don't. I don't do that, and I don't want to do that."

"Alicia," I said, trying to keep the panic from my voice. I swallowed hard as my stomach churned sourly. "We don't...we don't have to have a 'relationship.'" I made air quotes around the word. "I mean, we're dating. You know? We've never talked about the future. Let's just continue on this path."

"Where do you think this path leads?" She leaned a shoulder against the wall but didn't look at me.

I swallowed, having trouble with her cold and challenging tone. "I don't...I haven't really thought about it." It was a lie, and we both knew it.

"Yes, you have." Her voice was soft, almost gentle, and that made it so much worse. "You have thought about it. It leads to a relationship. And I can't have one. I don't want one."

My own anger began to bubble in my gut. I didn't like the feeling, but I was powerless to stop it. "Which is it? You can't have one or you don't want one? 'Cause those are two different things."

"Both," she said with a sigh. She seemed exhausted. So exhausted, like this whole topic was literally draining the energy from her body. "Look. We had fun. We had a good time. But that's all it was. A good time. And now it's over. Just let it go." She pushed herself off the wall as if that were the end of the conversation and walked past me toward the door to her office.

I followed her until we were standing in the doorway. "I'm sorry, just let it go?" I couldn't believe it. I couldn't believe that she'd said it. I couldn't believe she thought I could just do it.

Alicia stopped in front of the open door to Just Wright, her back to me, and hung her head.

"How can you say that to me?" I asked quietly, my eyes wide

with pain and sadness and, I'm sure, some of the panic that had now blossomed fully in my gut.

Slowly, Alicia turned to face me, took one step in my direction, and I was surprised to see her eyes filled with tears. "Please, Lacey." Her voice cracked then, and I wanted to wrap her up in a hug. "Can't you understand? Can't you *try* to understand? I can't do this. I'm sorry. I just can't. It's too hard. Please. I need you to leave me alone. I need you…to let it go. For me. *Please.*"

I blinked at her, and my eyes immediately welled up as I tried to swallow the painful lump that had settled in my throat. I knew what she was doing. I knew why she was doing it.

Nothing is permanent, Lacey…Anything can be taken at any time…

I just didn't know how to *stop* her from doing it.

In my peripheral vision, I could see Brandon, and I wondered if he was smiling in satisfaction. One tear spilled over and rolled down my cheek as Alicia backed up that one step, moving away from me. She cleared her throat, took another step back, went into her office, and shut the door with a quiet click while I stood there in the hallway feeling dazed, staring down at my feet.

It was all so simple, really. Alicia was scared. If she and I were in a relationship, she'd have to admit she cared about me. And losing something you cared about was painful. She'd suffered more than her share of that loss and was understandably terrified of it happening again.

If she didn't love anybody, then she couldn't lose anybody she loved.

Simple.

Practical.

Heartbreaking for both of us, and I had no idea what I should do next.

I glanced up and saw Mary standing in my doorway, her face conveying sympathy and worry. I made my feet move toward her.

"I…I need some air," I whispered to her as I passed, catching her nod out of the corner of my eye.

My legs felt heavy as I descended the stairs. My footsteps were slow, and they echoed in the emptiness. I was grateful nobody else was there; I had the flight to myself for the moment, so I took my time going down. When I got to the bottom, I stood there. I have no idea for how long. I just stood there, my vision blurred by the onslaught of tears that had—thank God—waited until I was no longer in view of anybody else before they pooled and spilled and rolled. The walls were gray. The railing was gray. The concrete floor was gray. The perfect color for the way I felt.

I need you to leave me alone.

Alicia's voice echoed through my head, and I actually flinched and looked around to see if she had followed me.

I need you to let it go. For me. Please.

I swallowed hard because if I didn't, the sob growing in my chest would be able to make its escape and I refused—*refused*—to let this rip into me while I was at work. Alicia had been frightened. That much was obvious. And despite my understanding of why she did what she did, I was still heartbroken. We had something. Something special. But I felt helpless because I was pretty certain we could bridge this—I wanted to say gap, but it now felt like an abyss—if we just tried, and I didn't think Alicia was willing to try. She'd made that pretty clear. Her fear overshadowed every other emotion she had. I *did* get it. I did. But I was at a loss as to my next move, and I felt desperate. Panicked. Hopeless. Devastated and untethered.

I knew I needed to respect her wishes. Knew she wanted me to let it go.

But how could I? How?

That awful feeling of falling hard for someone only to realize she didn't feel the same clawed at me like a trapped animal. My inner need for control had spun off its axis in a big way, because this was completely *out* of my control. I needed to think, to breathe. I needed to escape. To escape myself, escape this overwhelming…*awful*.

I pushed through the stairwell door and out into the bright sunshine, slightly blinded after going from the dimness of the stairwell to the brilliantly sunny afternoon. For a moment, I wished it had been raining and windy and cold, which would've made for a much more appropriate setting for me.

"Stupid sun," I muttered, as I stepped off the curb onto the asphalt, my brain a jumble of emotion.

I'm not sure if things would have been any different had I seen Nascar Kyle coming. I'm pretty certain I still wouldn't have been able to get out of the way. As it was, he hit me before I had any clue what was happening. That was probably a good thing.

Chapter Seventeen

B eep. Beep. Beep.

"...*three bruised ribs and a tib-fib fracture of her right leg, but we're most concerned about the concussion and brain swelling...*"

Beep. Beep. Beep.

"...*why don't you go home, Mom. I'll sit with her. You and Dad get some rest. I'll call you if anything happens, okay? Don't worry.*"
"*You all right?*"
"*Not exactly the way I wanted you to meet my parents...*"

Beep. Beep. Beep.

"...*how is she this morning? Oh, her color's a little better.*"
"*I thought so, too.*"
"*Mr. Chamberlain, want some coffee? I'm getting myself a cup.*"
"*That'd be great. Thanks.*"
"*She's nice, Scott. I like her. Your dad won't say so, but he does, too. She seems very...*"

Beep. Beep. Beep.

"...*that it's possible you can hear us when we talk to you, even though you're unconscious. Apparently, this is your body's way of protecting itself while your head heals. So, I decided I'm just going to talk to you whenever I can. The guys are holding down the fort at my office. Let's see. Mary's taking care of Leo, so don't worry about him. She's also taking care of your office and she brings him in, so he's been visiting with Gisele when she's not here with Scott. Speaking of those two, wow, huh? I never saw that coming. Did you? I mean, they don't seem like...*"

Beep. Beep. Beep.

"*...still here. She was here when Leanne left yesterday and the nurse said she's been here all night. Do you know her? Gisele seems to.*"
"*I told you, Mom. She's the one Lacey talked about at dinner.*"
"*The one she kissed?*"
"*That exact one, yes. She's Gisele's boss. They've known each other...*"

Beep. Beep. Beep.

"*...feels like it's been a long time, Doc. When's my baby girl going to wake up, goddamnit?*"
"*John, honey. Let the doctor talk.*"
"*I understand your concern, Mr. Chamberlain. The swelling in her brain has gone down considerably, which means the medication is doing its job. There's no need to...*"

Beep. Beep. Beep.

"*...it was a really nice day, but it's raining now. Kind of softly, if that makes sense. I like this kind of rain, especially at night. Soft, gentle, gives the air that scent that really tells you it's spring. And I love the sound of it, not really drops hitting the ground, but more of a whoosh, you know? If all of May was like this, I'd probably have an easier time of it. If it was a little gray and misty instead of sunny and cheerful and full of flowers.*
"*I miss my family, Lacey. I miss them every day, every moment of my life. It all feels so unfair that I'm still here. I mean, Ryan...I guess if I'm going to be honest, his death wasn't really a surprise. His sobriety*"

was actually the surprise. So, as horrible as it was to find him that day...as much as I'll never be able to scrub that sight from my brain... it wasn't shocking. Does that make sense? I mean, he was a drug addict longer than he wasn't. Though, let me tell you what a fun kid he was. We had a great time, me and Ryan. He was a jokester. He loved pranks. I can't tell you how many rubber spiders or snakes or lizards I found in my bed over the years. I screamed every single time and he fell over laughing every single time. It never got old, that joke. I remember this one time..."

Beep. Beep. Beep.

"...time, Lace-Face. Okay? You're worrying the 'rents. You're worrying me. I need you to wake up now. The doctor says you're gonna be fine, and I've got nobody to harass, so...and I really need to talk to you about Gisele. I mean...it's so weird. I've never felt like..."

Beep. Beep. Beep.

"...if this is your way of avoiding me giving you shit about your terrible eating habits, then fine. You win. I will never bring you another salad. Just...come on. Wake up. I miss you..."

Beep. Beep. Beep.

"...career woman all the way. She's the reason I had the guts to start my own business. Did I ever tell you that? I mean, as a high school principal, she didn't have a ton of small business experience, but she had drive. Man, she had drive. So when I was working for a big marketing firm and had all these ideas that I could never seem to get anybody to listen to, I'd tell my mom. And finally, one day, she says to me, 'Alicia. Baby. Why do you wait for these men to hear you? Do it yourself.' I just sat there. Literally, just sat there staring at her. I truly couldn't believe I'd never thought of that on my own. Talk about being slow on the uptake, huh? So I decided to take her advice, and that very day I started figuring out how to launch Just Wright. You'd have loved my mom, Lacey. You really would have. And my God, she would have adored you..."

Beep. Beep. Beep.

"...understand you're worried, Mr. and Mrs. Chamberlain. I promise you, your daughter is not in any pain and it's just a matter of time. She'll wake up when she's ready. Head injuries are tricky. I know it sounds clichéd to say that it takes time and all we can do is wait, but—."

"It takes time and all we can do is wait. Yeah, yeah. You suck at reassurance, doc."

"John. Please. He's just doing his job."

"His job is to make my daughter well again, goddamnit. How the hell am..."

Beep. Beep. Beep.

"...because I know that it's stupid. And convoluted. And messed up. But the three most important people in my life were taken from me, and I'm afraid to have that happen to you, too. I thought driving you away, keeping you at a distance was the best way to handle it, and I know that was wrong. So, so wrong, and I'm sorry. Please give me another chance, Lacey. Please...I can't...I don't know what...Okay. Fine. It's fine. You take your time. In the meantime, I'm just going to sit here and hold your hand and talk to you until you come back to me. Okay? You have no say in it. That's what I'm doing. So, if you ever want me to shut the hell up, you're going to have to open your eyes..."

❖

Pain.

Thirst.

Those were the first two things I became aware of. Pain. Everywhere. My head. My stomach. My leg. Burning, searing pain. I didn't open my eyes right away. Instead, I took stock of my body. More specifically, my body parts. From my aching head down, I did an inventory of sorts, feeling what I could feel, wiggling what I thought I could wiggle.

My throat was so dry, like sandpaper lined the inside. Swallowing was excruciating, and I squeezed my eyes shut against the awfulness of it.

"Hey. Are you awake? Lacey?" That was Scott. I was thrilled to recognize a voice. I felt him grab my hand. "Lace-Face, can you hear me? Squeeze my hand if you can."

"Dramatic," I rasped, hardly recognizing my own voice. "Is this an episode of *Grey's Anatomy?*"

His whoop of joy was so loud, I was pretty sure my head had split open. Then I realized that may have already been the case, as I was obviously in a hospital. I tried to clear my throat, but it wasn't working. "Water…" I said, hoping he understood me.

He did. "Okay, let me just check with the nurse and make sure it's okay."

I heard him leave the room. I still hadn't opened my eyes. Part of me was afraid to. I had no idea the extent of my injuries. Yes, I was pretty sure I could feel all my limbs, but wasn't phantom limb pain a thing? Wouldn't I still feel them even if they were gone? I was working on not only wiggling my fingers, but grasping the sheet so I could be sure both my hands were still intact, still functional.

The whoosh of the door was followed immediately by Scott's voice. "See?" he was saying. "She's moving stuff."

"Lacey?" This voice was vaguely familiar, but I wasn't sure why. Probably a nurse. "Lacey, can you hear me?"

"Yes."

"How do you feel?" she asked gently as I felt her fingers checking the pulse on my wrist.

"Like I got hit by a bus."

Scott snorted a laugh. "Not quite. But close."

I heard a humming and then my bed was moving slowly. She was sitting me up a small amount. "Can you open your eyes, honey?" The nurse again.

This was it. Now or never. I slowly opened my eyes, blinked many, many times to clear the blurriness, then squinted against the light, which felt like it was sending shards of glass into my skull. I groaned.

She used a little pen light to check my pupils, and if I'd had the energy to lift my arms, I'd have grabbed her by the throat. "I know.

It's going to be uncomfortable at first. You had quite the knock on your head. Just take your time. If it gets too much, close 'em back up." Mercifully, she finished. "She can have water," she told Scott. "But small sips. We don't want her to get sick. Throwing up with bruised ribs is no fun."

Bruised ribs? I thought. "Bruised ribs?" I asked.

"Three of 'em," Scott confirmed. "At least you didn't break 'em." He pressed the straw to my lips, and I looked up at him as I took a sip. I'd never seen him look so tired. Or so worried. Or so happy.

"I'll get the doctor," the nurse said, and left the room.

The water was like heaven sliding down my throat, and I sucked greedily until Scott pulled the straw away. "Easy, tiger. You don't want to puke. Remember?"

The deep breath I took then gave me a little preview of what that might be like, as it suddenly felt like I had barbed wire wrapped around my torso. I took one more sip and decided to let it be for a bit. That's when I noticed the cast on the lower part of my right leg. Awesome.

"I'm gonna text Mom and Dad. They're in the cafeteria." Scott pulled his phone from his back pocket, and I watched as his fingers danced over the keyboard. It took him much longer than necessary.

"Who else?" I croaked.

"Gisele. Leanne. Mary. Grandma. My boss."

"Long list."

"People have been worried."

"How long have I been here?"

"Three days."

Three days? Holy shit. I hardly remembered a thing. "What happened?"

"What do you remember?"

"Not much."

"Yeah, the doctor said that might happen." Scott pulled a chair close to the side of my bed. "You were leaving your office and you stepped in front of the little bastard with the Charger."

"Nascar Kyle?"

"Him."

"Nascar Kyle ran me over?"

Scott chuckled, then immediately apologized. "It just…sounds funny. But yeah, he kind of did. He said you weren't looking, but we all know he drives like a fucking maniac. The cops are charging him."

Weirdly, I felt bad for Nascar Kyle. He was just a kid. Well, okay, not exactly a kid. But it's not like he hit me on purpose. "Maybe that will make him more careful." Scott was as doubtful about that as I was; I could tell by the grimace he made.

"Anyway, Gisele was in the stairwell on her way to catch up to you when she heard the tires screech. She said she booked it down the stairs and out and you'd already been hit. You were unconscious." He swallowed hard, and I realized that the image he'd just painted made my brother a little bit ill. "She called 9-1-1, and they brought you here."

"How are Mom and Dad?" I could only imagine what they'd been going through. *Three days? Really?*

"Worried sick. Dad's been biting the head off your doctor on the daily." He grinned at me.

I returned it. "I bet. They're not working fast enough, hard enough, good enough."

"Exactly." Scott's smile faltered just a touch, and he reached for me, brushed my hair aside. "I was worried, too, Lace-Face. You scared us. I'm really glad you're okay." His eyes welled up.

It was a golden opportunity I couldn't resist. "Are you *crying?*" I asked. "Like, seriously crying? Bawling over your sister like a little tiny baby?"

He laughed outright and wiped the back of his hand across his eye. "Shut up."

Our gazes held. My relationship with my brother had always been swirly, like liquid through one of those funky straws I had when I was a kid. A little contention, a little affection, a lot of mocking/teasing/making each other miserable. But I felt like we'd grown up over the past month or two. Or maybe I felt like I had. Whatever it was, whoever had done the growing or changing, my brother loved me. I saw it on his face, I sensed it in the room. And I felt safe.

Before I could shake away the sentimentality to mock him some more, my parents burst through the door like a couple of typhoons, all happy gasps and thrilled smiles. My mother leaned over the bed and covered my face with about six dozen kisses, until I finally had to tell her she was smothering me to death. Thank God, the doctor arrived not far behind them and made them move so he could get close.

He introduced himself as Dr. Panjabi. He was a tall, very handsome man, either of Indian descent or maybe Middle Eastern; I wasn't sure. His aftershave was somehow comforting, and his dark brown eyes were soft and kind. He examined my leg, my torso, my head with a very gentle touch. When he finished, he stood up straight, made a couple notes on the tablet he carried, then made direct eye contact with me, which I found reassuring.

"Everything looks great, Ms. Chamberlain. We're going to keep you for another night or two, just to observe you for a little longer. You're going to need to keep those ribs wrapped for a couple of weeks and avoid any twisting or sudden movements. Which will be difficult anyway while you're on crutches." He gave me a wink, and I couldn't help but toss him a half grin. I liked him a lot. He made me feel comfortable. He touched my shoulder, gave it a squeeze. "You just relax and get some rest."

I nodded, which was a mistake, so instead told him I would do my best. Then he was gone and my mother was back at my side, her face too close to mine, her relief almost palpable—and the reason I let her stay so close.

The rest of the afternoon passed in kind of a haze. The pain meds made me woozy and sleepy, and try as I did, I couldn't stay awake once I got a fresh dose. I wanted to. I had visitors in and out on a constant basis. Leanne came in and reiterated everything Dr. Panjabi had told me, then assured me that he was good at his job. I understood that it was her way of feeling useful, of feeling like she was doing something to help, so I kept to myself that I'd drawn my own favorable conclusions about Dr. Panjabi. Leanne talked a good game, but I could see the relief in her eyes, very much like my mother's. Mary stopped by with a gorgeous bouquet of flowers and told me there were six more in the office from various clients with whom she'd had to cancel appointments during my hospital stay.

"I thought about sticking Leo in my purse and smuggling him in but wasn't sure that was such a good idea." She grinned at me.

"Probably not," I agreed.

"But don't worry. He's doing just fine. He's been wandering

through your office, though, wondering where you are, I'm sure. And he's been visiting next door regularly. Alicia's been carrying on complete conversations with him, according to Gisele." Everyone in the room chuckled...Mary, my parents, the nurse.

I didn't, though. At the mention of Alicia's name, I had a couple snippets of memories, a few things that clawed at the far reaches of my brain, but nothing I could grab onto firmly. And then my meds kicked in, and I didn't hear anything else Mary said.

When I opened my eyes again, it was dark, with the exception of a small lamp near one of the visitors' chairs. I had no idea what time it was, but there was a lone figure in the chair near the foot of the bed. I squinted until my vision cleared and saw that it was Gisele and she was scrolling on her phone. After a moment, she glanced up and smiled when she saw my open eyes.

"Hey," she said, very softly. "You're awake. Hi."

"Hi," I croaked, and as if reading my mind, she got up, grabbed my plastic water container, and held the straw to my lips. I drank greedily. "Thanks," I told her when I was done.

"How are you feeling?" she asked. Everybody asked that, and I knew they were being polite. Seriously, what else do you ask somebody who's in the hospital? What's your favorite color?

"A little better." It was true. My leg throbbed and my ribs still ached, but my head was finally beginning to feel less like there was a little construction team at work inside it with various tools. I let my gaze wander around the room. "You the only one here tonight?"

"Your parents just headed home about fifteen minutes ago. Scott's getting us coffee."

"You don't have to stay here, you know."

"I know."

I backpedaled, realizing how I'd sounded. "Not that I don't appreciate it. I do. Just...hanging out in a hospital room is beyond boring."

Gisele smiled.

"So...you and my brother, huh?" Her smile widened and she looked down at the sheet covering me. "Wait, is that blushing I see?"

She covered her eyes with a hand. "Stop," she said, but that big smile remained.

"He's a lucky man," I told her, and I meant it.

"I'm doing my best to take things slowly," she said. "But…"

"Yeah, Scott doesn't do anything slowly."

"I'm realizing that."

As I watched her, I had another flash of memory. Something Scott had said. I felt my brow furrow as I hunted for it.

"What?" Gisele asked. "Are you in pain? Should I get a nurse?"

"No. No, I'm fine." Then it hit me. "I remember almost nothing from the day of my accident, but when Scott was telling me what happened, he said you'd called 9-1-1 because you were the first person there, that you…" I searched for the words. "That you were on your way to catch up with me. Were we going somewhere?"

The way Gisele's smile faltered was so subtle, I'd have missed it if I wasn't looking right at her face. "No," she said, and toyed with the hem of the sheet. She was quiet for so long that I began to think that was all I was getting. Finally, she blew out a breath and said, "I wanted to make sure you were okay."

The door whooshed open then and Scott came in, carrying two white paper cups with the green Starbucks logo of joy on them. "You're awake," he said to me as he handed Gisele one of the cups, then bent to kiss my forehead.

"I am. And I'd kill for a latte right now."

"I can probably see if you can have some coffee, but I bet they don't want you having all the fixings…" He grimaced.

"S'okay," I told him. "I'm in the middle of talking to Gisele about my accident."

A look passed between them, and Scott pressed his lips together. Neither of them said anything to each other, but Gisele returned her focus to me.

"Why did you feel you needed to see if I was okay?" I asked her. "Did something happen?" I was struggling. You don't realize how hard it is not to be able to remember something until you're hunting through your own memories and can't find it. You know it existed. I mean, I obviously had an entire day, right? But I remembered almost nothing from it. Not getting up. Not going to work. Not driving or drinking coffee or answering phones. None of it. Dr. Panjabi had told me the memories would likely appear little by little, and he was right. Over the past half a day or so, snippets and slices and shards were beginning to appear in wildly random order, which was nearly as disconcerting as not being able to remember at all. I remembered Leo on Mary's lap. I remembered the molding in the hallway of my office building. I remembered the smell of peaches.

Before Gisele could answer me, the nurse pushed through the door wheeling her little Cart of Medical Paraphernalia, and Gisele popped up out of her chair as if ejected from it. "We're going to get out of your hair," she said and threw a look at Scott.

I was exhausted. Already. Which was incredibly frustrating. So I let them gather their things, knowing I had little energy to argue. They both kissed my forehead, and I took that moment to say, "Don't think you're off the hook. I know there's something you're not telling me."

Again, they exchanged a glance.

"Subtle, those looks."

Scott had the good sense to look sheepish.

"Go. I'll see you tomorrow."

The nurse that night, whose name was Karen, was gentle and kind. She took my temperature and my blood pressure, asked me some questions about how I felt, brushed my hair for me, and brought me vanilla pudding. It's possible I fell a little in love with her.

Getting a good night's sleep in a hospital is next to impossible. That's my takeaway from my time there. Somebody comes into your room every two hours or so and pokes and prods and sticks you, and by the time they've left and you've relaxed and started to drift back off, they're back to poke and prod and stick you some more.

It had to be somewhere around five or six in the morning when I finally drifted off. The light outside my window was softly crimson, the sun beginning its ascent into the late spring morning sky. I watched the hue change as my eyelids gave up the battle and then closed.

When I woke up a couple hours later, I felt heavy. Pummeled. Like I'd been beaten up in my sleep. Because in a way, I had. I remembered a chunk from that day. A discussion with Alicia. It was funny to me that I'd spent so much time and effort trying to recall a day that I now knew I'd have been better off forgetting altogether. I used so much energy to remember, and now I couldn't get it out of my head. It echoed. And it wouldn't stop.

"I can't do this. I'm sorry. I just can't. It's too hard. Please. I need you to leave me alone. I need you to let it go. For me. Please."

I refused to cry, mostly because I knew it would cause an epic headache I didn't need, given, you know, my *concussion and brain swelling*. But I could still hear the final "Please" in my head, the desperation and pain injected into that one word. I reminded myself of exactly what I knew about Alicia, of why she said what she did, and that seemed to help a bit as I told myself to just relax, to just breathe. I needed to feel in control of *something* as I lay in a hospital bed, unable to walk or eat anything more than pudding and Cream of Wheat.

I was gazing out the window trying not to think about her (and failing) when my parents arrived. My mom brought her usual cheer and warmth; it followed her like a cape she wore, and I found myself feeling the tiniest bit better just from seeing her face. But Alicia's voice still echoed through my head, try as I might to put a lid on it somehow.

"I need you to let it go. For me. Please."

When my eyes welled up, my mother took a quick step back like I'd burned her. "Oh, honey, did I touch your leg? I'm so sorry."

CHAPTER EIGHTEEN

They kept me in the hospital for two more days, and I was getting antsy. By the time Dr. Panjabi came in and told me I was being released, my eyes welled up with joy and relief and he simply kept his hand on my shoulder until I pulled myself together.

My parents were there to take me home. My dad filled out my paperwork while my mother helped me dress. I missed Leo so badly, it made my chest ache. The nurse had been helping me get around on crutches, and they now leaned against the wall in the corner. Once I was dressed, my mom got them for me, and I hobbled around the room, getting a feel for being upright. It was glorious. Difficult and painful, but glorious.

Scott and Gisele showed up as I sat on my bed waiting for my official release. My mom was in the hall, chatting with the staff that she'd come to know quite well, because that's how she is. Dad had gone to bring the car around. Scott went to say hi to Mom.

"They're springing you, huh?" Gisele asked, and looked a little bit uncomfortable. She hadn't been back since our last conversation, and it was obvious to me that she was still unsure how to proceed. But Scott coming to visit and then immediately leaving the room was a pretty big clue that she wanted to talk. I decided to let her off the hook.

"They are. Look, Gisele, you can relax. I remembered a little bit of the time before the accident. I know you were coming to check on me because of my last conversation with Alicia."

Gisele grimaced and sat down next to me. She studied her feet for a long moment, then slowly nodded. "That had to be hard. We all heard the gist of it. I'm so sorry…" She let her voice trail off as she raised her head and stared off into the room.

"It's okay." I shrugged. I stared at my hands as I asked quietly, "Does she know I'm here?" A beat went by, and I could feel Gisele's gaze on me, the weight of it. "What?" I said as I turned to her.

"Lacey…" Her brow furrowed. "You don't know, do you?"

"Know what?"

"She was here."

I gave her a look of what I was sure was befuddlement because that's exactly how I felt. "What? What do you mean?"

"Alicia. She was here while you were unconscious. Like, a lot. She stayed through the night. She stayed through all three nights."

I blinked at her. It was all I could do because I couldn't compute what she was saying. I had no memory of her, which I wouldn't, of course, because of being unconscious and all. "I don't understand."

Gisele took a deep breath. "It was loud, when you got hit. Screeching brakes and…" I heard her swallow. "When you hit. It made a horrible sound. Lots of people in the building heard it, including Alicia. She got to you only a minute or two after me."

I fought to stay with her story. It was the absolute weirdest feeling to have somebody tell you all about something that happened *to you* that you had zero recollection of. It freaked me out a little bit, and I could feel my heart beating harder in my chest.

"She and I drove to the hospital in her car. She drove like a madwoman. I'm honestly surprised we didn't end up in the room next to yours. And she kept saying things like, 'I'm so stupid. Why did I do that? This is my fault. I didn't mean it. I didn't mean any of it.' I knew she was talking about the conversation with you, but she wasn't really saying it to me, you know? So I didn't pry. I just let her mutter until we got here."

"And then?"

"Once you were admitted and your family got here, she went home. But she came back that night. And both other nights. The nurse said she stayed all night. Your mom probably saw her."

It didn't compute. I couldn't make it. "But she hasn't been here since I've woken up. How come?"

Gisele frowned, tipped her head from side to side in a gesture of uncertainty. "I can only speculate on that."

When she didn't, I raised my eyebrows expectantly.

She blew out a breath. "Guilt plays a big part in Alicia's world. I think you know that."

I nodded.

"I suspect she feels partially responsible for what happened."

"Well, that's ridiculous. She wasn't driving the car."

"True. But she upset you. She knows it."

I couldn't deny that. Since early this morning, memories had returned in trickles. A little snippet here, a tiny sliver there. One thing that was full-blown, though, was the memory of how much Alicia's words had hurt me. But that didn't mean I held her responsible for the accident, and I told Gisele so.

"I know. I'm just telling you what I suspect *Alicia* is thinking. I'm not saying it's rational." She gave me a small smile and Scott came into the room then, followed by my mother and a nurse with a wheelchair.

"Ready to blow this joint, Lace-Face?" Scott asked.

"You have no idea." I waved off any help and managed to use my crutches to get myself from the bed into the chair. The nurse was a large, bald man whose name tag told me he was James. Which was perfect because I pointed to the door and ordered, "Home, James."

He chuckled behind me. "Yes, ma'am."

I was able to put the whole Alicia thing aside for a while so I could focus on getting home. I needed a shower so badly, I wanted to see my dog, I was ready to eat something I actually had to chew. My mother insisted on staying the night with me and, while I put up a feeble protest, I was actually grateful to have her there. Mary had already dropped Leo at the house, so he was waiting for me, and if his excited barks and two-legged jumping were any indication, he'd missed me as much as I'd missed him. Mom kept him from ending up either clubbed by crutches or squashed flat by his falling mommy, who was still learning to navigate on said crutches.

The house smelled a little bit stale from being unoccupied for days. "Mom, can you open a couple of windows?"

"I can. I'm going to scramble you some eggs, too. Okay?"

Eggs sounded like absolute heaven, and I sat carefully back on the couch and let her wait on me. Let me offer up a piece of advice: never bruise a rib if you can help it. You'd be shocked how important an uninjured torso is when it comes to doing things like, oh, I don't know. Moving and sitting?

I ate. Slowly, but I ate. I had to give my stomach a little time to adjust to actual food. Plus, the medications I was on didn't always sit well. But the eggs tasted divine, and I ate every last bite. Well, not *every* last bite. The last bite was for Leo, and I gave it to him right off my fork. Mary would've been proud of me.

I tend to do a lot of my deepest thinking in the shower, but such was not the case that night, and that was a good thing. I needed my mother's help in a big way; it made me feel like a kid again, which was simultaneously heartwarming and mortifying.

She must have seen it on my face because she made an expression that read *Really?* and said, "I pushed you out of my vagina, fed you from my own breast, and changed your poopy diapers, Lacey."

"I know," I whined, "but it's still weird to have you seeing my boobs."

She shook her head with a grin.

We put a garbage bag over my leg and did our best to keep it out of the spray altogether. Unwrapping my ribs wasn't hard, but washing my torso without putting any kind of pressure on them was, and tears sprang into my eyes more than once. My biggest reasons for showering, though, were to wash my hair—which had become stringy and flat—and to shave my armpits.

"You've started to look like Scott," my mother joked when I lifted one arm.

"You're hilarious," I told her. She shaved while I used my other hand to balance and keep myself from dropping into a heap in the tub.

"Wait until you've had your cast on for a few weeks. Then you'll *really* look like him."

"Mom!" When I said it, it had three syllables. My mother laughed.

None of it was easy, but we did it, and by the time I was out of the tub and standing on the small rug with a towel wrapped around me, we were both out of breath.

"Well. That was fun." I leaned against the vanity while my mother took a seat on the lid of the toilet. "But I feel so much better. Thanks, Mom."

My mom smiled. "Welcome."

By early evening, I was beat. Going to bed before nine seemed ridiculous and made me feel old, but my body had had enough. My leg throbbed, my ribs ached, my head was pounding. Mom shook out the pills I needed—mostly pain meds at this point—and helped me into my pajamas. I couldn't get the bottoms over my cast, so I had to settle for bikinis and my favorite, super-worn Temple T-shirt that I'd stolen from Leanne a couple years back. Once I was in bed, my leg propped on a pillow, Leo curled up near my good foot. I smiled; it was like he knew to be careful, not to bump my bad leg.

"Okay?" Mom asked.

"I think so."

"All right. I'm putting your phone right here. Can you reach it?"

I stretched my arm out to the nightstand easily. "Yup."

"I'll have mine right with me and my volume is turned up loud, so if you need anything, text me. I'll be right next door." She bent down and kissed my forehead before heading to the guest room, and again, I felt like a child being taken care of. This time, instead of mortifying me, it warmed me from the inside.

"Thanks, Mom." I wondered how many more times I'd say that. A lot, I suspected.

"Try to get some sleep." As she reached the doorway, she stopped with her hand on the light switch. "I'll pop back by in two hours just to poke you awake, okay?"

"Ha ha. Don't you dare."

Her chuckle followed her down the hall.

And then I was left alone with my thoughts. I'd waited ever since I'd spoken with Gisele to be able to analyze the things she'd told me, but I also knew I was going to be fighting with the meds. I was utterly exhausted—I couldn't remember ever being so tired, and I'd pulled all-nighters more than once during tax season—and my eyes didn't want to stay open.

"Alicia. She was here while you were unconscious. Like, a lot. She stayed through the night. She stayed through all three nights."

Gisele's words rolled around in my head, and I realized I'd forgotten to ask my mother whether she'd seen Alicia. I actually toyed with the idea of texting her the question, but it was as if my body rebelled against my brain, not allowing me to lift my arm and reach for my phone. I released a long sigh, knowing I wasn't going to be able to fight sleep and also knowing I probably shouldn't. It's not like any of this was going anywhere. All these thoughts would still be there when I woke up.

Leo let out one of those doggie sighs, the ones they release when they've settled in for the night. The ones that are a combination of "My day was so hard" and "I'm so happy to be next to my person." It made me smile, and I decided to take a page from his playbook and just let myself fall into relaxation.

Didn't take long.

❖

"...this is your body's way of protecting itself while your head heals. So, I decided I'm just going to talk to you whenever I can..."

"...you'd have loved my mom, Lacey. You really would have. And my God, she would have adored you..."

"...I miss my family, Lacey. I miss them every day, every moment of my life..."

"...I thought driving you away, keeping you at a distance was the best way to handle it, and I know that was wrong. So, so wrong, and I'm sorry. Please give me another chance, Lacey. Please..."

Unlike a TV movie, where the heroine has a significant dream that jolts her awake, pops her eyes open, makes her gasp, my rise to wakefulness was gentle. I simply opened my eyes and lay there, playing the words over and over in my head.

Memories. They had to be. Right?

I was still on my back, my leg still on the pillow, Leo snuffling softly in his sleep against my thigh. I ached, a combination of my injuries and the fact that I'd been lying in the same position for—I turned to look at the digital clock on my nightstand—nearly six hours. While I realized it was the first time in a while I'd gotten a stretch of sleep longer than a couple of hours, I really needed to move. I wanted desperately to roll onto my side but knew my bruised ribs would have none of that. When I did try to move, my breath hitched as every muscle in my body seemed to seize up. I'd grown stiff as I'd slept, and moving at all was going to take some effort.

I knew I should call my mom for help, but it wasn't even three in the morning, and I wanted her to sleep. The struggle was slow, frustrating, and painful, but I somehow managed to get myself upright, maneuver to the bathroom to relieve myself, take more meds, and head back to my room. I liked the idea of sitting on my couch and watching bad, middle-of-the-night television, but the stairs seemed a bit too daunting to attempt on my own, especially in the dark. I settled for getting myself somewhat comfortable sitting up in my bed and clicking on the small TV on my dresser.

Confession: I love to channel surf. It doesn't really fit my personality of liking everything just so, because when you channel surf, nothing stays. Things constantly change. You'd think that would drive me nuts, but it doesn't. Instead, I find it somewhat mesmerizing to continually change the picture I'm seeing. That being said, there isn't much to settle on at 3:00 a.m., so I just kept hitting the channel up button. As I did so, I dug back into my brain to the lines I'd remembered in my sleep. I replayed them, rolled them around, examined them from different angles. Gisele had said Alicia was at the hospital, that she'd stayed through three nights, and it only made sense that the things I was remembering were things she'd said to me. It's not like my mind would invent that kind of thing, right? The fact that I could only hear her in my memories, that I didn't actually *see* her at all, sort of confirmed that for me.

Alicia had talked to me while I lay unconscious.

Not only had she talked to me, she'd apparently shared with me. She'd talked about her family, something she'd never done before. Something I got the impression she hardly ever did.

I let it swirl around and around. Alicia had opened up to me. Granted, I was unconscious at the time, but I'd take it. It meant a lot. It meant everything.

All the swirling must have exhausted me because the next thing I knew, the sun was streaming in through my window. The TV was off and the remote was on the nightstand. Leo was gone and my bedroom door was open.

And I smelled food.

My mouth filled immediately, letting me know just exactly how hungry I was. Before I could utter a word, Leo came rushing in and jumped onto the bed—I held my breath, expecting him to run over my cast, but he didn't—shockingly—and I could hear footsteps on the stairs. My mom came in with a tray loaded down with breakfast. French toast, coffee, and orange juice.

"Good morning, sunshine," she said, her voice full of cheer. She set everything down and helped me to sit up higher. "What time did you get up?"

I regaled her with my middle-of-the-night adventures.

"Lacey," she said.

"Uh-oh. Stern Mom Voice."

"I don't like that you did all of that by yourself. What if you'd fallen?"

"I didn't."

"But you could have."

"But I didn't." We had a stare-down for a couple of beats until we both burst into laughter. I then had to hold my stomach as pain seared through my torso. "Ow, ow, ow."

"See what happens when you try to outsmart your mother? God punishes you."

She sat with me while I ate—her French toast is one of the most joyous foods on the planet, I swear—and then she helped me change out of my pajamas. I picked out an old pair of yoga pants I didn't care about and she cut the right leg up to knee length so I could wear them over my cast. I pulled my hair back into a ponytail, as I was in no mood to deal with styling it. I stood in front of the full-length mirror, balanced on my crutches.

"Stunning," I said as I checked out my reflection, let my eyes take in the butchered pants, the long-sleeved Nike T-shirt that had to be ten years old, the dark circles under my eyes, and the slight gray pallor of my skin. "I am absolutely stunning."

"Yes, you are," Mom said and kissed me on my temple.

I spent the next two days on the couch as visitors came and went. Flowers arrived. Candy appeared. People brought pizza and casseroles, and I smiled and said thank you while I wondered how many people they thought lived here. But my dad came by to hang, and between him and Scott, they did a good job of paring down the ever-growing food supply.

Leanne stopped by on Thursday and watched two episodes of *Friends* with me, sitting next to me on the couch, quoting the lines along with me. She looked like she wanted to say something the entire time she was there, but she left with the same expression, so whatever it was went unsaid.

My phone dinged constantly, texts flying in fast and furious. Even Amy sent me a sweet note and well wishes, and not long after that, an Edible Arrangement showed up from her. Again, my dad and brother went to town, shoving chocolate-dipped fruit in their faces like they hadn't eaten in days. I smiled and shook my head.

It was weird, though, because the whole time my family was there, surrounding me with their love and their jokes and their overstaying, I thought about Alicia. I thought about how she'd had this same thing: two parents and a brother. And how she simply didn't have them anymore. It put a lump in my throat, and all I wanted to do was wrap my arms around her and keep her safe from any more hurt.

After dinner on Friday—or dinner *time*, as my family had been stuffing their faces all day—my dad headed home. Scott left about twenty minutes later and it was just me and Mom again. We watched TV in silence together for a while before she turned to me.

"How's your bladder?"

"Very, very full," I told her, dreading the simple task of using the facilities. Not for the first time, I wished my small house had a powder room on the first floor.

Mom stood up and held out her hand. "Let's do this."

Once I was as settled as I could get on the toilet, given my cast, my wrapped torso, my crutches, and every other obstacle I had, I waved her away. "Okay. I got this. Go."

"Call me if you need help."

"I will wipe my own ass if it kills me, thank you very much."

That cracked her up for some reason, and her laughter followed her down the stairs as I shook my head and grinned.

I was just finishing up my business when the doorbell rang. My first thought was, *Oh, my God, please no more. I can't force any more smiles. I'm too tired.* But I strained to listen and heard nothing but hushed voices. Curious, I got myself to my feet and hobbled slowly down the hall to the top of the steps.

"I'm not sure she's up for any more company," my mother was saying. I couldn't see anybody, so they must be standing at the door. Mom's tone was an odd mixture of sympathy and uncertainty.

"I understand that. I don't blame her."

Alicia! My eyes flew open wide, and I had no idea what to do. Part of me wanted to launch myself down the stairs just to lay eyes on her. Another just wanted to cry. With relief. With joy. With missing her.

There was a long moment of silence, and I pictured my mother debating whether or not I could handle seeing her. I assumed Scott must have given her details but made a mental note to check on that later. If she didn't know, she needed to. And I could already hear her words, had an immediate vision of her comforting me, telling me it would be okay, that she understood my pain, that maybe I could try... just try to see things from Alicia's perspective, how opening her heart to somebody might be intensely difficult for her, given what she'd gone through. My mom is that person, the one with the gentle soul, the one who can feel the pain of others, who would take it on for them if she could. It suddenly occurred to me just how much Alicia could probably benefit from talking to Mom rather than me, and it tugged up one corner of my mouth.

"Mom," I called down the stairs. "I'm okay. Let her in."

There was a beat of silence before anybody started moving. My mother appeared at the bottom of the stairs, followed by Alicia.

Goddamn her, she looked gorgeous. I assumed she'd gone home after work, as she wore a light-colored pair of jeans and a navy blue T-shirt with a V-neck, subdued colors for her, but she was beautiful. Even from the top of the stairs, I couldn't keep myself from letting that blue gaze snag mine, and we held it for a long moment as my mother climbed the staircase to help me down.

"You sure you're up for this?" she whispered as she took one crutch from me so I could use the railing.

"Mm-hmm." I nodded, and we descended slowly.

Alicia looked a little lost, and I felt the sudden urge to keep her safe. She moved out of our way and scooped up Leo as Mom helped me hobble to the couch, then slowly lower myself. She slid the ottoman over and helped me prop my casted leg up on it.

I looked up at Alicia as she absently scratched my dog under his chin and looked exactly like the proverbial deer in headlights. "Hey," I said. "I'm really glad to see you."

"Yeah?" she asked, and gave me an uncertain smile. "How are you doing?"

I took a deep breath and blew it out. "Well, aside from the broken leg, aching ribs, and constant headache, I'm great. You?" I chuckled and waved at the couch next to me. "Sit. Please."

"Can I get either of you anything?" Mom asked. We both shook our heads. "All right. Let me know if you change your mind. I'll be in the kitchen."

She squeezed my shoulder as I softly thanked her. When she was out of sight, I turned back to Alicia.

"It's so good to see you," she whispered, and I watched as her eyes filled with tears. Her smile lit up the room. I swear to God, it did. And then she gave a small chuckle and I couldn't take my eyes off her. I was *so happy* to have her sitting next to me.

"You know," I said, pulling at a string on the chopped-up leg of my yoga pants, "if I knew all it would take to get you to open up to me was for me to jump in front of a car, I'd have done it sooner."

Her laugh was like music, and it grabbed me, shook me, made me listen. Made me feel. I had such a mix of joy and relief in that moment.

She sobered. "You heard me? In the hospital?" She seemed surprised. Wary. Uncertain.

"I must have. I remembered some of it last night, but it's choppy. Bits and pieces. Out of order. You told me about your family."

"I did." Alicia looked down at Leo, who hadn't left her side since her arrival.

I nodded, doing my best to absorb it all.

"Look, Lacey, I need to tell you that I'm sorry." It looked like her search for words was actually painful, and my heart ached for her. I held up a hand, stopping her.

"There's no need. I understand."

"You do?"

"Yeah. I do." God, it felt good to tell her that. I smiled at her and held her gaze for what felt like a long time. Then I pushed myself up a bit so I sat taller. "Okay, here's what we're going to do," I said. "You and I? We're going to get to know each other."

"Okay." She looked slightly confused, but to her credit, went with it.

"My meds kick my ass, and I don't last long. I've had a hundred and fifty visitors today and I'm exhausted and need to rest. Can you come back tomorrow for dinner? Can you do that?"

"Absolutely."

"Six thirty?"

"Okay."

"Bring Chinese."

A smile snaked across her face. "I will."

"We'll talk."

"We'll talk." Her nod was vigorous. She stood, Leo in her arms, and looked down at me for a moment like she wasn't quite sure what to do next. Finally, she gave one more nod, handed me my dog, and smiled. "Tomorrow."

CHAPTER NINETEEN

I didn't think it was possible to have too many well-wishing visitors when you were under the weather—or, you know, recovering from being run over by a moving vehicle. But it was Saturday, so friends and family who didn't have to work decided to come by en masse and say hi, bring flowers, candy, and yes, more food. I actually toyed with texting Alicia and telling her to forget about the Chinese, but changed my mind. Sharing Chinese food was something I now associated with her, and I didn't want to give it up.

My grandparents left mid-afternoon, and I was shocked by how tired I was. My worry about falling asleep on Alicia was valid, but I had no time for a nap, as my two aunts showed up twenty minutes later. I pushed through the exhaustion because I was suddenly very aware of how lucky I was to have so much family.

"What do you need from me tonight?" my mom asked once the last visitors had left around 5:30. My father sat on the other end of my couch muttering at the TV, but he turned to look at us.

"Can you stay long enough to let her in?"

"Of course." Mom hesitated. "You don't want me to stay overnight?"

I tilted my head to one side and smiled tenderly at her. "You've been so amazing, Mom. You really have. I don't know how to thank you."

"But you don't want me cramping your style on your date." I'd filled her in on some of the details of Alicia's life, the things I thought she needed to know before casting judgment. Her eyes had filled with tears when I told her. That's my awesome mom. Now she gave me a wink, and I hoped my sigh of relief wasn't too obvious. "It's no problem, honey. Dad and I will get out of your hair once Alicia gets here."

"You sure you're gonna be all right?" my father asked. His voice was gruff and he kept his focus on the television, but I was touched anyway.

"I'm sure."

He nodded, gave a small grunt, and that was the end of the discussion.

The truth was, I'd learned to maneuver around pretty well on the crutches. My ribs were still very sore but felt a little better than they had just a few days ago, so I had to believe healing was happening. My headaches were finally easing up. It was time for me to take my house, my life back, even if Alicia hadn't been coming for dinner.

I changed into a nicer shirt, a long-sleeved, cream Henley, but was stuck with the yoga pants. Mom had grabbed me a couple cheapo pairs so we could cut the leg off them, too, as I was stuck in that cast for at least eight weeks. I styled my hair for the first time since I'd returned from the hospital, and I even applied a little makeup and a spritz of coconut body spray. I was giving myself one last check in the mirror when I heard the doorbell, and Leo started barking.

I inhaled very slowly, let it out even more slowly.

"I got this," I said to my reflection.

I made my way down the stairs to find my parents gathering their things, them, Alicia, and Leo all crammed into my front entryway like they were in an elevator and couldn't get out of each other's way. Alicia met my eyes over the top of my mother's head and smiled at me. She was in jeans again, and a red button-down shirt with the sleeves rolled up to just below her elbows. Her hair seemed extra wavy, her eyes bright. God, I was giddy just to see her face.

"You're sure you're all set?" my mom asked, her purse over her shoulder and her eyes worried. She sidled her way toward me.

"I'm sure."

She wrapped her arms around me and hugged me gently, then pressed a kiss to my forehead. "You call me if you need anything. I'm a ten-minute drive away. Promise?"

"I promise. Thanks, Mom." I looked past her. "Bye, Dad."

He waved and made his way out the front door. My mother gave me one last look of concern, then she gave Alicia a smile and squeezed her shoulder before following my father out. The door shut behind them with a click and then it was just me and Alicia, standing about ten feet apart, Leo on the floor looking from one of us to the other as if waiting to see who would move first.

"So," Alicia said and held up two white bags. A brown one was tucked under her arm. "Hi. Hungry?"

"Surprisingly, I am."

She moved into the kitchen, and I followed her.

"Whoa," she said, as she stopped in her tracks at the sight of all the food spread across my counter.

"I know, right? People must think while I'm recovering, I should just stuff my face. So, I am." I gave her a lighthearted chuckle. "I'm so grateful and I don't want it to go to waste. But my waistline is going to be in trouble when this is all over."

"No, it's not," Alicia said, and her gaze did a quick slide over my body. "You have nothing to worry about. Trust me."

I felt my cheeks heat up and tried to smother a smile.

Alicia held up the brown bag. "I wasn't sure if you're allowed…" She pulled a bottle of wine from it.

"I'm not supposed to, but I don't think one small glass will hurt."

"Let's hope not. You've had enough pain for a while."

"Agreed."

We worked together—well, Alicia worked, and I pointed to where things were—and once the food had been dished out, we moved into the living room so I could prop my leg up. Mom had brought over a couple of TV trays, so we used those and ate in front of the television like two ten-year-olds in the eighties.

"Tell me about your dad," I said, suddenly enough to surprise me as well as her.

Alicia blinked at me, took a beat to gather herself, I figured, and then spoke. "He was kind. Probably too kind. He did a lot of things for a lot of people."

"Like favors, you mean?" I watched her as I ate a bite of my spring roll.

She nodded and gazed off into the room. "If you needed something, help or money or a ride, my dad was the one you called. He'd drop whatever he was doing to help a friend."

I liked the soft wistfulness in her voice. "He sounds great."

"He was." She ate some rice. "Tell me about yours."

"My dad is the epitome of the tough guy with a heart of gold. He's abrasive. He grunts instead of actually answering you with words." Alicia chuckled as I described my father. "He thinks technology is a fad. But he's a big teddy bear. There's no place I feel safer than in my father's arms."

I saw Alicia swallow as she looked at me, and then one corner of her mouth tugged up. "That's awesome."

"How was work this week?"

We talked like this for a while, just touching on normal, sometimes mundane things that people talk about. I asked questions and Alicia answered them and after an hour or so, it almost felt like we were back to being comfortable together. Only this time, it was more equal. She told me about two new pitches she'd given last week, how she thought each went, what she had lined up next week. I told her that I hoped I hadn't fallen too far behind and how thankful I was that my accident hadn't happened a month earlier, as that could've been devastating for my business.

This is nice.

That thought kept scrolling through my head as the evening went on. I tried not to dwell on it. Instead, I simply tucked it away.

"Want to watch a movie or something?" Alicia asked once she'd cleaned away our dishes and refilled her wineglass. I was still on my first, nursing it slowly to make it last. "Or I could go, if you want. You look tired." Her tone told me she didn't actually want to leave, which made me happy, but the fact she was willing to go if I asked her to was kind of terrific.

"No, stay. Please? I'd love a movie. I just should probably take my meds first." I made a move to get up, but her hand on my shoulder stopped me.

"I'll get them. Tell me where they are."

Ten minutes later—after we'd both been amused at my washing my drugs down with a mouthful of wine—we settled onto the couch to watch a movie. Leo was on my right, tucked between my thigh and the arm of the couch. Alicia sat on my left, close enough to share the ottoman, our thighs brushing. And as the movie went on, we somehow seemed to inch closer together until my eyes started to grow weary, and I leaned my head on Alicia's shoulder. She shifted so her arm was around me and I snuggled up against her. It was heaven, though I tried not to think about it. "Tried" being the operative word.

The next time I opened my eyes, it was fully dark. The TV was off. Leo was snoring next to me. I felt warm and safe and loved. I lifted my head from Alicia's shoulder, and she was looking at me.

"Hi," she whispered.

"Hey. What time is it?"

"It's after midnight. I think we should get you up to your bed. It can't be good for your ribs to sleep in this position all night."

I didn't have the energy to argue with her. Plus, she was right. My torso had begun to ache from being in a sitting position for too long. I nodded, and slowly, we stood from the couch and made our way upstairs, Leo on our heels. I relieved myself, changed into a pajama top, then let Alicia help me into bed. Leo was already curled in a ball at the foot of it, his eyes closed, and I envied how he could simply drop off to sleep in four and a half seconds.

"Okay?" Alicia asked quietly once I was settled.

I nodded.

She bent to kiss my forehead, but I moved my head at the last minute and caught her lips with mine. She pulled back, the confused hesitation clear on her face even in the night. I wanted her to stay. God, how I wanted her to stay.

"Come back tomorrow?" I asked, trying not to sound desperate even as that was exactly how I felt.

Her confusion changed to relief and she kissed me softly once more. "Definitely."

"Bring breakfast."

"Your accident made you bossy, you know that?"

"Better get used to it."

"Uh-oh." Her shoulders moved as she laughed softly, then continued to stand there and simply look down at me. Our gazes held for a long moment, and even in the dark, I could feel it, the near intimacy we shared. In that moment, in that very specific point in time, I knew we were going to be okay. It was a weird feeling, alarming in its depth, and more than a little surprising to me. Not something I was ready to share. But I felt it. In my heart.

"Until breakfast." Alicia ran a fingertip down my cheek, then turned and left.

I waited until I heard her car pull out of my driveway and down the street. But instead of going over every word that had been said through the evening, instead of analyzing every little thing, I closed my eyes and breathed deeply. And despite my wishing it was time for breakfast already, sleep took me immediately.

I slept like a baby.

❖

My eyes popped open at 6:45, and I woke up with extra energy and a very positive attitude toward the day. The sun was starting to peek in through my closed blinds. A check of my phone told me it was heading into the seventies today. "It's gonna be nice, Mr. Leo," I told my dog, as he gingerly stepped near my head to give me kisses, and I marveled at how he instinctively knew not to stand on my torso like usual.

Still not terribly sure about showering on my own, I gave myself a very thorough sponge bath and managed to wash my hair in the bathroom sink. I made a mess, and my ribs were screaming afterward, but I got it done. After that, blow-drying and styling was a breeze. I donned the damn one-legged yoga pants—sadly understanding that a favorite wardrobe item of mine would be banished from my drawers forever once that cast came off—found a decent long-sleeved shirt in olive green, and hobbled my way downstairs.

I barely got my coffee made when the doorbell rang and Leo barked. I glanced at the clock. 8:25. Was somebody in a hurry to come over? I hoped so, because my stomach was full of butterflies and anticipation.

Alicia looked amazing. I thought that every time I saw her, but she never *didn't* look amazing. Today, she wore dark denim capris, a white short-sleeved shirt that buttoned down, and a lightweight scarf in various shades of blue draped gently around her neck. White Keds were on her feet. She looked casual and comfortable, but decidedly feminine and soft. I wanted to throw myself into her arms, but I managed to maintain some control.

"Coffee?" I asked. At her raised eyebrows, I laughed. "I know, I know. Stupid question."

Alicia set a bag of bagels on the counter and took a couple out, along with a container of honey walnut cream cheese. "Hungry?"

"I am. But…" I stopped making coffee and turned to her. "Maybe you can take me for a walk later? I won't be able to go far."

"Or fast."

"Or fast, ha ha, but…I could use some fresh air and sunshine. And a little exercise."

"You got it."

We took our coffee and breakfast to the couch—a spot I used to adore, but was rapidly becoming sick of—and sat, my leg propped on the ottoman. Leo took up the spot next to my foot, staring at us as we ate.

"What's on your agenda for today?" I asked Alicia as I chewed my cranberry orange bagel and tried not to moan in pleasure.

"This," Alicia said simply and took a sip of coffee.

I don't know why I was surprised, but I was, and I sat there looking at her while I chewed. She finally let out a half laugh.

"Why are you looking at me like that? Do I have something on my face?"

"You're giving up your whole Sunday for me?"

Alicia cocked her head like a dog that heard a high-frequency sound. "Of course I am."

I didn't know quite what to say to that, so I nodded.

Alicia set down her coffee and turned so she faced me. "Look, Lacey." She glanced down at her lap, wet her lips, and seemed suddenly nervous. "I've had a lot on my mind since your accident. A lot to think about. I was going to wait. I was going to rehearse it in my head a bit more, to be honest, but I guess this is as good a time as any." She moved so her gaze was on the door to the backyard, and she was quiet for so long, I wondered if that was all she was going to manage to say. When she finally looked at me, I was taken aback to see unshed tears in her eyes. "There's something about you, Lacey. Something…" She looked back at the door and cleared her throat. "I tend to keep people at arm's length. Brandon and Gisele are exceptions. Everybody else is kept at a distance. And that's worked fine for a long time. It's been just fine. But you…"

I wanted to touch her. I wanted to say something, to reassure her.

But I was afraid if I moved, if I spoke, it would break this spell. Alicia was opening up to me, and it was almost like I could see it happening, could see her being split down the middle and expanding, light pouring out. I kept quiet, but my attention stayed riveted on her face.

"You drew me in immediately. That first day when you were all huffy and annoyed." She glanced at me with a grin. "There was something then. I don't know what it was, but it pulled at me. And I wanted to be around you all the time. That's why I was always popping in, bringing you wine and stuff."

"You can pop in with wine any time you want."

Her smile widened, then faded. "The little voice was in the back of my head, but I was having so much fun getting to know you that I was able to keep it in its little compartment for a long time." She looked in my eyes. "I don't know if you have a little voice, but they can be *really* hard to ignore."

"What was it saying to you?" I asked quietly.

"The same thing it always says. 'Don't get too close. It won't go anywhere. You'll lose her, too, just like you lose everybody.'" Her tears finally spilled over and rolled slowly down her cheeks.

"Oh, God, Alicia." I put my breakfast down and scooted as close to her as I could get with my cast. My arm around her shoulders, I squeezed her to me.

"It's silly and ridiculous, I know," she said, through her tears. "I'm a smart girl. I've read enough books. I'm aware of how blatantly obvious it is what my mind is doing to me. But in the moment? Sometimes, it just…slices through me like an actual razor blade. I can almost feel myself bleeding all over the floor."

I pressed my lips to her temple and held her tightly, my heart breaking for the pain this beautiful soul of a woman had been handed already in her young life.

"And then, after you came over on the anniversary of my mother's death and held me while I cried, that voice had a field day." She furrowed her brows at me. "It's like another person living in my head. And he sees what's happening and does what he can to sabotage it. You know? Like, I loved that you held me that night. *Loved it.* Nobody has ever held me like that because I've never let anybody. And it's like he saw that and got jealous and planted the seeds for me so the next morning, my first thought was, 'I need to put a stop to this thing right now, before I get hurt again.'" She shook her head. "It's so obvious and so typical and so…goddamn destructive. And I just couldn't fight it. I wasn't strong enough." She looked at me again and her voice was nothing more than a whisper. "I'm sorry, Lacey. I'm sorry I hurt you."

"It's okay," I whispered. "I get it. It took me a while to fully grasp it all, but…I need you to stop beating yourself up over my accident. Can you do that? Because it wasn't your fault. God, Alicia, you lost your entire family." I could feel how wide my eyes were as I said it. "Of course you want to protect yourself. Of course."

Her eyes welled up, but she didn't interrupt. She let me go on.

I took both her hands in mine. "I get you, Alicia." I said it firmly, with quiet determination because I *needed* her to hear me, to understand. "Okay? *I get you.*"

Her face in that moment…I'll never forget it. The combination of relief and love as her tears spilled over and coursed down her cheeks… it will stay with me forever.

"I'm still sorry I hurt you," she whispered.

"It's okay," I said with a shrug, exaggerating the nonchalance. "I'm tough. You didn't hurt me that much. You know what did hurt?"

"Being run over by a car?"

"Yes. *That.*"

We both started to chuckle, shoulders shaking as we held each other. Then the chuckles grew into full-blown laughter, and before we knew it, we were crying for a happier reason.

"Stop," I pleaded, arms wrapped around my middle. "Please. Stop. Laughing hurts."

Alicia instantly stopped laughing and reached a hand out, obviously uncertain whether to touch me. She let her fingertips brush my stomach. "I'm sorry."

I took her hand, brought it to my lips, and kissed those fingertips. "It's totally okay. I'd much rather laugh with you and have a little pain than see you look sad. So stop being sad, okay? At least about us. Because I think you and I? We're kind of awesome together."

"Do you know what you made me realize?"

"Tell me."

"How very, very lonely I was."

I swallowed down the lump in my throat, tightened my grip on her hand. "Oh, sweetheart…"

Alicia's expression was hesitant. "I've got a lot of baggage, you know."

"I'm aware." I made sure my face was open. I didn't care about her baggage. I wanted her to be with me. "Big suitcases don't scare me."

"I've got a couple of trunks, too. And a storage locker."

"Still not scared," I said. "Have I never mentioned my bellhop fantasy?"

Alicia's grin broke through like sunshine after a summer rainstorm. "Who doesn't love a woman in uniform, right?"

"Exactly. Me, in a burgundy pantsuit and cute little hat, carting around all your baggage while you tip me? Come on. That'd be awesome."

Alicia's grin broke into a full-on laugh. Our gazes held, and it occurred to me that I would never get tired of looking into the deep blue of those eyes, especially when they looked like they did right then. A beat passed, and Alicia took my hand, held it in hers, looked down, studied it. When she raised her eyes again and looked at me, *really* looked at me, I felt a warmth deep inside. A comfort. A certainty. She had trouble with the words; I knew that. It only made sense that she would. But I also knew what the words were, and they were right there, on her face, in her eyes. I felt them. Solidly. For now, that was enough.

A wave of sheer, blissful contentment washed over me as I reached out and rested my palm against her face, stroked my thumb across her cheek. I smiled softly at her and whispered, "I know, baby. I love you, too."

About the Author

Georgia Beers is a Lambda, Foreword Book of the Year, and Goldie award–winning author of lesbian romance. She resides in upstate New York, where she was born and raised. When not writing, she enjoys too much TV, too little wine, not enough time at the gym, and long walks with her dog. She is currently hard at work on her next book. You can visit her and find out more at www.georgiabeers.com.

Books Available From Bold Strokes Books

A More Perfect Union by Carsen Taite. Major Zoey Granger and DC fixer Rook Daniels risk their reputations for a chance at true love while dealing with a scandal that threatens to rock the military. (978-162639-754-5)

Arrival by Gun Brooke. The spaceship *Pathfinder* reaches its passengers' new homeworld where danger lurks in the shadows while Pamas Seclan disembarks and finds unexpected love in young science genius Darmiya Do Voy. (978-162639-859-7)

Captain's Choice by VK Powell. Architect Kerstin Anthony's life is going to plan until Bennett Carlyle, the first girl she ever kissed, is assigned to her latest and most important project, a police district substation. (978-162639-997-6)

Falling Into Her by Erin Zak. Pam Phillips, widow at the age of forty, meets Kathryn Hawthorne, local Chicago celebrity, and it changes her life forever—in ways she hadn't even considered possible. (978-163555-092-4)

Hookin' Up by MJ Williamz. Will Leah get what she needs from casual hookups or will she see the love she desires right in front of her? (978-163555-051-1)

King of Thieves by Shea Godfrey. When art thief Casey Marinos meets bounty hunter Finnegan Starkweather, the crimes of the past just might set the stage for a payoff worth more than she ever dreamed possible. (978-163555-007-8)

Lucy's Chance by Jackie D. As a serial killer haunts the streets, Lucy tries to stitch up old wounds with her first love in the wake of a small town's rapid descent into chaos. (978-163555-027-6)

Right Here, Right Now by Georgia Beers. When Alicia Wright moves into the office next door to Lacey Chamberlain's accounting firm, Lacey is about to find out that sometimes the last person you want is exactly the person you need. (978-163555-154-9)

Strictly Need to Know by MB Austin. Covert operator Maji Rios will do whatever she must to complete her mission, but saving a gorgeous stranger from Russian mobsters was not in her plans. (978-163555-114-3)

Tailor-Made by Yolanda Wallace. Tailor Grace Henderson doesn't date clients, but when she meets gender-bending model Dakota Lane, she's tempted to throw all the rules out the window. (978-163555-081-8)

Time Will Tell by M. Ullrich. With the ability to time travel, Eva Caldwell will have to decide between having it all and erasing it all. (978-163555-088-7)

Change in Time by Robyn Nyx. Working in the past is hell on your future. The Extractor series: Book Two. (978-162639-880-1)

Love After Hours by Radclyffe. When Gina Antonelli agrees to renovate Carrie Longmire's new house, she doesn't welcome Carrie's overtures at friendship or her own unexpected attraction. A Rivers Community Novel. (978-163555-090-0)

Nantucket Rose by CF Frizzell. Maggie Jordan can't wait to convert a historic Nantucket home into a B&B, but doesn't expect to fall for mariner Ellis Chilton, who has more claim to the house than Maggie realizes. (978-163555-056-6)

Picture Perfect by Lisa Moreau. Falling in love wasn't supposed to be part of the stakes for Olive and Gabby, rival photographers in the competition of a lifetime. (978-162639-975-4)

Set the Stage by Karis Walsh. Actress Emilie Danvers takes the stage again in Ashland, Oregon, little realizing that landscaper Arden Philips is about to offer her a very personal romantic lead role. (978-163555-087-0)

Strike a Match by Fiona Riley. When their attempts at matchmaking fizzle out, firefighter Sasha and reluctant millionairess Abby find themselves turning to each other to strike a perfect match. (978-162639-999-0)

The Price of Cash by Ashley Bartlett. Cash Braddock is doing her best to keep her business afloat, stay out of jail, and avoid Detective Kallen. It's not working. (978-162639-708-8)

Under Her Wing by Ronica Black. At Angel's Wings Rescue, dogs are usually the ones saved, but when quiet Kassandra Haden meets outspoken owner Jayden Beaumont, the two stubborn women just might end up saving each other. (978-163555-077-1)

Underwater Vibes by Mickey Brent. When Hélène, a translator in Brussels, Belgium, meets Sylvie, a young Greek photographer and swim coach, unsettling feelings hijack Hélène's mind and body—even her poems. (978-163555-002-3)

A Date to Die by Anne Laughlin. Someone is killing people close to Detective Kay Adler, who must look to her own troubled past for a suspect. There she finds more than one person seeking revenge against her. (978-163555-023-8)

Captured Soul by Laydin Michaels. Can Kadence Munroe save the woman she loves from a twisted killer, or will she lose her to a collector of souls? (978-162639-915-0)

Dawn's New Day by TJ Thomas. Can Dawn Oliver and Cam Cooper, two women who have loved and lost, open their hearts to love again? (978-163555-072-6)

Definite Possibility by Maggie Cummings. Sam Miller is just out for good times, but Lucy Weston makes her realize happily ever after is a definite possibility. (978-162639-909-9)

Eyes Like Those by Melissa Brayden. Isabel Chase and Taylor Andrews struggle between love and ambition from the writers' room on one of Hollywood's hottest TV shows. (978-163555-012-2)

Heart's Orders by Jaycie Morrison. Helen Tucker and Tee Owens escape hardscrabble lives to careers in the Women's Army Corps, but more than their hearts are at risk as friendship blossoms into love. (978-163555-073-3)

Hiding Out by Kay Bigelow. Treat Dandridge is unaware that her life is in danger from the murderer who is hunting the woman she's falling in love with, Mickey Heiden. (978-162639-983-9)

Omnipotence Enough by Sophia Kell Hagin. Can the tiny tool that abducted war veteran Jamie Gwynmorgan accidentally acquires help her escape an unknown enemy to reclaim her stolen life and the woman she deeply loves? (978-163555-037-5)

Summer's Cove by Aurora Rey. Emerson Lange moved to Provincetown to live in the moment, but when she meets Darcy Belo and her son Liam, her quest for summer romance becomes a family affair. (978-162639-971-6)

The Road to Wings by Julie Tizard. Lieutenant Casey Tompkins, Air Force student pilot, has to fly with the toughest instructor, Captain Kathryn "Hard Ass" Hardesty, fly a supersonic jet, and deal with a growing forbidden attraction. (978-162639-988-4)

Beauty and the Boss by Ali Vali. Ellis Renois is at the top of the fashion world, but she never expects her summer assistant Charlotte Hamner to tear her heart and her business apart like sharp scissors through cheap material. (978-162639-919-8)

Fury's Choice by Brey Willows. When gods walk amongst humans, can two women find a balance between love and faith? (978-162639-869-6)

Lessons in Desire by MJ Williamz. Can a summer love stand a four-month hiatus and still burn hot? (978-163555-019-1)

Lightning Chasers by Cass Sellars. For Sydney and Parker, being a couple was never what they had planned. Now they have to fight corruption, murder, and enemies hiding in plain sight just to hold on to each other. Lightning Series, Book Two. (978-162639-965-5)

Summer Fling by Jean Copeland. Still jaded from a breakup years earlier, Kate struggles to trust falling in love again when a summer fling with sexy young singer Jordan rocks her off her feet. (978-162639-981-5)

Take Me There by Julie Cannon. Adrienne and Sloan know it would be career suicide to mix business with pleasure, however tempting it is. But what's the harm? They're both consenting adults. Who would know? (978-162639-917-4)

Unchained Memories by Dena Blake. Can a woman give herself completely when she's left a piece of herself behind? (978-162639-993-8)

Walking Through Shadows by Sheri Lewis Wohl. All Molly wanted to do was go backpacking…in her own century. (978-162639-968-6)

Freedom to Love by Ronica Black. What happens when the woman who spent her life worrying about caring for her family finally finds the freedom to love without borders? (978-1-63555-001-6)

A Lamentation of Swans by Valerie Bronwen. Ariel Montgomery returns to Sea Oats to try to save her broken marriage but soon finds herself also fighting to save her own life and catch a murderer. (978-1-62639-828-3)

House of Fate by Barbara Ann Wright. Two women must throw off the lives they've known as a guardian and an assassin and save two rival houses before their secrets tear the galaxy apart. (978-1-62639-780-4)

Planning for Love by Erin Dutton. Could true love be the one thing that wedding coordinator Faith McKenna didn't plan for? (978-1-62639-954-9)

Sidebar by Carsen Taite. Judge Camille Avery and her clerk, attorney West Fallon, agree on little except their mutual attraction, but can their relationship and their careers survive a headline-grabbing case? (978-1-62639-752-1)

Sweet Boy and Wild One by T. L. Hayes. When Rachel Cole meets soulful singer Bobby Layton at an open mic, she is immediately in thrall. What she soon discovers will rock her world in ways she never imagined. (978-1-62639-963-1)